PROPHECY

PRAISE FOR THE GIFTEDVERSE

This one kept me interested from the very beginning. With a lot of drama, intrigue and some magic, it's fast paced and entertaining.

...This trilogy is action packed from start to finish with love and loss along the way... From first book to last, the Owens women will keep you fascinated.

Packed with excitement, danger, adventure and a roller-coaster ride of emotions. I couldn't put it down until I finished it!..

Wow. That is all I can say about this book. It kept me on my toes waiting to find out what came next. It was well-written with a lot of character and world building.

THE GIFTEDVERSE SERIES

In reading Order:

The Owens Chronicles

Prophecy

Destiny

Legacy

The Gifted Chronicles

First Life

Second Chance

Third Eye

Companion Volumes

Annabelle

Etta

Find out more at

www.giftedverse.com

PROPHECY

THE OWENS CHRONICLES BOOK ONE

AMANDA LYNN PETRIN

For everyone who supported me along the way...

Get new release updates and exclusive content when you sign up to my mailing list.

Copyright © 2019 by Amanda Lynn Petrin
Cover by 100Covers

Available Formats: Regular and Large Print
Ebook: 978-1-9991886-2-7
Paperback: 978-1-9991886-7-2 978-1-9991886-3-4 / 978-1-989950-21-0
Hardcover: 978-1-9991886-6-5 / 978-1-989950-20-3
Case Laminate: 978-1-989950-13-5 /978-1-989950-19-7

PROLOGUE

I can still remember the very first time I met Embry and Gabriel, two mysterious men who came out of nowhere and inserted themselves into my life. The details were fuzzy, more like a dream than a memory, but I knew they were important. I always felt special when they came to see me, even if I didn't know why. I was so young that I didn't understand the gravity of the situation, or how these men would eventually become my dark knights in shining armor, keeping me safe from all the scary characters from my nightmares...

I was five years old and Grams had just died. She had been the one taking care of me ever since 'the cancer' took my mom away. I used to make Grams look under my bed almost every night because I thought 'the cancer' was a monster, like the boogeyman. They always talked about it in hushed voices, and I knew it was the reason my mom left me. Instead of admitting there was nothing that she or anyone else could do to protect me from it, Grams humored me with a flashlight and some herbs that she would leave under my bed, to make sure it wouldn't come while I was asleep. She would go through different phases, sometimes putting salt by the windowsill as a protective barrier, other times hiding garlic in the closet. The smell was terrible, but it made me feel safe. Grams convinced me that burning sage to cleanse the house and all of her other tricks could help ward off 'the cancer' and other misfortunes. I didn't realize they were old wives' tales until 'the cancer' ripped Grams from me as well.

I hadn't counted, but it looked like there were hundreds of people gathered in the manor I grew up in. It was unnerving when I had never met a single one of them before. The manor was big enough that every curious mourner could lurk in their own room and I would never run into them. However, the East and West Wings were roped off, so everyone was crowded in the parlour. Mr. and Mrs. Boyd, the groundskeeper and his wife, were in charge of me until someone else could be found to take me in. Neither my mother nor my grandparents had any siblings or relatives to mention, and I knew nothing about my father, other than a blurry picture of a man whose face you couldn't see.

Mrs. Boyd was always vocal about her opinions, such as how horrible it was that the townsfolk were using Grams' funeral to gain access to our elusive manor. There were real estate agents and lawyers wandering as far as they could, trying to get lost on their way to the restroom, sniffing around for clues as to who was inheriting the property and whether they were likely to sell. Mrs. Boyd made certain none of them felt welcome, and a few of them literally retreated from her steely gaze. She had always been fiercely protective of us, and her fiery red hair, though slightly graying, made it clear she was not the type of person you wanted to mess with. I was grateful it meant no one dared come near me, but I could still hear their whispers.

I would never have called Grams suspicious or eccentric, but that was how the strangers in my home described her. They spoke as though they knew her and her crazy old woman behaviors, but they didn't know about half of the odd things we did. I could only imagine what they would say if they knew we ate strawberries and jumped into the creek for summer solstice, had soul cakes instead of trick-or-treating for Halloween and filled the house with fresh cowslip. Not to mention the bonfires. Or the locket. In movies, girls wore lockets with pictures of people they loved, whereas my locket was incredibly old and sealed shut. Grams had wanted me to wear it all the time, but it smelled funny, so she said it was okay as long as I wore it around the end of October. She never elaborated on the purpose of the locket, or what she was protecting me from, and she did get most of her information from books and movies, but she ingrained in me from early on that something terrible would happen if I didn't follow these practices. When she died, I saw it as proof that none of it was real, but then again, maybe I just hadn't tried hard enough to do everything she taught me.

The townspeople knew none of that. They only knew that Grams was a recluse who never mingled with the outside world. A few people had come to visit us once or twice over the years, but we never left the manor and after my mom died, there were no more visitors. Mrs. Boyd did our grocery shopping and her husband took care of any errands we had.

Whenever Mrs. Boyd suggested I needed playmates my own age, Grams would remind her that I had Samuel, Mr. and Mrs. Boyd's fifteen-year-old-son. Sam had none of his mother's fierceness, and tended to make me laugh more than anything, particularly when he got angry, which was rare. His hair was ginger and reminded me more of a carrot than of fire, which suited his personality perfectly.

In an attempt to avoid the strangers, I secluded myself on the stairs, past the velvet rope Mrs. Boyd used to show our 'guests' where they weren't welcome. I was perfectly content there, playing with Grams' antique dolls. They lived on a shelf in my bedroom, too high for me to reach, because they were old and fragile. As Grams would say, "They're meant to be looked at, not played with." Sam had taken them down for me that morning as a special treat. On occasion, Grams would bring them down as props for the stories she would tell me about the lives they had lived. I loved these stories about adventures and courage, even though they never ended with the dolls living happily ever after. "It's not about that," Grams would tell me. "It's about the kind of women they were, the things they overcame with their strength and bravery." She made sure my heroes wouldn't be princesses whose sole ambition was to marry the prince by the end of the story, then live happily ever after.

Other than Beth, whose hair barely reached her chin, the dolls all looked the same, with big green eyes and lots of curly brown hair. I had to look at their clothes to tell them apart; Annabelle looked like a pilgrim with her bonnet, Rosalind had the big, poofy bottom to her dress, Cassandra wore a straight gown in bright colors with white gloves, and Elizabeth had a flapper dress. Grams said you could recognize them by their smiles, but I assumed she was teasing because the smiles all looked the same to me. They were strong and confident, but also a little sad.

My favourite part was that each doll had a crescent moon birthmark on the back of her neck, right below the hairline. You had to lift up their hair to see it, so Grams didn't know about it until I showed her. I liked it because I had one too, in the exact same spot. Mr. Boyd tried to rub it off once, when Grams put my hair up in a high bun for a ballet lesson, but Mrs. Boyd told him it was just something that ran in my family.

"Does that mean the dolls are real?" I had asked Grams excitedly.

"They're just dolls," she brushed it away.

"But they look like people who are related to me," I specified.

She looked at me in that way where she tried to be stern, but failed miserably. "They're made to look like your ancestors," Grams reluctantly agreed.

"Did you know them?" My eyes grew wide.

"They all died long ago," she sounded sad.

"That means that all of their adventures..." My brain tried to remember every story I had been told.

"They're just stories, Luce."

I WAS LIFTING up their hair to see the birthmark when a man, dressed all in black, knelt down in front of me. His sandy blond hair was still wet, as though he had tried to make it look presentable, but it was sticking out all over the place. Mine always got really frizzy, which made Grams think I hadn't brushed it when I had.

"That's a pretty doll you have there." He picked up the white bonnet I dropped when lifting her hair and handed it back to me. "What's her name?" His voice was kind, with the hint of an Italian accent, but his eyes were dark and intense. Not exactly scary, but unlike anything I had seen before.

"Annabelle," I answered, which made him smile. "And this is Beth and Cassie and Rosie," I introduced him to the others. The isolation I grew up in at the manor meant that I hadn't encountered enough strangers to be warned not to talk to them. Although even if I had, I would have made an exception for him. He made me nervous, not that he gave me any reason to be, and he felt familiar, as though I had met him before.

"And what is your name?" he asked me.

"Lucy." The shyness in my voice led him to turn around and see the other man who had caught my attention. His hair was dark brown and straight, but his eyes, that he hadn't taken off me since he came up the staircase, were the same as the first man's. He was listening intently to our conversation, but made no attempt to join it.

"It's nice to meet you, Lucy," the first man continued, turning back to me. "I'm Embry Dante and this is my friend, Gabriel Black." He said 'friend' in a way that told me they weren't.

The introduction provided an opportunity for the other man, Gabriel, to come closer. He also knelt down to my level and extended his hand, so I could shake it. Up close, his eyes were even scarier, but I wasn't afraid.

"I've never seen her so young before," Gabriel told Embry, looking me up and down. The statement confused me, as I had only ever been younger.

"How did you know my Grams?" I asked, sensing these weren't townspeople looking for access. They had gone past the velvet rope, but instead of looking like they got caught while exploring, they acted like I was the one they were looking for. They must have been Grams' friends. Or more likely my mom's.

"We're old friends of the family," Embry explained, not looking all that old to me. He was older than Sam, but younger than any adult I knew.

"Did you also know my mommy?" Grams knew so few people, that anyone who knew her would have known my mom as well, especially if they were friends of the family. I remembered so little of my mom that I was always asking people to tell me stories, but it made Grams sad, and the Boyds insisted they had already told me all the stories they knew.

"Of course I knew Marilyn," Embry told me while someone in the hallway caught Gabriel's eye.

"Lucy, you need to eat something." Sam came over and extended his hand, expecting me to follow him to the room where the food was set out. He had looked at the men with curiosity when he walked by them, but focused entirely on me once he got close.

"They knew my mommy," I argued with him, not ready to leave.

"This area is off-limits to guests," Sam told my new friends. "I'll bring you to her room later if you come with me now," he tried to bribe me. It was a tough decision. I could stay there and talk to men who might know stories I had yet to hear about my mother, or I could take Sam up on his offer and spend hours going through my mother's things, wearing her clothes and possibly hiding something in my blankie to treasure later. I carried it with me everywhere, so no one would suspect anything if I slipped a photograph or some jewelry into the creases of the pearl-colored material. Grams was always worried I would break things, which was why the dolls lived on the shelf that was too high for me to reach.

"Okay," I reluctantly agreed, taking Sam's hand to get up from the steps. "Will I see you again?" I asked Embry, looking around, but Gabriel had vanished while I was talking to Sam.

"I'll be around," he assured me before Sam brought me to the dining room, where his parents were waiting.

"Come here sweetie, I made a plate of your favorites." Mrs. Boyd motioned me over, took me into her lap, and handed me a plate with deviled eggs, Swedish meatballs, hot dogs wrapped in bread and bacon, as well as little cheese cubes. I knew she had also bought a tub of cookie dough ice cream for me to have later, once all the strangers were gone.

"Where was she?" Mr. Boyd asked Sam. He was tall and fair and usually wore dirt-stained overalls, but now looked uncomfortable in the stiff black suit his wife made him wear.

"On the stairs, talking to some guys I've never seen before. I got the feeling they were hiding something," he told his father, stealing one of my cheese cubes with a smile, knowing I would forgive him.

"Everyone here today is hiding something. None of them have seen the inside of this house in years, if at all," Mrs. Boyd added her two cents.

"They knew Grams. And mommy," I inserted myself into their conversation.

"What were their names, sweetie?" Mrs. Boyd asked me, playing with my hair. Sam didn't have any siblings, but she liked having a girl around, and I definitely didn't mind.

"Embry and Gabriel," I said with my mouth full. "I like them."

Mr. and Mrs. Boyd exchanged a glance before she took me off her lap and asked Sam to watch me while she went to take care of something.

I TRIED to ask Sam where they were going, but he didn't seem to know any more than I did, so he let me finish eating, then brought me to the backyard. His girlfriend, Deanna, showed up not long after and played hopscotch with me. Sam wasn't biologically my brother, but he had been there my whole life. Grams had rarely let him have friends over because they were always too loud or 'had a look about them', but even she had liked Deanna. Her auburn hair was cut just below her ears, but she still knew how to do French Braids, and would do mine sometimes when Sam had homework to do. Grams liked her because she was always smiling.

Eventually, Deanna and Sam snuck out to the garden swing to do 'grown-up things' which I knew meant kissing, leaving me alone.

I SAW Embry and Gabriel by the fountain, so I went over to try and talk to them some more. I was sure Embry would answer questions about my mom, and maybe even tell me some stories. Unfortunately, Mr. and Mrs. Boyd had found the men as well, so I stayed close enough to hear, but far enough that I wouldn't be seen.

"My family has been taking care of Lucy's for a long time, Mr. Dante, and I know who you are." There was a warning in Mrs. Boyd's tone, like when she was yelling at the animals that ate out of the garden.

"Then you know why we're here." Embry sounded serious, like it was important business that had brought him to the manor. Everyone seemed to know what was going on, but I didn't have a clue.

"Martha, you can't believe your father's stories? He was a drunk." Mr. Boyd didn't trust the two men, or believe their story, whatever it was.

"I never believed them before, Curtis, but he is not a day older than in the painting from the East Wing, or the picture from Miss Helen's bedroom." That was where I knew him from.

The manor had four wings, but I couldn't tell you which one was which, except for the East Wing, because I wasn't allowed to be there. This meant I had been dozens of times and seen the life-size portraits of my two new friends. Miss Helen was my great-grandmother, who died before I was born, so I never felt the urge to explore her bedroom, which was also in the East Wing.

"That painting could be of anybody. It's hundreds of years old," Mr. Boyd argued.

"It could, but it isn't. We understand that it's difficult to fathom, but we are exactly who we say we are, and we're here for Lucy." He didn't sound mean, but I could tell that he was going to get his way. I didn't think they were going to hurt me or anything, but at the same time, I didn't want to leave the manor, or Mr. and Mrs. Boyd.

"You'll take that girl over my dead body," Mr. Boyd said with anger, but it still made me smile. He was strict, and often talked to Sam and I like we were soldiers in his army rather than children, but deep down, he was a softy. He was the one who would sneak me a cookie when Grams said I wasn't allowed to have dessert.

"We don't want to take her," Gabriel said as if it were preposterous. "What would we do with a five-year-old girl?"

"We want to come by every once in a while and make sure she's safe," Embry spoke calmly, convincingly, until he used the wrong words.

"She'll be perfectly safe with us." Mr. Boyd sounded hurt by the accusation.

"Of course she will. We don't doubt that you are fully capable of raising her with as much love and affection as her own mother would have, but we want to stop by sometimes and see how she's doing. We made a promise a long time ago, to look after this family, and it is imperative that we stick to our promise," Embry implied they would keep coming whether we liked it or not.

"I don't trust you," Mr. Boyd said before I heard his footsteps drifting away. I was about to go back to Sam and Deanna, but Mrs. Boyd wasn't done.

"What are you exactly? I mean...are you demons? Angels? Warlocks?" she asked, intrigued.

"You read way too many novels," Gabriel laughed, sounding bored.

"There's no name for what we are, though there are some historical references to The Gifted. Some people like us live normal lives and die just as they would have without it."

"I thought you were invincible, or immortal?" she inquired.

"We just stick around until our job is done. We linger until our unfinished business is taken care of, like purgatory. We have something to live for, something we need to accomplish, so we live," Embry explained. "There are some people like us who don't even know what their purpose is. Leonardo da Vinci kept making invention after invention, waiting to discover the one that would finally let him join the ones he loved."

"And you live to protect the descendants of the woman you loved?" she verified, unimpressed by whoever he'd mentioned.

"It was her dying wish that we take care of her daughter," Embry explained, the emotion clear in his voice.

"And she said she would come back," Gabriel spoke up, letting everyone know why he was still hanging around.

"There's no such thing as vampires and demons and werewolves and goblins and all of those things?" Mrs. Boyd sounded disappointed.

"Not that I've encountered." Embry laughed warmly, but Gabriel looked like he wasn't so sure.

"We should have this conversation when Lucy isn't listening in." Gabriel looked right to where I was standing.

I stepped out of my hiding spot behind some bushes, and he looked at me in a way that let me know I had done something wrong, but then he smiled. It was the tiniest of smiles that barely lasted a second, but I was sure I saw it. Like breaking the rules might be something he approved of.

"I thought I told you to wait in the kitchen with Sam?" Mrs. Boyd asked me in her motherly tone, trying to determine how much I had heard.

"Deanna came so they went to the yard, but I wanted to see Embry and Gabriel," I explained.

"Come here sweetie, we'll get you back inside." Mrs. Boyd picked me up so she would be sure I went with her. As she walked past the fountain, she paused. "We're taking care of her until, or unless someone else comes around to claim her. I don't mind you coming as long as Lucy still wants to see you, but the minute I start feeling about you like my husband does, you won't be invited back," she warned.

Embry nodded as we walked away. I tried to look back and wave at them, but we rounded a statue and they were gone.

"How much of that did you hear?" Mrs. Boyd asked me while we made our way back to the guests.

"All of it, I think," I said, letting my head rest on her shoulder. She smelled clean, like soap, but also like cookies and food. Being up in her arms made me feel safe. As long as she held me, Embry and Gabriel wouldn't have to worry, because nothing bad would ever happen to me. I knew I was wrong, even then, because Mrs. Boyd held me in her arms for most of the time that my grandmother was sick, and she still died, just like my mom.

"One day this hiding and sneaking around is going to get you in trouble," she said, rubbing my back so I would fall asleep. She didn't sound mad, and she usually found it funny when I snuck up on her in the kitchen.

CHAPTER ONE

"I can't believe our little girl is graduating." Deanna helped me fix my cap over my long brown curls, which she tried to tame for the occasion.

"You're not even 10 years older than me," I reminded her. We celebrated her twenty-seventh birthday a couple of months before my eighteenth.

"And I'm your little girl!" five-year-old Clara pointed out, barging into her parents' bedroom and putting herself between me and Deanna at the mirror. You wouldn't think we were related if you saw us individually, with Deanna's platinum pixie cut and Clara's strawberry blonde pigtails, but when I looked at the 3 of us together in the mirror, we were a family.

"Lucy is our big girl and you're our baby girl," Sam explained, making me roll my eyes. His mom died when I was twelve, then his father three years ago, making Sam my legal guardian. He was an amazing dad to Clara, but I still saw him as a big brother.

"But who is your favorite girl?" Clara was all about favorites these days, ever since Deanna went back to work. It was only part time, a day or two every week, but she loved being a social worker and helping people. Clara wasn't used to sharing her mom with anyone but me, and kept making sure she was still the favorite. I found it adorable.

"I love all three of my girls more than anything else in the world," Sam answered without answering, which got Clara to sigh loudly for effect, oozing attitude. I appreciated his sentiment, but it had been thirteen years since I was anybody's favorite, and I was okay with that. Most of the time.

"You're my favorite sister." Clara turned to me. She knew we weren't really related, but I had been there every single day since she was born.

"And you're my favorite little sister," I assured her.

She pouted at that, but I shrugged and looked up at Deanna, who became my big sister long before she became Sam's wife and, ultimately, my guardian. "I'll put this back on after lunch," Deanna assured me, gently removing the cap now that we knew how it would look.

"What time are we eating at?" I asked.

"I told everyone 12," Sam shared. He literally meant everyone, but no one would show up. A few kids used to come to my birthday parties when I was little, so their parents could explore the manor and see if the rumors about us were true, but they gave up when they realized the eccentricity died with Grams. Keisha was the exception. She moved to town halfway through sixth grade, when everyone else already had their best friend, except for me. I wasn't bullied, but people rarely went out of their way to make me feel welcome or accepted. Neither did Keisha, to be honest. She just showed up with so much confidence and strength that when she said we belonged, I believed her.

"I better start making the cake." I got up and followed Sam and Deanna out of the room.

"Do you want to play hide and seek?" Clara asked, following me.

"I can play now, and she can come join us?" Deanna offered on her way down the stairs.

"Does that mean I'll have to lick the spoons all by myself?" I pretended that was a daunting task.

"I can lick the spoons?" Clara asked in a whisper, looking over to her mom. Deanna liked to warn us about the salmonella we could get from cake batter.

"Of course," I told her with confidence. I was barely allowed to leave the property as a child, but the house was always stocked with cookie dough to deal with heartbreaks.

"Let me get my hat." Clara stopped midway down the stairs and ran back up.

I followed her to her bedroom, decorated with princesses and unicorns, and waited while she sorted through her toy chest to find a baker's hat. She loved playing dress-up and helping us cook, so it was the perfect birthday gift for her. Embry nearly replaced me as her favorite when she opened it.

I MADE the cake batter with Clara and let her lick all the spoons and mixers, but I saved a few spoonfuls from the bowl for myself.

"Now cookies?" Clara looked up at me, her face all sticky with chocolate icing from when she tried to lick the middle of the mixer spoons.

"Now I go set the table while you wash up," I corrected her. "We can make cookies next Sunday." I never understood the harm in a 'sugar rush' until we introduced Clara to chocolate.

I went to the dining room and set seven places for my Graduation Party. Sam, Deanna and Clara were a given, and Keisha said she would come for an hour or so between her two parents, who divorced a month into our sophomore year. Gabriel would run off with something important to do as soon as the cake was done, but Embry would make up for him by staying an entire week to hang out.

By 12:30, Sam, Deanna, Clara, Keisha and I were sitting at the dining room table, waiting while the smell of delicious food kept wafting in, making my mouth water.

"You did invite them, right?" Clara asked like maybe her dad had been silly and forgot to tell the other guests about the party.

"I did," he assured us.

"And?" I asked.

"Embry said he wouldn't miss it for the world. Gabriel looked at me like I was talking a foreign language and said he would see."

"Sounds accurate," I conceded. Gabriel was like that brooding teenager whose parents forced him to attend an event about 90 percent of the time, while Embry was the big brother I would run to whenever he showed up. Which was often.

"Maybe you told him the wrong date?" Keisha ventured after I tried Embry's cell phone again and was sent straight to voicemail.

"Or they thought this was a dinner party?" Deanna played along, but we hadn't had dinner celebrations since Clara was born. She had a tendency to fall asleep at the table if anything started past 6 o'clock.

"I'm hungry." Clara looked around the table to her parents, then back to me when they shrugged to let her know it was my party, so my decision.

"We can heat some up when they arrive," I assured her, letting Sam and Deanna know I was okay with us eating without them. There were a million reasons why they could be late or unable to come, but few that explained why they hadn't told anyone and weren't answering their phones.

Sam, Deanna and I went to the kitchen and made five plates

of Sloppy Joes. The table was decked out with hot sauces and chili for Deanna, ketchup and relish for Clara, who treated it like a hamburger, and mountains of shredded cheese for Sam and I. Keisha ate hers as is, with a fork and knife, opposed to the 'sloppy' part of the meal.

I smiled at Clara, who loved being able to make a mess of herself with food, but my mind was on the two empty chairs.

"You okay?" Sam asked while we brought the empty plates to the kitchen.

"Gabriel never said he was coming," I said as if I hadn't expected him to.

"True," he agreed, but no matter how unenthusiastic Gabriel was sometimes, he was always there for milestones and big events.

"And maybe Embry doesn't like the idea that I'm growing up, or that I'm going off to college instead of staying here forever," I shared what had originally been a fear, but was now a better alternative to something bad happening to them.

"You think he didn't show up just to spite you?" he questioned my logic.

"Do you have a better suggestion?" I would take disappointing them over 80 percent of the scenarios running through my mind.

"He forgot the date. Got a new phone and couldn't figure out how to use it. He was speeding and the cop brought him to the station because he couldn't provide a valid driver's license. He got held up on his way because he stopped to rescue orphans from a burning building and his phone was lost in the fire," he gave me a list of somewhat plausible explanations where Embry wasn't hurt or mad at me.

"Thank you," I smiled at the last one, because it was very Embry.

"Anytime," he assured me.

"I hope it's a simple misunderstanding." I let out the breath I was holding and tried to release some of the tension that wasn't letting up in my shoulders.

"How many messages under the table?" he let me know I hadn't been as sneaky as I hoped.

"A million texts and three calls," I admitted. "But I'm sure they're fine," I brushed it off.

"They always make it back to you," he reminded me.

"Exactly," I agreed with absolutely no conviction. Even if I was worried about them, I didn't want Sam to worry about me.

"We're ready for you!" Clara and Keisha called.

"Let's go, High School Grads." Sam ushered me to sit beside Keisha, where they put the candle-lit cake.

"For they are jolly good fellows, for they are jolly good fellows..." Clara and Deanna sang. Sam asked, "Really? That's what we're going with?" before joining in.

"This is so unnecessary." I shook my head at them, but I was grinning ear to ear as Keisha and I blew out the candles.

"You girls are going to be amazing," Sam said, locking eyes with me so I would know he meant it.

"You'll knock them all dead," Deanna encouraged.

"Then bring them back to life." Sam looked pointedly to his wife, reminding her that I was going to be studying Medicine in the fall, where the hope is that I keep people alive, not kill them.

"Obviously." She rolled her eyes and smiled.

"I love you guys." I ignored the tears.

"Yeah, thank you Mr. and Mrs. Boyd." We all inadvertently cringed when Keisha thanked them. Ever since the first time she came over, she insisted it was impolite for her to call them by their first names, but Mr. and Mrs. Boyd were Sam's parents, so it sounded weird to us.

"We can do it all over again once Embry and Gabriel get

here," Deanna assured me when my eyes ventured to the empty chairs again.

"We'll try to come up with a more fitting song for round two," Sam agreed, getting a playful slap from his wife.

"I'll have to pass on round two. My dad is taking me for ice cream." Keisha got up from the table.

"How long is he in town for?" I asked. He moved to Providence after the divorce so his visits, though few and far between, were always extra special.

"He's moving me into MIT after prom, then traveling for the rest of the summer."

"How's your mom taking it?" Deanna asked.

"Me leaving or him being there?" Keisha asked in a way that told us neither of these were suiting her mom so well.

"It's a 15-minute drive," Sam pointed out.

"How are you feeling about the 30 minutes to Harvard?" Deanna shot back.

"Point taken," he agreed.

"And it won't be 15 minutes. She got a grant to go do research and dig stuff up in England."

"She finally said yes?" Her mom was always being asked to lead research expeditions all over the place, but she always said no to opportunities I would have jumped on.

"She says you can come with me at Thanksgiving if you want."

I turned straight to Sam, but all my hopes died when I saw his expression. "We'll have to talk it over," he told Keisha.

"You've got time," she assured him before Clara and I walked her to the door.

"Will you be at Lucy's graduation?" Clara asked.

"I kind of have to be. I'm giving a speech," Keisha shared.

"How come?" Clara looked at her like giving a speech was the last thing anyone should want to do.

"She's smarter than everyone else." I rolled my eyes before smiling at my best friend.

"By like half a percent," she argued.

"It still counts," I assured her.

"All that to say I will see you both later," she told us. "And thank you Mr. and Mrs. Boyd!" she called back to the kitchen.

"Anytime, sweetie." Deanna poked her head into the hallway.

"CAN WE PLAY TAG NOW?" Clara asked once we were back in the dining room, wolfing down her last few bites of cake.

"Of course," I sighed while Deanna smiled at me, knowing I was only pretending it was a chore. I loved hanging out with Clara and would miss her dragging me out for adventures once I was on campus in the fall.

"You're it!" She touched me before running off as soon as I opened the door to the backyard. I used to have to run at a snail's pace and pretend I couldn't catch her, but she was getting better, and sometimes I only barely caught her.

"Do you think Embry is okay?" she asked once I had her up in my arms, having trapped her in the maze that used to be our apple orchard.

"Of course he's okay. He's Embry," I told her as if she had nothing to worry about, but my heart had been tight in my chest ever since Sam suggested we sit at the table instead of waiting for them in the doorway. Gabriel usually showed up right on time, but he was never late, and I couldn't remember the last time Embry wasn't hours early for a party. Something was off.

"You're not worried at all?" Clara asked, making me feel terrible, because I knew she would trust me if I told her there was nothing to worry about.

"Nope. I'm thinking about all the cake we can have if they don't come," I teased, tickling her before running off.

. . .

"You're so fast today!" I said when she caught me. I wrapped my arm around her shoulders so we could head back to the manor to get ready.

"I'm always fast." She ducked under my arm and ran ahead of me to prove her point. If only I'd had her confidence at that age, I would have spent a lot less time worrying, and a lot more time doing things. Like standing up for myself and making friends, things I didn't do until Keisha showed me how. Clara had her grandmother's fierceness, her dad's kindness, and her mother's social skills. She was what I wanted to be when I grew up.

Once inside, I changed into the gorgeous yellow dress Deanna got for me to wear underneath the gown, and let her put the cap back on. Sam often said the luckiest day of his life was when he was the first person Deanna met when she moved to town with her dad, and it was one of mine as well. Sam had always been one of my favorite people, but Deanna had quickly become the best friend/sister I never got to have. Because Sam lived at the manor with my crazy family, a lot of the kids at school didn't take the time to find out how awesome he was. Deanna walked into the grocery store when he was helping his mom out, literally fell into his arms in the produce aisle and left with his heart. Luckily, he'd made an impression on her as well. I was still waiting for someone new to move to the neighborhood and stumble into the manor, which might be the only way I could meet him before he found out that I was 'that weird Owens girl' to everyone in town.

When we got to school, Sam and Deanna took Clara to get seats while I found my graduating class in the library. There were eighty of us, mostly the same students I met on my first day of kindergarten. I was amazed at all the kids my age I had as friends, until they went home and their parents told them to keep their distance. Mrs. Boyd would say, "People are afraid of what they don't know," which wasn't very comforting, even back then.

"We made it." Tennison came over to me while someone from administration tried to line us up alphabetically, leaving behind the cheerleaders he'd been talking to. Other than Keisha, who came much later, Tennison Montgomery was the only student who talked to me when the teachers weren't requiring it, which they rarely did. He had been my best friend on that first day of class, when I showed up all nervous because of so many new faces. He said he liked my curly hair, but I always thought it was the homemade brownies Mrs. Boyd sent me to school with. He sat with me at snack time until around second grade, when he became the boy every girl had a crush on. He would still volunteer to be my partner for school projects, with other kids acting like he was taking one for the team, but we would meet up way more than the projects required. Sam recommended I ditch anyone who was only nice to me when other people weren't around, but his dad used to tell me that not everyone could be brave and fearless. Some did the best they could, until they got brave enough to act the way they felt inside. I was all for giving him a chance as long as he wasn't mean to me, and he never was.

"Was there any doubt? It's not like we went to war." Keisha was utterly unimpressed, and felt the same as Sam about him.

"It's something you say. I just meant congratulations. To both of you. You guys slayed it," he said before one of his teammates called him over.

"We slayed it?" Keisha asked me. "You're literally the only person who signed my yearbook."

"I'm the only one you asked," I reminded her. "And you're valedictorian. I'm the runner-up. Academically, we did good."

"Academically, we slayed it." I shook my head at her before falling in line.

WE WENT OUT onto the football field once we were in order, with families in the bleachers. It took forever before they called out my name, and I was only two-thirds of the way down the list.

"Congratulations Ms. Owens." Our principal, Mr. Higgins, handed me my diploma before shaking my hand, while I scanned the audience. It was easy to find Sam and Deanna, who both stood up and cheered, with Clara on Sam's shoulders, looking like she had just woken up. It was also easy to find the empty space beside them, for Embry and Gabriel, who didn't show.

"LEFTOVER CAKE?" Sam asked, wrapping an arm around me once the ceremony was done and we were able to go home.

"I think I'm good," I told him.

"Did Lucy say no to cake?" Deanna pretended to be shocked. It wasn't that I had it all the time. We tried to limit the sugary and unhealthy foods, but if there was cake, I was always going to have some.

"I'm tired, and I'm helping Keisha pack tomorrow." She got accepted to a super intense program at MIT, designed for people who were going to become astronauts or cure cancer or something equally impressive. This meant they expected her to spend the summer taking extra courses, so she could start off on the first day smarter than 99.9 percent of the population.

"You still need to have dinner," Sam pointed out.

"I will. I just don't need the whole round two thing," I explained.

"Sounds reasonable," he agreed, but he was mostly playing along so we could pretend the lack of celebration was because I was tired, not because half the guests never showed up.

CHAPTER TWO

I spent the next week enjoying the beginning of summer holidays. For me, this meant reading books that were on my college syllabus rather than the high school curriculum. It may not have been entirely due to the manor and Grams' eccentricity that I had so few friends.

Like clockwork, Clara would come to my room every day at 3 and ask if I could come play outside. The one time I tried to say no, she reminded me that I was leaving her in September and it might be our last chance to play before I forgot all about her. Come Saturday, however, she didn't even bother to ask.

Part of me wanted to stay home and enjoy the weekend with Sam, Deanna and Clara, or spend one last day with Keisha before she was off to dorm rooms and college, but another tiny part of me, that I usually kept buried deep inside, was excited. I watched movies and read books about the high school experience. If they taught me anything, it was that prom was a night that could change everything. I didn't expect it to make a difference for me in the long run, but for one night, I wanted to get dolled up with my hair all fancy, wear a pretty dress and be like everybody else. I didn't even need the fairytale ending of finding my prince at the ball, I just wanted to be invited. Not that I admitted any of that while Deanna, Clara and I sat in the living room, doing each other's nails.

"Make sure your phone is charged. I want a million pictures," Deanna warned me, adding a second coat to my right hand. The color was called Blush, and it was the perfect amount of pink to be elegant without reminding you of Barbie.

"I'm surprised you decided not to chaperone," I called her on how overprotective they liked to be. I also knew that she'd filled out the application, but we came back from the shopping trip with a dress for me and nothing for her.

"Mr. Higgins implied that I was better at breaking rules than enforcing them."

"That's completely..."

"Accurate," she cut me off before I could come up with a lie. "But I'm old now and way more responsible and it's a volunteer position. You don't turn people down."

"He hurt your feelings," I understood.

"Only because I voted against setting his toupee on fire as our senior prank, and I can't go back and change that."

"What's a toupee?" Clara asked. We were letting her use a super cool nail polish stick that peeled off, in case she got it in the wrong places. Unfortunately, she insisted on wearing the green one, which left the slightest green tinge, just enough to make her fingers look infected.

"It's something people wear on their heads when they don't have hair. Like a wig, but only for one spot," I explained to her, because Deanna's eyes went wide, like she forgot her daughter was in the room when she made that statement.

"Wouldn't it hurt if you put his head on fire?" Clara looked up at her mom, so innocent, that Deanna's face went red instead of answering.

"I'm sure they weren't going to do it while he was wearing it," I assured Clara, making Deanna's face go even redder. After spending four years with Mr. Higgins, I couldn't exactly blame her, but I wasn't the type who was invited to or consulted on the senior prank. Deanna, on the other hand, had been a wild child, once upon a time. She was still a free spirit who didn't always follow conventional rules, but she did have her own lines that she would never cross.

ONCE MY HAIR WAS DRY, Deanna helped me put it up into the most gorgeous bun I have ever seen. My hair was curly, which I loved, but it was also unruly, so any updo usually came with a halo of fuzz around my head. She managed to tame it so there was no frizz or flyaways, just beautiful twists that met in an elegant knot at the back of my head.

"The finishing touch," Deanna said, taking something fragile and dainty out of a black velvet box.

"I think the tiara is a bit much," I argued once she opened it to reveal a delicate silver band encrusted with diamonds and indicolite. According to Grams, her great-great-many-times-great-grandmother had worn it when she met the Queen of England.

"But you're a princess!" Clara argued, overruling me.

"It's bad enough you convinced Sam to let you skip the Debutante Ball and your introduction to society. Your grams would never forgive me if I didn't at least make you look the part of a lady at prom." She slid the tiara into my hair, so it rested on the top of my head. I rolled my eyes like it was annoying and embarrassing, but Clara was right; I looked exactly like a princess. And I wasn't even wearing the dress yet.

MAKEUP WAS interesting because I never wore any. I dabbled with BB creams and foundation whenever I got a breakout, and used mascara the few times we went to a restaurant in town or if there was an event, but that was it. Deanna didn't need makeup with her perfect complexion and miles of eyelashes, but she had been a teenage girl once and now referred to my face as her canvas. I vetoed the use of the torture device she called an eyelash curler, but she only agreed when I didn't respond well to the eyeliner or mascara or anything that went close to my eyes.

She had me facing her instead of the mirror, so by the time I saw myself, I got the full effect of looking at a face I could tell was mine, but didn't look anything like me. I teared up, trying to stop it because I knew it would ruin Deanna's work, but I looked exactly like my mother. Or at least the version of her that lived in my head and was a combination of actual memories, the dolls and an older-looking me.

"It's perfect," I smiled up at her expectant face, which broke into a smile as well.

"I didn't want to do much. You never wear anything, but I thought it would be nice to bring out how beautiful you are," she told me.

"You have to say that," I reminded her.

"Nope, me being related to you is entirely voluntary, therefore I am not biased. I could even be mean to you and make you do all my chores because evil stepmothers are socially acceptable."

"In fairy tales," I pointed out.

"Either way, I think you're awesome and 100 percent the belle of the ball."

"I have an overwhelming urge to lock you in the basement until you're forty-five, so I'm gonna say she's right." Sam came in with Clara, who wasn't interested in the makeup if she wasn't the one wearing it.

"Let her out when she's thirty. I want grandbabies," Deanna teased.

"You guys are ridiculous," I pointed out.

"Aren't you glad you're stuck with us?" Deanna smiled at me.

"Overjoyed," I agreed, pretending to be sarcastic, but I loved them and was grateful for everything they did for me.

"Ready for pictures?" Sam asked, holding an old camera we'd had since I was a child.

"Just missing the dress." I looked to Deanna. We had all gone shopping together, but Deanna was the only one in the store with me when I found it, and she insisted it should be a surprise for everyone else until tonight.

I WENT UP to my room and took the garment bag from my closet, catching a glance at myself in the mirror. I looked different than I had ever looked before, and yet so familiar. Like someone I had met in a dream...

"Need help?" Deanna walked in and pulled me from my thoughts. I was holding the deep blue material in place, but hadn't secured it yet.

"With the zipper," I agreed, giving her my back. She did the clip before pulling up the zipper, which went effortlessly.

"So?" I asked, turning to face her.

"Clara was spot on. All this time you've been a princess," She told me.

"It's prom, this is what everyone looks like," I argued.

"You're mesmerizing," she refused to let me dismiss the compliment.

"You're like a Queen!" Clara exclaimed, coming close. "Can I hug you?"

"Of course," I assured her, but I could see where the uncertainty came from. The gown was gorgeous and intricate. I wouldn't know where to touch it.

"Babe, we're ready!" Deanna called, so Sam appeared in the doorway.

"Any chance you'll stop growing up if I ask?" he tried.

29

"In my head, you're still fifteen, and you better not tell me otherwise," I let him know I understood.

"I can still see you as the little six-year-old with the pigtails and the blankie you carried everywhere. Whenever something went missing, it was always hidden in there."

"Because you wouldn't let me take things away from where I found them," I defended myself.

"Even then you were a rule-breaker," he said with a smile.

"Let's get this over with." I shook my head at him. We all knew I followed the rules and curfew. The most rule-breaking I did in high school was read ahead in textbooks and write longer assignments.

"All the pictures." Deanna had a mischievous grin before they took pictures of me alone, then pictures of me with Clara, with Deanna, with Sam. We went downstairs and took more of all those pictures before Sam set the timer and we made about a dozen attempts at a full family photo before we succeeded.

"Am I good to go now?" I looked at my phone and saw I had 20 minutes before I was supposed to meet Keisha outside the yacht club.

"Come on, I'll drive you." Sam handed the camera to Deanna.

"I can drive," I argued.

"Not in those heels." Deanna shook her head, knowing I had very limited experience wearing high-heeled shoes.

"I'm sure you can, but I'll drop you off and come pick you up whenever you want."

"I can also take my car and drive home whenever I want," I pointed out.

"If I remember correctly, the best way to leave prom is either on the school bus to the Foundry, or in the limo to the house of some cool kid whose parents are out of town."

"And you're endorsing those options?" I asked, knowing that Tennison's parents left for Belgium right after graduation. I was pretty sure I could get Keisha and me an invite, but I doubt we would be welcome.

"I trust you more than I trusted myself at that age," he shrugged his shoulders. "I want you to have fun and enjoy your last moments of high school before the real world comes in."

"You're like every high school movie that thinks prom is some magical night?" I asked, eager to hear his take on it.

"No, I'm someone who was a teenager and knows there's nothing magical about prom." He looked over to Deanna with a knowing smile. "But this is your last night to hang out and have dance parties with Keisha before you both go to separate schools. And you look amazing in that dress."

"Magical proms," I shook my head.

"Confidence looks good on you," he told me.

"If only I had more," I agreed.

"You're perfect the way you are," he assured me.

WE SPENT the drive talking about his prom, which was a fiasco, except for the 5 minutes at the end. "And then she said 'yes,'" he finished as we pulled into the yacht club, explaining the earlier smiles.

"On the night everyone else is worried about prom king and queen, you were asking Deanna to spend the rest of her life with you?" I shook my head at him, but I also loved it.

"No, I knew she wanted to spend forever with me, it was asking if she'd marry me that was terrifying. My parents were hardcore Catholics if you remember, and Deanna was a free spirit who didn't want to be tied down."

"How did you get her to say yes?" I asked.

"I told her I never wanted to own her or tame her, I just wanted her to take me along for the ride."

"I had no idea you were this romantic," I smiled at him.

"I have many surprises you'll have to stick around and see," he said mysteriously.

"I'm still living on campus. I need to get out there," I warned.

"I know. This is me making sure you'll come home for Thanksgiving and Christmas and Easter and..."

"I wouldn't miss them for the world," I assured him.

"Not even for England?" he asked in a way that implied he felt the same.

"Would you let me go?" I turned it on him. I had never been anywhere further than our Beach House in my life.

"Have fun tonight, Luce." He knew the question was rhetorical. "Show them what they've been missing." I used to get so upset when I realized that the kids at school were mean to him. He was the coolest kid I had ever met, and they had no idea what they were missing out on.

"OH MY GOD! YOU LOOK AMAZING!" Keisha exclaimed when I got out of the minivan. Not the most glorious mode of transportation, but she was one of the only kids standing outside, and my reputation was non-existent to begin with.

"Look at you!" I reciprocated. "Did you get lost on your way to the Oscars?"

"I thought I'd pop in before going to my real party," she played along. Whereas my dress had volume and screamed princess, hers was long, black, sleek, and showed off a lot more skin than she usually did.

"I really appreciate it. I would be lost in that jungle without you."

"It's senior prom. We have to go, or we'll regret it forever, telling ourselves it could have changed our lives, and all of our dreams would have come true, if only we had gone."

"No regrets," I smiled at her, pretending she was doing this only for potential regrets, rather than because we secretly dreamed of fitting in and being a part of it all.

"Let's do this," she smiled back.

WE HEADED into the yacht club and found the dining hall had been converted into a combination of a movie set and a Royal Ball for our theme of Once Upon a Time in Hollywood. It looked like everyone else chose Hollywood over fairy tales for the dress code, meaning gowns with swooping necklines and side slits, but I in no way regretted my dress.

I was lucky that people at school tended to ignore me more than the bullying I saw in most high school movies. Keisha had decided I was all she needed friend-wise, but it wasn't because anyone had been mean to her. She wouldn't have allowed it. She had a heart of gold, but also a tendency to put you in your place if you tried to belittle someone. I loved watching the shocked faces on some middle graders when they tried catcalling her, but it was less fun when I said something negative about myself and she launched into a lecture. Still, I absolutely loved her for it.

WHEN THE MEAL plates were cleared, they put the music louder. We loved dancing, even if we had no idea how to do it. Grams had taught me ballet when I was little, before she got sick, but that was the extent of dancing lessons I'd received. Any other dancing experience came from Keisha and I hanging out in each other's rooms, usually using a hairbrush to pretend we were singing along to songs from the 60s, 70s, 80s, and the occasional one from Spice Girls or Britney Spears. All this to say we looked like a trainwreck on the dance floor, but I couldn't care less.

"Not him again." Keisha turned away when Tennison walked towards us.

"He's nice, stop it," I warned. She was not a fan of how all the girls were into him, or how he played into it. I appreciated the way he never let popularity dictate how he treated me. Sure, we hung out less, but he was always nice to me.

"Hey Lucy, Keisha," He greeted both of us with a smile.

"Hey Tennison," I acknowledged him, nudging Keisha to do the same.

"I was wondering if you wouldn't mind dancing with me, just for a song?" he asked me, more nervous than I had seen him since our Spanish oral presentation last year.

"Sure," I accepted, getting a slight eye roll from Keisha, who went back to our table.

"We don't have to dance," he told me once she was gone.

"Is everything okay?" I asked. They weren't playing a traditional slow song I would dance with him to, but it would be less weird to dance than to stand in the middle of the dance floor.

"I need your help," he admitted. "I want to ask Keisha to dance with me once there's a slow song."

"Then why didn't you ask her instead of me?" I asked.

"Because she thinks I'm annoying and full of myself." I couldn't argue with that statement, so I let him keep going. "When she turns to you and asks if I'm serious, tell her yes. When she asks if this is a Carrie prank, tell her no, that she is beautiful inside and out and she's funny and strong and fierce and smart and keeps people on their toes and is exactly the dream girl I described to you on our first day in kindergarten."

I was about to tell him I wasn't going to lie to my best friend, when I remembered the conversation he was referring to. "You were talking about Buffy the Vampire Slayer," I argued.

"Yes, but other than actually slaying vampires, is there anything that wasn't accurate?" he asked. I thought about it, comparing his description of Buffy to how he had just described Keisha. Beautiful, funny, fierce, smart...

"You said you wanted a girl who kicks ass," I called him on it, but I was fully on board. I had a suspicion she hated the way he was with other girls and the way they fawned over him because she thought he was better than that. And they liked him for his hair rather than his brain.

"Were you not there at the spelling bee? Or debate meet? Or when Mr. Baltrek called Tiny Tim a cripple?"

"All this time?" I asked him with a smile. The Tiny Tim incident was a week after she arrived in our sixth grade class.

"Do you see anyone else who is anything like her?" he asked.

"Nope," I agreed, trying not to smile so much. I didn't know if Keisha was watching and didn't want to spoil it for her.

"You'll help me?" he asked.

"I'll do what I can," I agreed.

"Thank you," he smiled, looking relieved before taking me in for a hug. "It's kind of full circle, you being my sidekick on the first and last day of school."

"I feel like I have to mention it though; break her heart and I will kill you."

"I know," he assured me.

"You too?" Keisha asked when I got back to the table, before wiping the smile off my face.

"For old time's sake. He's nice," I reminded her.

"Sometimes," she agreed. "Other times I think he's a babbling idiot."

"Most guys are," I teased before we went back on the dance floor.

TENNISON MOVED OFF and on the dance floor, with different groups of friends, but always gravitated towards us, waiting for them to play a slow song. I was about to suggest he go and request one, when the music to 'You and Me' by Lifehouse began.

"I love this song," Keisha said, hinting that she wished we could stay and dance to it.

"Could I have this dance?" Tennison came over and extended his hand.

"Luce?" She turned to me when I didn't answer, annoyed that she was losing her dance partner.

"He's asking you," I argued.

"Making the rounds?" she asked like this was the exact behavior she had come to expect of him.

"More like building up the courage," he shrugged it off, but I could tell he was nervous.

"Is this a Carrie prank?" she asked me, figuring he was nervous because he was about to do something huge and terrible.

"Nope," I told her, smiling. He had known that was exactly where her mind was going to go.

"But he danced with you," she pointed out.

"So that he could dance with you," I agreed.

"That makes no sense."

"Give him a chance," I told her before retreating. She still looked like she wasn't sure, but she trusted me enough to go with it. They looked awkward at first, dancing with a lot of space between them, until she looked up and asked something. His answer took a long time, but by the end of it, they were both smiling and talking while dancing.

"THEY'RE CUTE," Danny Kinks commented, coming to stand beside me. He was a few years ahead of me and had quite the reputation. He brought our school to State every year he was on the team, but took his Junior year off. The official story was a torn ligament, but Tennison said something once that made me think it was an attitude problem that got him benched.

"They are," I agreed, wondering who he came with.

"Danny," he said with a smile, putting his hand on the wall behind me. Guys leaned onto lockers to talk to girls all the time on TV, but I didn't like how he was towering over me.

"Lucy." I gave him a polite smile and spotted his name tag. It made a lot less sense to have him chaperoning than Deanna, if you asked me.

"But now who are you going to dance with?" He came closer, so there was only an inch between us.

"I can wait my turn," I assured him, slowly inching away.

"Doesn't make sense, a pretty girl like you all alone on the sidelines. I'll dance with you," he said as though he was doing me a favor.

"I'm not much of a dancer," I argued, trying to get by him.

"Of course you are." He abruptly brought his other hand up to the wall, making me flinch. There was an arm on either side of me, the wall behind me and him in front of me. All I could smell was the whiskey and cigarettes from his breath. I scanned the room, but couldn't see any teachers or other chaperones, and Keisha had her eyes closed while she leaned into Tennison.

"I really don't feel like it, I..." I tried to stay polite and act normal, but he was making me incredibly uncomfortable.

"This might loosen you up," he offered, pressing his flask to my mouth, but I managed to turn away. It had the same notes of whiskey as his breath, minus the cigarettes.

"I would really like to get back to my table," I tried, but he leaned his forearms on the wall, bringing himself a lot closer.

"I'll bring you back when I'm done with you." He had the kind of smile that was reveling in my discomfort.

"Please let me go," I asked as politely as I could, trying to sound confident and strong, but I was terrified, and he knew it.

"What will you give me if I do?" He took a swig of his flask. I took advantage of the space that created, moving before his drunken faculties could react.

"I need to use the ladies' room," I told him, sliding under his arm and rushing to the one place he couldn't follow me into.

"I'll be right here," he called after me. I could hear the smile in his statement. He knew I was trying to escape and he wanted to let me know I wasn't getting away that easily.

I HAD LEFT my clutch on the table while I danced with Keisha, so I couldn't call her. Once my heart slowed to a normal rhythm I remembered that she was dancing with Tennison, her fairytale prom moment, and I would kill anyone who took that away from me, even if it was me. I could borrow the phone of the next person who came in and call Sam or Deanna, who would be there within 15 minutes. I was fairly certain Danny chose me because I was alone and friendless, so even if Deanna was the one to get me from the washroom, he wouldn't dare do anything. But that would mean bothering them, being the damsel in distress, and letting my entire graduating class watch me get escorted from prom by my guardians. That was not going to happen. Not tonight.

All I wanted to do was go home, change into my pajamas and curl up with a warm tea and a book on anatomy or systems. There was the possibility that Danny would get bored and leave, but I had no way of knowing without going back out. There was also a chance that the alcohol in his flask was strong enough to convince him to come into the washroom to get me. Which was not a chance I was willing to take.

I saw the window was open to let in a breeze and remembered how I used to sneak in and out of our kitchen window, so Mrs. Boyd wouldn't know I was gone. At the time I thought I was so smart for tricking her. I never considered that sneaking out to play in the mud brought damning evidence of its own.

I sighed and looked at myself in the mirror before going back to the window. We were on the ground floor. It didn't look like it would be difficult to take out the screen. The manor was only about an hour's walk from the yacht club, meaning I would be home long before curfew, but close enough that they wouldn't ask questions and be concerned.

"I'm really doing this," I said out loud to myself, looking around to see if there was a better option, but the bathroom offered no solutions. I shook my head at myself before removing the bug screen and leaning it against the side of the window.

I did not feel like a princess as I bunched up the bottom of my dress and hoisted myself onto the ledge of the window. Luckily, it was big enough that I could turn to get my legs through, because I would have fallen on my butt otherwise.

Once I was out, with my heels sinking into the muddy ground, I reached in to get the screen and place it back. I couldn't put it in properly, but at least it looked a lot less suspicious if Danny sent anyone in looking for me.

I was looking back at the yacht club to make sure I hadn't been followed, that Danny Kinks was still in the hallway waiting for me, when I collided with something a lot softer than a tree, but much harder than the clear path I was traveling towards.

CHAPTER THREE

They were here. Or at least one of them was, but Gabriel never came by without Embry.

"Get in the car," he said with his serious intensity. He acted like there was nothing unusual about me climbing out of a bathroom window in a prom dress, but I still felt like I had done something wrong.

I followed him to a beat-up Tercel, which was not a car I had seen him driving before. I had barely shut the door when he put the car in drive and started moving. He wasn't going more than a couple of miles over the speed limit, but he was clearly in a hurry.

"I'm sorry," I told him, assuming I had done something wrong by the look on his face. I had no idea if it was talking to strangers, climbing out the window, or going to prom in the first place...all I knew was that something was upsetting him.

He turned as if he was going to say something, then went back to the road for the rest of the drive. He barely even glanced in my direction, except to make sure I was okay after he made a sudden stop to avoid a raccoon.

I tried to hurry behind him as he walked straight into the manor, looking over his shoulder like he expected Clara to jump out at us from the bushes. He opened the door without knocking and waited for me to go in first before calling, "Samuel!" in a tone that suggested he might be in trouble as well.

"Embry!" Clara called, rushing down the stairs to us. She was disappointed when she realized it was only Gabriel, but kept coming until she saw his face. Gabriel would sometimes let her jump into his arms, but tonight she didn't even try.

"Where is your father?" Gabriel asked her, making it sound like an interrogation rather than a question.

"Where's Embry?" she asked, suddenly small.

"He'll be here shortly," he placated her with a quick answer. "Where is your father?" he repeated.

"What's going on?" Sam asked, coming down the stairs.

Gabriel gave him a look before they both went to the kitchen.

"Aren't you supposed to be in bed?" I turned to Clara when they made it clear I wasn't welcome to follow.

"I thought Embry was here," she defended.

"You still have to sleep." I pointed my finger at her, knowing she would laugh.

"Gabriel looks mad," she told me.

"I'm sure your dad will calm him down," I said hopefully.

"Do you think Embry will be here when I wake up?" she asked.

"Gabriel said shortly," I shrugged my shoulders to let her know I didn't have any extra information.

"Maybe we can play hide and seek with him," she suggested through a yawn.

"I'm sure he would be happy to." I gave her a smile I only half-believed. *Gabriel wouldn't lie to her*, I told myself, but the uneasy feeling came back when I remembered that I had spent the past week lying to Clara because I didn't want to worry her.

ONCE CLARA WAS TUCKED in bed, hopefully sleeping, I called Keisha from the house phone to let her know I was okay and Gabriel brought me home. I could hear Tennison in the background, as well as the smile in her voice.

"You can come see me anytime at MIT. And we can do lunch every week."

"It's a 20-minute walk. We'll have study sessions and sneak into each other's libraries. It'll be awesome," I assured her before Tennison asked who she was talking to.

"I so would have regretted not coming," she told me before we said our goodbyes.

I WENT BACK DOWNSTAIRS and waited in the hallway to be allowed into the conversation of the kitchen. Gabriel had looked intense and scary at the yacht club, which was the only reason I was waiting in the hall instead of barging in and demanding answers. I was shaken when he showed up, but he had no reason to be mad at me. I had every right to know why he missed my graduation and ignored my calls. I spent an entire week thinking something terrible had happened to them. I still wasn't sure if that was the case or not. He was mad, or upset, which told me he either didn't agree with me going to college in the fall (even though I chose the closest one), or something serious was going on that he thought I was too young to handle.

After what felt like an eternity, the voices stopped, so I decided that was my cue to come in. They were both standing by the kitchen table. While Sam at least glanced in my direction, looking apologetic, neither of them said a word.

Gabriel was solemn, like the first day I met him almost fourteen years ago. It was definitely not good news. I also got the feeling it had nothing to do with my going to Harvard.

"Gabriel?" I asked, going closer to him, trying to catch his eye.

"Why don't you go see Deanna in the studio for a little bit?" Sam suggested when Gabriel stayed silent.

"What is going on?" I asked Gabriel, not at all impressed with his game. I hadn't seen him in months, he hadn't come to my graduation and now he was avoiding me. "Where's Embry?" I hoped he might answer if the question wasn't about him. Embry didn't usually go this long without a visit, and he always texted or called when he couldn't make it. Until last week.

"He's coming," Gabriel said with so little conviction, I worried that he might not be avoiding me so much as trying to find the words to tell me my death magnet struck again. It was the most likely explanation. That something happened to Embry. It explained him not coming to my graduation and ignoring me. Why else wouldn't Embry be here, apologizing profusely?

"Lucy, could you please give us a moment?" Sam asked of me. There was a pleading desperation in his voice. That, paired with me no longer knowing if I wanted to know what was going on, made me oblige.

I was on my way to the back door when Gabriel spoke, stopping me in my tracks.

"She shouldn't go outside. I'll bring her to the plantation. We can't let anyone else in." His talking showed an improvement, but he was talking to Sam as if I wasn't even there, and not making much sense.

"What do you mean?" I asked at the same time as Sam.

"Shouldn't Deanna and Clara go with her?" He looked

43

worried, which I liked about as much as Gabriel's aloofness. I kept my hand on the door because if there was something dangerous out there, we should get Deanna back inside. The studio was basically a gazebo, and I doubt paintbrushes would be useful in a fight.

"I don't think they're at risk once Lucy is removed, but you could set them up at the beach house if it will make you feel safer," Gabriel offered.

"Once I'm removed? What the hell are you guys talking about?" I let go of the handle and focused on my anger, not wanting them to know how annoyed and hurt I was. Not to mention terrified.

"Not like that," Sam tried to reassure me.

"Like what?" I asked.

"We need to leave the manor and take you far away, where you can't be found," Gabriel said like it was supposed to make sense, looking down at his hands instead of up at me.

"Found by who? For how long?" I asked the first of dozens of questions that were forming.

"Indefinitely."

"No," I flat out refused. "I have college and orientation and a chance to start over as something other than the weird Owens girl and…"

"You're going with Gabriel," Sam overruled me. "You can defer and go next year, or once it's safe, but I am not losing you so that you can feel normal," he added when I looked at him with shock, but that only made it worse.

"Lose me?" I asked. "Neither of you are making any sense."

"A long time ago, I made a promise to protect you and keep you safe. Up to recently that meant checking in on you and making sure you were okay, but now it means taking you away from here." Gabriel looked up to me at the end.

"Who did you promise?" I asked him, trying to understand. He and Embry had shown up out of the blue at Grams' funeral and inserted themselves into my life. They said they were old friends of the family, but there had to be more to it.

"Annabelle," Gabriel said simply.

I looked to Sam before coming back to Gabriel. "My doll?"

"She was a person before she was a doll. I'm sure Evelyn told you."

"My ancestor," I agreed. "Grams told me fairy tales about her from an old book."

While most girls were raised on Cinderella, Snow White and Sleeping Beauty, my grandmother had recited stories from an old, leather-bound book. My mom might have read me the normal stories before she died, because I knew enough to ask my grandmother why her princesses never found their princes or lived happily ever after. "There are much more important things than finding a prince," she'd say before continuing her tales. She would open the book to the right page, but she'd tell me the story like she had been there, or rather like it had been told to her a thousand times. She would tell me about Rosie saving soldiers from a mudslide, Beth singing on stage at a speakeasy, Cassie meeting the Queen and Annabelle bravely crossing oceans...I knew them all, but Gabriel couldn't have met them.

"The Chronicles," Gabriel agreed.

"Is that what the book was called?"

"No, it's what it is. Annabelle started it when she left England, and the major events have been recorded in it ever since."

"And I guess Rosie, Cassie and Beth filled in the rest?" I rolled my eyes, naming my other ancestral dolls.

"Some more than others," he agreed. "Rosie's was mostly stories she told us because she never had to deal with the dangers..."

"What dangers, Gabriel?" I cut him off. "The Annabelle my doll was named after lived in the 1600s. Rosie was there on the first Independence Day, so I doubt she told you anything." Gabriel looked at me like he was wondering how much he should tell me, while Sam didn't look confused or surprised about these tall tales Gabriel was telling. It was like he took it all as fact.

"I was born here in 1662. I met Annabelle the day she arrived and have loved her every minute since. Before she died, she asked me to keep her daughter safe, so that is what I have been doing for centuries," Gabriel emphasized the last word. "Most of the time I stay in the shadows and watch from a distance, but every once in a while, one of you will look like her and then we do what we have to, so he can't get you."

"He?" I needed clarifications.

"The Big Bad who is after you," Sam shared.

I turned back to Gabriel. "You and Embry have been protecting me and my dolls from a guy who wants to hurt us..." I tried to sum it all up.

"The women the dolls represent," Gabriel corrected, which made the story even less plausible. He looked relieved that I was getting it, whereas I was trying to point out how crazy he sounded.

"They lived centuries ago," I reminded him, not believing that he was born in 1662 and had been hanging around for centuries to keep me safe.

"Correct," he stuck to his story.

"And you believe him?" I turned to Sam. It didn't make sense that he was going along with it.

"My mom did," he admitted. "My dad hated them, but even he told me that if ever a time came where you were in danger and they showed up, I was to let them do whatever they needed, because keeping you safe is why they're still alive."

"You're my guardian angel?" I asked Gabriel. I still found it ludicrous, but while Sam might have gone along with a prank,

Gabriel had rarely been anything but completely serious. As far as I knew, he didn't even have a sense of humor.

"Cassie tried calling us that, but I'm no angel."

"What are you then?" I was still skeptical. "A vampire? Do you have horns that sprout at night? Do you ride around on a broom?"

"This is serious Lucy." Gabriel wasn't yelling at me, but I could tell he was on a short fuse.

"You're the one who's implying you're immortal."

"I'm not immortal. I'm sticking around because I have a job to do," he argued.

"Protecting me."

"Yes," he agreed. "Which is why we have to leave. Now."

I was about to argue, but Sam spoke before I could. "Why don't you go upstairs and pack up some things." I wanted to say no and keep asking questions, but he gave me that look, where he was pleading and needed me to do it, so I sighed before reluctantly going up the stairs, shaking my head at the two of them.

"Pack light, but for a long time," Gabriel advised, which was much easier said than done.

My room, like me, had changed a lot since I used to beg Grams to show me the dolls and read me their stories. The teddies and costumes were replaced by books, and the walls held posters of skeletal structures and anatomy instead of Beauty and the Beast decals. The dolls were still up on a shelf that was no longer too high for me to reach, but it had been ages since I had taken them down.

I tried to imagine Gabriel interacting with them, the women from my family who died centuries ago, but that was a lot easier when I was a child who believed in magic. I wondered where the old book had gone. I had asked for their stories at first, but

Sam said he didn't know any, and Mrs. Boyd ran out of them pretty quickly.

I figured the best way to comply with Gabriel's instructions would be to limit myself to whatever I could fit in my backpack. I packed it like I would for a sleepover at Keisha's, the two times that happened, then added my tiny old photo album. I doubted Gabriel would see the point, but it had all the pictures I had of my mother and Grams, the one picture I had of my father, as well as a few of Mr. and Mrs. Boyd. It wasn't something I took out frequently, but if we were going to be gone indefinitely, just the two of us, I got the feeling I might be homesick. Gabriel had been popping into my life sporadically since he showed up when I was five, but he had always been more reserved than Embry.

I put the copy of Gray's Anatomy that Sam had given me for graduation and some medical journals into the part that was for laptops. I was scanning the room to make sure I hadn't forgotten anything when Deanna walked in. She used to knock, even when the door was open, and wait for my permission to come in, but eventually she decided I was family, and family doesn't need permission. She never once acted like my mother, and I wouldn't want her to, but I appreciated having something like an older sister since she married Sam. She hadn't expected to have to raise a fifteen-year-old a couple of years into her marriage, but she stepped up to the plate like there was nothing she wanted more.

"I finished the laundry while you were escaping through bathroom windows." She gave me a look while putting a pile down on my bed. She must have seen the guys before coming up. "I didn't want you to forget this." She took my old blankie from the top of the pile and handed it to me. It was thin and white, made from a bamboo-like material, the kind that keeps you cool if you wear it in the sun, but warm if you're cold. It had a purple threaded border and my name in eggplant on the corner, with a pink heart underneath.

"I don't..." I was about to tell her that I was basically a grown woman and didn't need my blankie anymore, but she looked at me like she wasn't going to believe it.

"I'm not going to remind you that I was already dating Sam when you went through that phase where it never left your sight, or that it lasted two years and only ended when you thought you lost it and Martha suggested you keep it on your bed," she said, doing exactly what she said she wouldn't. "But if you're going somewhere far from those of us who love you, I want you to have it."

"Did they tell you what's going on?" I asked her, putting the blankie into my backpack.

"Sam filled me in," she agreed.

"And?" I waited for her to be the voice of reason.

"Years ago, when Sam first told me about it, I thought he had gone mad. Then I talked to Embry and...I'm glad they're looking out for you."

"Embry confirmed Gabriel's story of them being over three-hundred years old and put here to protect me?" I asked, hoping she would crack and admit it was all a joke.

"They don't get any older, Luce." She could tell I was having trouble accepting it. "Ask Embry about it when he gets here. He spent hours answering my questions."

"Is he even coming?"

"I don't think Gabriel would lie. About something like that," she added when I raised my eyebrows.

"Are you afraid?" I asked.

"I have it in my mind that Embry and Gabriel are invincible and the best at whatever it is they do, so I'm going to go the Beach House, make sandcastles, eat seafood, then hopefully come back and help you pack this all up for a dorm room."

"That's it?" I asked. The boys were way more scary and serious about it.

"That's it," she agreed.

"It was never because I needed a blankie. I knew it wouldn't keep me safe or any of those foolish kid reasons," I defended myself from her earlier comments. "My mother made it for me when I was a baby."

"I know," she assured me, like she understood, before going back to her own packing.

"I WANT TO GO WITH LUCY!" Clara was pleading as I came downstairs with my backpack. The ears from her bunny onesie flew as she shook her head, pouting through all her freckles.

"Sweetie, you, me and mommy are going on a trip of our own. You're going to have all kinds of fun!" Sam tried to calm her down and act like this was an exciting adventure.

"Please Lucy, please!" She ran over and wrapped her arms around my legs.

"Clara, if you let go of my legs, I'll make you chocolate chip cookies," I offered as a bribe, knowing they were her weakness.

"But how will I get them?" she asked, wise beyond her 5 years of age.

"I'll give them to your daddy and he'll bring them to you," I promised, looking to Sam for confirmation. He looked to Gabriel, who didn't look convinced, but nodded anyway.

"Promise?" she asked her dad, knowing he had more of a say than I did.

"I promise," he agreed. Clara let go of me and ran into his arms, but there was a guilty look to him that made me doubt his keeping his word, at least not for a while.

"I'm ready," I told Gabriel, who had stayed quiet throughout this whole debacle. It wasn't just me he was acting indifferent to…he was a lot nicer to Clara the last few times he came.

Without saying anything, Gabriel effortlessly picked up an oversized suitcase I had never seen before. He walked to the garage while I said goodbye to the people who had long ago become my family. I knew Sam was bringing his wife and daughter to the summer house and Gabe was taking me to the old plantation, things we did every year, but I felt the same as Clara.

CHAPTER FOUR

"The black one," I told Gabriel once I got to the garage and found him trying to decide which vehicle to take. We had a collection of expensive vintage cars from my great-grandfather, but Sam bought me a newer one when I got my driver's license, making sure it had all the best safety features, like the mini-van he was strapping his daughter into.

I watched Deanna's minivan drive out, then punched in the alarm code, got into the passenger's seat and let Gabriel take me to the plantation. My family had lived there for generations, until Cassie married Alan Roosevelt and we moved into the manor. I still spent a couple of weeks there every summer with Embry, but I hadn't been since it was remodeled last Fall.

"Speak," I said while we drove through the wooded trails. Most people would feel safest near a city, or in a place where you could walk to your neighbor's without it taking you an hour, but the plantation was completely isolated. There was the forest between the plantation property and the manor, then acres of land between it and any neighboring fields. It would be easy to keep track of any incoming visitors, but outside help would be extremely hard to come by.

"There's nothing to talk about," he dismissed me, keeping his eyes on the road.

"How about, 'Hi Lucy, it's been a while! How was graduation? It's good to see you too?'" I gave him suggestions.

"It's best if we stay quiet," he warned, still not looking at me.

I leaned over and turned the radio on to whatever station annoyed him the most. I didn't particularly enjoy the techno station either, but I could practically see the vein pulsing in his forehead while he forced himself to keep on ignoring me instead of making me change it. I would find it funny if I wasn't so worried and annoyed with him.

WHEN WE GOT to the house, he parked and got out of the car.

"What are you doing?" I asked. It could have been some prank to leave me alone in the middle of nowhere, but he left the key in the ignition.

"The house was retrofitted in case something like this ever happened. They had your DNA so you have free roam of the house, but everyone else needs to be given permission for each room."

"Like vampires need to be invited into your house? Or like booby traps and trolls?"

"With a high-tech computer security system. Embry and Sam know more about what happens if someone isn't invited in, but I got the impression it was more like loud noises and laser beams." He wasn't amused by my question, but it sounded just as reasonable as the rest of his story. I wanted to point out that getting dissected by laser beams was way more intense than being yelled at by an alarm, but Gabriel walked away from the car and motioned for me to drive up.

I tried to move into the driver's seat as gracefully as I could in my prom dress, but there was a lot of tulle and it was tight in places that made this incredibly difficult.

I stopped in front of the garage and wondered how I was going to get it to open. I was about to try 'Open Sesame' when a dark grey box came out of a hole in the ground, adjusting itself to be at my eye level.

"State your name," a computer-animated voice rang out.

"Lucy Owens," I said, but nothing happened. "Lucine Suzanne Owens." It was on my birth certificate, but no one ever called me by it. Except when Mrs. Boyd had been upset, or wanted to make sure I listened to her.

"Vocal Recognition Achieved. Move closer."

I saw the screen had switched to a handprint, so I put mine down and waited for it to say, "Digital Imprint Approved. Look here."

Here was a vague description, but the handprint was replaced by a red dot, so I moved closer and stared into the screen.

"Welcome Lucy, please proceed."

The garage door opened, and the inside looked the same as it always had. It was big enough for two cars, but half the space was taken up by bikes and toboggans and junk that hadn't been used in my lifetime. The major difference was a grid made from tiny green lasers. I bit my bottom lip as I drove through it, half-expecting it to chop me into tiny pieces like in Resident Evil.

I looked back to Gabriel, who called out, "I'll patrol tonight. Shut the door and get some sleep."

IT WAS EASIER SAID than done. He watched as I shut the garage door, but once I was in the house, other than the little computer screens that showed an analysis of every ChapStick and pack of gum it found when scanning the car, everything was dark.

I was always more afraid of the unseen than of the creatures that lurked in the night, but I was currently wishing that whoever put me into the system would have put Embry and

Gabriel into it as well. Yes, it made sense to not let other people in if there was some evil guy trying to kill me, but the guys protecting me should be allowed to follow me in.

I tried to find the light switch, so I could look for a user's manual that would allow me company, but they moved the switches when they remodeled. I knocked over what sounded like a vase, and the crash nearly made my heart stop. For the third time tonight, I was terrified. I didn't like not knowing things and Gabriel's ridiculous story made me feel like it was just as likely that a zombie would crash through the window as a burglar or a ninja assassin.

I found a light switch just as something else fell, either from the wind or some side effect of my stumbling around, but my heart felt like it was going to leap out of my chest. I quickly walked to the front of the house, turning on every light on my way. As soon as I got close, I ran to the front door and wrenched it open, calling out to him, "Gabriel!"

He had been off in the woods, but got to the porch before I even finished his name. "What's wrong?" he asked, looking into my eyes with all of the intensity I could remember from his visits. He used to come every time Embry did, or at least summers and most holidays, but I either did something or he got bored and stopped coming right after my eighteenth birthday.

"I understand that you want me to stay here alone, but is it really breaking the rules if you stayed on the balcony tonight?" I asked of him, suddenly nervous. Embry was the easy-to-talk-to one who would understand that the last thing I wanted to do after being ripped from my home because my life was suppos-edly in danger was to spend the night in a huge, mostly un-lived in house, alone. I would prefer Embry or Sam or Deanna, but Gabriel could do the trick if he stopped running away.

He looked angry that I had made him worry and rush to my side for nothing, but I think he understood, though he hated it.

If he didn't want me to imagine the worst and scare myself into a heart attack, he either had to give me more information, or stay close.

"Just tonight," he warned before walking away.

"THANK YOU," I told Gabriel, handing him sheets and pillows through the French doors that led to the balcony from my bedroom. The thought had occurred to me that he agreed because the balcony could be a liability otherwise, but I was comforted all the same.

"You should get some sleep," he said dismissively, keeping his eyes on the bundle I had given him.

"Gabe, could you please just tell me who this Big Bad is? And why you're being cold and distant? Are you going to hurt me? Will I hurt you? Are you keeping a secret and you're worried I'll get you to tell me? Give me a reason," I asked, putting a pillow and blanket for myself on the bean bag near the balcony. This wasn't the first time I'd had someone camp out here, although last time it was Embry who stayed on the balcony with me. At the time, he'd said he wanted to see the stars, but now I was thinking it might have been to keep an eye on me, like Gabriel was doing now.

"He knows you're here," he told me simply, like it was something I should understand.

"I've always been here. Grams kept me locked up in the manor. The Boyds let me get out sometimes, but they still keep me close. We've been here for generations," I reminded him, starting to take out the bobby pins that kept my prom hair in place.

"He checks in on your line every once in a while, but a lot less than we do. I knew the moment I saw you, even if you were younger, that he would come after you. Because you look like Annabelle."

"Like all the dolls," I realized. One for each of us the Big Bad hunted.

"We've kept an eye on every woman in your family, but you, Beth, Cassie and Rosie were the only ones who looked like Annabelle."

"Because we're related." I knew the dolls looked the same, but Grams could always tell them apart. She liked to call it a family resemblance.

"Identical," he argued. "Down to the very last freckle. The only differences are the ones you make, or don't. Scars, haircuts, tattoos...but every dimple, everything about you is her." He looked at me with a different kind of intensity, filled with pain.

"He's been hunting her since the 1600s and now he's after me." I nodded like this made sense and wasn't terrifying.

"He hasn't made a move yet, but he will."

"How do you know he knows?" I pressed.

"He's recruiting."

"An army?" I could picture those old Uncle Sam posters shouting, 'We Want You!'.

"He has the ability to control people who are like me and Embry. If he touches you, it forms a bond and he can manipulate you, even if he's far away. People like us are disappearing."

"What do you mean by people like you? Immortals?"

"Some people like us live a normal life and then die without coming back. It's only if you die before you accomplish what you're meant to do. There's no official name, but some call us The Gifted." He revealed that he wasn't invincible, he just came back to life whenever he died.

"And they're all protecting people?" I asked of The Gifted.

"No, but we all have something to do. Some of them are poets or authors or great figures in history. Scientists and explorers. It's an insurance policy to make sure the world doesn't go without whatever their talents are. Embry likes to tell it like they all had great tasks to accomplish, but Einstein also created the hydrogen bomb, and Hitler did a whole lot of shitty stuff before he finally got it right."

"Einstein and Hitler?" I asked, to which he nodded. "I'm pretty sure Hitler didn't get anything right."

"He lost his way and became the dictator he was born to defeat, but he did accomplish his task eventually." I waited for him to smile, or tell me he was teasing.

"When he committed suicide?" I asked, making sure that was what he was implying.

"There are many ways to get something done, and not all of it is pretty. The pharaohs turned their people into slaves to get the pyramids, we used nuclear power as a weapon instead of an energy source...not all contributions are worth it." He sounded bitter, but I couldn't tell if it was over the horrible things that happened on the way to discoveries, or the pointlessness of his contribution.

"And if my Big Bad controls these people, he can use them forever, making them commit murders, as long as they never do what they were supposed to?" I verified, not liking it one bit.

"It won't work forever. Once you discover what it is you need to accomplish, the drive is almost impossible to say no to. Some people tried to avoid their calling so they could live forever, but it doesn't work."

"Is he like you? The guy who is after me?"

"Yes."

"And what he needs to accomplish is to kill me?" I confirmed. There had to be a worthwhile reason for me to die if the universe was giving him an insurance policy for it. How horrible was I going to become?

"I don't know what he needs to accomplish. I don't know if he's working on something else and happens to want revenge over some slight from Annabelle..."

"But he's definitely trying to kill me, and you and Embry are staying alive to protect me from him?"

"Among other things," he agreed.

"Is Embry okay?" I asked, worried that maybe he was one of the people being recruited, which would mean the end game for me. Even if Embry and Gabriel weren't exactly friends, they would still lay down their lives for each other, which meant that if Embry was sent to kill me, both of us would let him. Or at least I would.

"He's on his way," he assured me. "He hasn't been recruited, he's just taking his time to be safe. We believe the bond breaks and has to be re-established every time you die, so Embry would be a prime target. And in case it doesn't, we can't risk getting too close to you." He implied that they'd been under his control before.

"Do you know why he wants to kill us, or what Annabelle did to him?" I asked, taking advantage of him answering me, but it was one question too many, as he sighed.

"Get some sleep, Lucy." He let me know the conversation was over.

I let out a loud sigh, to let him know I was annoyed too, and wasn't happy with everything he was keeping from me. Still, I wasn't going to press after he had conceded to partially explain it to me.

I WENT over to the walk-in closet and managed to untie the bow at the bottom of my back, which loosened the gown enough that I could wiggle and step out of it. *Magical proms*, I thought to myself, though this was not at all what I had imagined. I found a pair of sweatpants and T-shirt and put them on, still trying to wrap my head around everything I was supposed to believe now. True, Embry and Gabriel didn't look any older, but neither did Sam. Younger me would have believed all of it. She believed in fairy tales and magic, but the only way my life compared to a fairy tale was the castle-like manor and people dying around me. Which was cancer, not magic.

I WENT BACK to Gabriel and tried to get comfy on the beanie bag, playing with my pillow and blankets, but I knew I wasn't going to sleep anyway. I was used to losing people after my mom, my grandmother, Mrs. Boyd and Mr. Boyd, but Sam had always been there for me. He was like a big brother before his parents took me in, before I even met Gabriel or Embry, and now he felt so far away, with his family possibly in danger, because of me.

I kept glancing at Gabriel, who wasn't moving, but couldn't be comfortable on the ground like that. I wondered if he had old bones and a bad back, even though he didn't look to be older than his early twenties. His skin was tanned, but otherwise flawless; no wrinkles, no cuts, and no bruises. I was wondering if he was sleeping, which was almost impossible, when he said, "You could always sleep in the bed," with his eyes still closed.

"I'm fine," I assured him, deciding to lie on my side. It wasn't exactly comfortable, but I didn't want him to make me leave if I moved around too much.

I concentrated on watching him sleep for a while. He was the more intimidating of the two. The one who never warmed up to most people, but asleep like this, with his dark hair a mess, his face peaceful…it almost made you forget how he could get when he was awake.

CHAPTER FIVE

A nnabelle held her daughter close and walked into the church with purpose, her head held high. This was not a defeat, she reminded herself, this was coming home. She had waited until the last of the stragglers had gone inside to make sure that no one would try and talk to her. She was slightly surprised, but also expecting it when her usual spot was empty, even after she hadn't attended in years.

It was only once she sat down and placed Margaret on her lap that she allowed herself to look up, just a quick glance, barely a second, to see if he was there. As soon as she lifted her head, her eyes locked on his, and she had to turn away. That little moment was enough to make the emotions rush back, and the tears threatened to overwhelm her. Whether out of habit or simple inattention, when turning to avoid Gabriel, her eyes rested on Embry, who looked so happy to see her that she had to turn away from him as well.

Annabelle could feel eyes on her during the entire service, with the hairs on the back of her neck sticking up, but she managed to convince herself that it wasn't them; the boys she had loved. She knew that the entire congregation had reason to be staring at her, gossiping about how she had returned after five years, without a husband, but with a daughter. They would be wondering what happened to bring her back, *why she left in the first place, if there ever was a husband, if he deserted her, died or was coming with the rest of their household.*

WHEN THE SERVICE ended and people made their way outside the church, Annabelle followed Father Brown to the side of the altar.

"I was surprised when you asked to see me, Miss Owens," he said, eying Margaret, waiting for her to correct him on her name.

"It's Mrs. Hathorne now," she assured him, noticing that he exhaled and smiled, the relief obvious on his face.

"Your letter mentioned a baptism?" he asked.

"Yes, for Margaret," she agreed, looking down at the sleeping child, who smiled when her mother kissed her forehead.

"This has not yet been done?" Father Brown inquired, worried about what kind of heathen his parishioner had married. She had perhaps left town, but a shepherd never gave up on his flock.

"Yes, she has, of course," Annabelle assured him.

"I'm afraid I don't understand what you're asking of me."

"There were some rumors about the priest in the town where we were raising Margaret. I would hate to think my child would not..."

"Of course," he understood, cutting her off, not wanting to hear about any rumors that would tarnish the reputation of the church. It was enough to have rumors of witchcraft floating around, he didn't want to dignify them with a denial, or even admit to their existence. "Will your husband be joining us?"

"I'm afraid he is no longer of this world," she said, bringing her hand to her heart.

"I am glad you are turning to God for solace in your time of mourning. The baptism can be as soon as next Sunday."

"I appreciate it, Father," Annabelle said before making her way out of the church. A few women had stayed to eavesdrop on the conversation, and others were waiting to speak to the priest as well, but most people had gone back to their fields, or Sunday activities. She knew better than to expect that Gabriel and Embry would have gone home *after she returned to town without so much as a word to either of them.*

Embry was to the right of the door, playing with his niece and nephews as if he hadn't a care in the world, though he glanced up almost as soon as she walked out, and smiled. He kept playing with the children, but it would be rude if she didn't go see him now, and no matter how things had ended when she left, he was still one of her closest friends.

"You're like a vision after so long in the dark," he said dramatically after whispering something to his niece once Annabelle was in front of him.

"You haven't changed at all." She had been nervous about seeing them again. The warm smile Embry offered made her want nothing more than to let him take her in his arms and tell her everything would work out. Embry was so optimistic that he would believe it, and she would be forced to do the same.

"You have," he said. "I mean, you're as beautiful as ever, but this little lady and I have yet to be introduced."

"Margaret," she smiled. "My daughter and the absolute love of my life."

Embry nodded, then said, "She's beautiful," but looked at Annabelle in a way that made her heart beat faster than normal.

He continued to smile at her, and she got the feeling he could keep at it all day, but she could feel herself blushing. She could only imagine what her mother would say if she could see her. Of course, her mother wouldn't have approved with the direction she took the conversation in either. "I'm sorry I left," she told him, hoping he understood how truly she meant it.

"We don't have to get into that," he assured her, but he looked away, and she knew it was because she had hurt him, and he didn't want her to see that.

"I have felt terrible about it. I should have explained myself and..."

"I wouldn't do well to pine over a married woman anyhow." He resumed his smiling, but there was a question to the statement.

"*A widow,*" *she corrected him a moment before realizing life here would be so much easier if she had said her husband was on a ship back to Europe or some excuse that left her unavailable.*

"*Then we might effectively have some talking to do.*" *The happiness this brought him nearly broke her heart, but she couldn't bear to mislead him either.*

"*I would love to have you and Gabriel over for some tea this afternoon, but you must understand that Margaret is my priority.*"

"*As it should be,*" *he assured her, but not in a way that implied he understood her meaning.* "*And I would love to join you for tea this afternoon. Although I'm afraid Gabriel might not be so inclined.*" *He nodded to a spot behind her, so she turned around and saw a young woman openly flirting with Gabriel under the watchful eye of who must be her mother. Her heart literally stopped as she watched them, or at least it felt like it did. Gabriel was the perfect gentleman, smiling and making her laugh, this young girl who was smitten with him, but Annabelle consoled herself by deciding that the smile did not reach his eyes. Those beautiful brown eyes that she was convinced followed her the moment she turned away.*

"*He can bring his friend if he likes. It's simply an afternoon among my oldest and most beloved friends.*" *Annabelle hoped she managed a polite smile, but every time she heard that girl laugh, it felt like a knife was being twisted around inside her chest, eviscerating her heart.*

I WOKE UP WITH A START, a feeling of fear and heartbreak overwhelming me. I'd been having a dream that felt so real, but I knew I wasn't me. It was like I was experiencing it from inside the person it was happening to. This wasn't the first time. While I had long ago resigned myself to them, I now knew that Sam and his parents were wrong to tell me they were just dreams, nothing to concern myself with. The dreams were memories. Not mine, of course, but my ancestors'. I used to think it was my brain revisiting the stories Grams had told me; elaborate masquerade balls, romantic entanglements and European adventures. Given everything I found out yesterday, I knew I was visiting Annabelle's memory. They had always been so vivid and exhilarating, but this time the memory wasn't so pleasant.

I TURNED to the spot where Gabriel had spent the night and only saw the blanket and pillow, neatly folded as if they hadn't been used. I brought them inside, then stepped onto the balcony, knowing he wouldn't be too far.

This was one of my favorite spots on the plantation. It was high enough that you could see everything. If I went to the left side, I could see the meadow leading to the creek, with the little row boat I always begged to go out on. I had convinced Sam to take me out once, but I spent the whole time telling him about the scene in the Notebook with all of the swans. He spent his time laughing at me, until the rain came down in buckets, like in the movie. He swore, which he wasn't supposed to do in front of me, but it only made me laugh harder while he tried to row us back to the dock. We were both soaking wet. He told me I would have to do the rowing next time, but we never went out again.

In front, all you could see were trees. Big, weeping willows I used to associate with Pocahontas. For years after Grams died I would go out there and talk to the biggest one I could find, pretending that she was talking back. Embry found me once. I knew Grams wasn't really in the tree, but I wasn't ready for him to tell me that. Luckily, he was the type of grown up who understood those things, so he sat with me and pretended he could hear her too. By the end of it, I was wondering if maybe she actually was in the tree. Embry also used to pretend he could see our manor from the balcony, even though it was at the other end of the forest. I thought he had way better eyesight than I did. I would test him, asking what color the curtains were, how many windows…he would squint really hard as if he was trying to see further, then would answer the question. I was amazed by him. It never occurred to me that he had been coming to the manor for years, and knew these details about it, just like I did.

The view to my right held less pleasant memories, but the cemetery was still beautiful. I vaguely remembered my grandmother bringing me there to see my mother's grave, but after she died, Mrs. Boyd only brought me there once or twice, saying I could pay my respects without having to spend the day in a cemetery. Still, every time I found myself in this house, I would come out here and look upon the big white marble statues of angels and saints. Even from my balcony, I knew exactly which one was my mother's, and my grandmother's, but I didn't know most of the others. It was our family plot though, so they were all from the long line of women I came from.

Most cultures value male offspring, putting so much stock into heirs that would carry on the family name. In my family, whether by choice or by design, we were all women. I couldn't tell you how far back it went, but so much as I could tell, it was only ever the daughters who went on to continue the line, keeping the name of Owens and passing it on through generations. The only men who had tombstones in our cemetery were either their husbands or their sons who died in infancy, sometimes a little older, but never having children of their own. I tried to ask about it, to see if there was a reason or if we were a long-lasting fluke in nature, but the closest I got was Mrs. Boyd telling me the women in my family were stronger than most men. Considering how all the women I grew up with were buried in that cemetery, I wasn't sure how accurate she was.

It didn't surprise me that the cemetery was where I spotted Gabriel, standing solemnly in front of one of its oldest tombstones. I had followed him to it once and asked him who Annabelle was. I was maybe eight, and it hadn't occurred to me that it was the woman my doll was named after. That was when I found out that if I wanted to know about the past I could ask Embry, but never Gabriel. He was upset that I asked, shocked that I didn't know, and looked at me in a way that made me feel like I had no right to even utter her name. That should have tipped me off that when he said he was an old friend of the family, he meant long before my grandmother, but I never expected him to be from the 1600s like Annabelle.

Gabriel had come to me that night and apologized, stiffly, making me think Embry was the one who told him that I was just a child who didn't know any better and that he should make amends. It was a long time before I would ask him anything else.

I HAD PACKED SOME CLOTHES, but I knew the closet here was stocked. We stayed at the plantation when Embry came every summer, to give Sam and Deanna a break from me. I quickly changed into a blue polka dot halter dress and tried to wrestle my curls into a bun before going to see Gabriel. He was still standing in front of Annabelle's tombstone.

Her name was starting to fade, but the crescent moon carved into the stone on top of it was as clear as day. Even with my hair in a bun it was still long enough, and the elastic low enough, that you couldn't see my birthmark. He hadn't mentioned it when he was going on about freckles last night, but I got the impression he knew a lot more than he was sharing with me. Under the faded name were the years she lived, 1664-1692, and a golden plaque to cover where it used to say she was a criminal who was burnt at the stake. It now read, "Beloved mother and dearest friend, my heart is yours until we meet again."

"When was the plaque added?" I asked, fishing for information. I had always assumed the plaque was put there by someone who loved her, like her husband, who meant that he would be with her once he died. Now, with all the information I was learning, I got the impression Gabriel added it. He probably believed that she was going to come back to him some day, and they would be together in this world. Just pick up where they left off. Except Embry liked to hang out by the tombstone as well. It wasn't exactly going to work for the both of them, but I guess you wouldn't dwell on how she could only come back to one of them when there were bigger obstacles in the way. Like how she had been dead for centuries.

"You shouldn't be out in the open like this," Gabriel warned, turning away from the stone and walking to the opening in the wrought-iron fence, knowing I would follow even though he didn't so much as glance in my direction.

"We would hear if there was anyone within a mile of this place," I reminded him, looking around and seeing nothing out of the ordinary, only hearing animals and leaves dancing in the wind. Even squirrels would have sent the birds into a flying frenzy.

"If we heard them, would you have time to run to the house, get inside and lock yourself into the bunker before he got to you?" he asked, like he trusted the ultra-modern security system about as much as he trusted my athletic abilities. From what I could tell, the plantation house was safer than the White House. Still, Gabriel sounded like he trusted the trees and secret hiding places better.

I hadn't seen the remodeling yet, but 'the bunker' used to be a huge room in the basement that was made of some incredibly strong metal and installed generations ago as a bomb shelter. It also had all kinds of religious symbols and protective drawings on every inch of it, which Embry had told me were blessed. As a child, I thought Embry was teasing. Now, I wouldn't be surprised if the pope himself had blessed the metal sheets. I accidentally locked myself in it once, and although it took less than 20 minutes for someone to let me out, I still thought of the bunker as more of a tomb than a safe haven. Hopefully the danger would never come close enough for me to have to go in it.

"You haven't been back in a while, but I was on the track team this year," I tried for some of the banter we had in the past, but his face was a mask, emotionless.

A few summers ago, Embry would have smiled and asked "You?", teasing me for my lack of athleticism, while Gabriel would have sat there, pretending not to listen or care, with a smile spreading, until we would finally get him to participate. Today, all he managed was, "Get inside and try to figure out how to let me into the house, but not Control or your bedroom. I'll make sure no one has breached the perimeter."

"Be careful," I warned him as he set off. He walked around and made sure no one could get close, but anything with the perimeter was also code for spending hours in the woods. Either to be alone with his thoughts, or to get away from me, I couldn't be entirely sure.

I went back to the house and finally took a look at the renovations that had been done. Most of the rooms looked the same, albeit with a tiny black computer screen, except for what used to be an empty office. It now looked like the command station for a space launch. I assumed this was the 'command' Gabriel had warned me not to give him access to.

It took me a while to find the manual for the system, mostly because I had expected it to be a book instead of a computer file. My biggest issue was figuring out the passwords, which seemed to have been chosen by Sam, as well as coaxing myself into the pin prick on my finger to confirm my DNA. The ocular scan, my fingerprint and all of these security measures were absurd. I still wasn't sure the entire thing wasn't an elaborate and expensive prank.

Once I figured out how to give other people access to

specific rooms, I made the Control room and my bedroom off-limits to anyone but me, no matter what. Then I went to the kitchen to see what food I had to work with. The fridge was full of water with some coffee and Gatorade, while the pantry had a whole lot of canned goods and granola bars. It would do for now, but one of us had to go to the store.

I opened a can of fruit salad and went to wait for Gabriel on the porch. I was eating the last spoonful when he showed up, his face not revealing much, so there probably hadn't been any sign of Embry.

"I figured out how to let you in. I need some of your blood to give you access to the house, then your fingerprints and an ocular scan to get you past the foyer," I said offhandedly, giving him the second fruit salad I'd brought out. "It's not bad," I told him when he looked at it with confusion.

"I'll have to get groceries," he said, surprising me by sitting beside me on the porch swing.

"I can make you a list. I got a lot better at cooking since the oatmeal." I once made him the most pasty, chunky combination of oats, milk and god knows what. I was eight at the time, so he couldn't hold it against me. "Clara says my mac and cheese is the best she has ever had." I noticed a small smile creep across his face before he remembered to hide it. "I was thinking, if you keep acting like you're mad at me and pretending you don't care, then I won't be able to tell if ever he does take over you, but if you're nice and we go back to our friendly banter, then I'll realize that it's not you when you start being mean," I suggested, hoping I had found a way to use the threat of my safety in order to con him into being nicer to me. Or at least to acknowledge me when I happened to be in the same room as him.

"Or it might be easier if you don't get close to me, either way," he said, getting up although he was nowhere near done his fruit salad.

"How come it's always one step forward, ten steps back with

you?" I asked, getting upset instead of being quiet and letting him go, like I usually would have done. I didn't generally like confrontation, as you could tell from my escaping prom through a bathroom window. Plus, Embry was usually there to fight my battles for me.

"Lucy, why are you so bent on being friends? I'm not Embry," he said, half self-deprecating, half to hurt me.

"No, but if you're going to keep acting like this, then maybe I would rather you get controlled. He might at least pretend to be nice." I wasn't entirely sure why I was so mad at him. He wasn't being as distant as yesterday, and this was how he always acted. Gabriel usually hung around while saying nothing, but Embry would talk. If you sit around people having a conversation long enough, you can't help but participate every once in a while.

After 'lunch', I programmed Gabriel into the house. I enjoyed stabbing his finger to get DNA more than I should, especially when he disappeared to 'secure the perimeter' as soon as I was done. I got a book from the library and spent the rest of the day reading on the balcony, which was as close to reading in the field as Gabriel was going to let me.

CHAPTER SIX

Over the next couple of days, we got into a routine, where Gabriel would spend most of his time reading old books from the library, or going to 'check the perimeter' and disappearing for hours on end.

While he was gone, I also read books from the library. Most of them were non-fiction, and in addition to medical textbooks, there were some on aviation, fashion, photography, biographies...I could read all day, every day, for the rest of my life, without running out of books. Gabriel would come back for most of the meals I made, politely thanking me for it before going off on his own again, but he hadn't been at breakfast Sunday morning.

I DIDN'T LIKE IT, but I took advantage of his absence to do a little science experiment I had been planning. I was still mostly convinced everyone was overreacting about this Big Bad, but in case they weren't, I might as well help out.

There was a tiny, dilapidated shed on the property that held turpentine, rusty gardening tools, an old, defunct lawn mower

Mr. Boyd used for the cemetery when I was little, and fertilizer. It was an old fertilizer you couldn't find in stores and people were supposed to have returned ages ago, but Mrs. Boyd had a stockpile she would use for her garden.

I wasn't comfortable having those levels of ammonium nitrate in such high quantities next to the house now that we were possibly expecting an invasion, so my first thought had been to get rid of them. Then I remembered what Mrs. Benson taught us in Physical Science, when someone asked how you can make a bomb with something that's 'just dirt'. She hadn't given us a recipe, but it couldn't be that hard to figure out.

One by one, I took out the bags and spread them along the edge or what we considered the plantation house yard. Beyond it was still our property, but it was mostly fields that hadn't been worked in at least a century.

I had enough to make a thick line all around the house, except for once I got to the creek. The meadow surrounding it was still in its wet stage, which meant it shouldn't light up anyway.

Once I was done, I brought the bags of evidence and buried them in the bottom of the garbage bins, underneath the household waste.

"YOU'RE BACK," I said, surprised when I walked into the kitchen and found Gabriel there, making himself a sandwich. I quickly slipped my dirty hands into my pockets and hoped he wouldn't notice.

"What do you mean?" he asked. I had the hardest time not smiling when I saw he was cutting off his crusts. Mrs. Boyd used to do the same for me, until her husband told me I could be as strong as him if I ate them. I eventually found out that wasn't true, but at the time, the lie had worked.

"We're the only two people for miles. I notice when you

leave in the middle of the night, or pretend you're 'searching the perimeter,'" I pointed out, using air quotes for the last part before burying my hands back into the pockets.

"I'm keeping you safe," he defended his intentions, oblivious to my mistake.

"I have no doubt about that, but you're still running off all the time and I don't know where you are."

"Did something happen?" he asked, concerned.

"No," I admitted, sort of wishing something had, so he wouldn't leave again. "But what is going on? You're not leaving long enough to get out of town, so where are you going?"

"That's none of your business."

"Gabe..."

"Stay in your parts of the house. No more roaming around outside." He gave me what felt like a punishment for asking. "I'm going to check the perimeter," he said before going off without looking at me.

I watched him head off into the woods, the least likely route anyone would take to come and find us. He went past the cemetery, so I knew he wasn't going to see Annabelle. If I wasn't so worried he would be mad and yell at me for being reckless, I would follow him to figure it out.

WHEN I FIRST MET THEM, I was used to this. Embry would play with me and talk, answering any questions I thought up, while Gabriel would lurk in the background when he visited, mostly acting like he didn't care.

It wasn't until I was about seven that I first saw the side of Gabriel that made all of this ignoring me so hard. I had spent the day in the yard with Embry, who never complained about playing tag or hide and go seek for hours. Gabriel had gone off to the East Wing when he arrived to find Embry already there, and I hadn't seen him since. When Embry finally decided he had to go take care of something that wasn't me, I decided it was time for me to find out what Gabriel did with his time at the manor.

As a child, I thought the house was made specifically for me, because there were all kinds of little hidden passages between the walls for me to play in. Of course, the house was built hundreds of years before I was born, but I still made use of the passage ways every chance I got. They came in handy that day as I weaved through the rooms of the East Wing, trying to find which one Gabriel was hanging out in.

He was in what looked like a study, with a huge painting of a woman on one of the walls. Her hair was long and brown and curly, exactly like what I imagined my mother's to be when I tried to remember her. Of course, I now knew the painting was of Annabelle, and if I took out my mother's picture, I could point out all of the differences, but going off of memory alone, I often pictured them as one and the same.

I couldn't see what he was looking at, so I ventured into the next room. It had once been a bedroom, but was now used mostly for storage, based on the mountains of furniture covered with white sheets. I could make out a couch against the wall, underneath the weird grid thing you could slide to see into the other room. My bedroom used to be next to my grandmother's, so when I would have nightmares, she would keep it open and talk to me when I woke up in the middle of the night. Gabriel left his side of the grid open, so I could see him once I managed to open my side as quietly as I could.

He was looking at a book of old drawings. By old, I meant they were so faded that it took me a few minutes before seeing it was the portrait of a woman, Annabelle again by the looks of it. He was tracing the lines of her face with his fingers as if it could bring him closer to her.

He looked nicer and more vulnerable than I had ever seen him before, but there wasn't much else to see, so after about ten minutes, I got up and abandoned my 'spy' mission. I figured I would find Embry and convince him to play with me again. I moved the metal grid back into place as slowly as I could to ensure it wouldn't make a sound. I thought I was safe, until my knee bumped into the coffee table, and something under the sheet fell over.

Gabriel and Embry could be paranoid about strange noises, so he was definitely going to come and check. I debated for a second whether I would have time to get back to my passage-way, before deciding to go back on the couch and pretend to be asleep, just as the door opened and Gabriel came in. I knew I wasn't allowed in the East Wing, but I didn't think he did.

I had grown up playing this game with Sam, of pretending to be asleep, so I knew my breathing would be convincing, but I was worried. Gabriel and Embry always knew things there was no possible way they could know. I concentrated on my breathing like my life depended on it. He had never been violent or punished me, so I wasn't afraid of what he would do if he found out. But I was worried he would like me even less than he already did.

Instead, I heard his footsteps stop in front of me, before his hand brushed the hair out of my face, to make sure my eyes were closed. I passed his test, but I was so nervous I almost stopped breathing when he picked me up in his arms and carried me all the way to my own bedroom. He put me down on top of the sheets, then he put my blankie over me, tucking it in at my sides.

I could feel him, standing in front of me, before he bent down and kissed my forehead. When I opened my eyes to peek, he was gone. I couldn't tell if it was me he didn't want knowing he had a heart, or if it was everyone else, but that was when I found out he did, and that as long as he didn't think you were watching, he would show it.

. . .

I NEVER USED it against him, or let him know I knew, but every once in a while, if Embry had been gone for a long time or I was feeling particularly vulnerable, I purposely curled up on a couch where he was sitting and tried my best to fall asleep. I couldn't be sure, because actually falling asleep meant I didn't know how much of what happened was real and how much of it was a dream, but I think he liked it too.

Sometimes, even when I was sleeping in my bed and had no idea Gabriel was even in the country, I would wake up convinced that he came to talk to me. I could remember snippets of conversation that it would be impossible for me to make up. Whenever I confronted him, to see if the conversations were real or figments of my imagination, Gabriel acted like there was nothing out of the ordinary and made me feel like I was losing my mind.

I TRIED to ask Embry about it once, to see if he thought it was possible that Gabriel might sneak into my room sometimes and talk to me while I was sleeping. After reassuring him multiple times that all he did was talk, Embry told me it wasn't likely.

"Unless he talks to you as someone else, and does it when you're sleeping, to make sure you can't hear," Embry proposed.

"No, everything I can remember him saying was to me," I argued, having expected him to either tell me I was imagining things, or that Gabriel was weird sometimes. I did not expect an inquisition.

"Long conversations?" he asked.

"No. Mostly sitting in silence, then saying a few words, then more silence."

"And you're not dreaming it?"

"That's what I'm asking you," I reminded him.

"Well, he is socially awkward. Maybe he thinks this is bonding," he said as a joke, but I felt there was more to it.

.   .   .

77

AT THE PLANTATION, there was no chance of him visiting me at night without my knowing. He was making me sleep in my bedroom, with all doors locked and barricaded, while he slept somewhere else. If he so much as tried to open my door, a bunch of alarms would go off and alert everyone within a five-mile radius. And possibly slice him to pieces. The plantation had its fair share of spare bedrooms, but I didn't think he was sleeping much these days. When I got up in the morning, there was no trace he even slept at all.

CHAPTER SEVEN

After a few weeks at the plantation, Gabriel was getting annoyed with me, or worried, which meant he had to spend as little time as possible in my vicinity. I had stopped asking questions and tried to pretend this was like any other visit, but apparently being nice and normal also unnerved him, so we settled into the most annoying silence. He might find that easier than arguing and bickering, but I felt a fight would be a welcome distraction.

That might be why I went to read on the dock instead of the balcony. Gabriel had gone off into the trees, pretending he was running security instead of running away from me. There was a possibility I would be back inside by the time he returned and none would be the wiser, but it was equally likely that he would come back and find me gone, panic, see me on the dock, come yell at me, then maybe understand that he couldn't lock me up and ignore me. I hadn't quite decided which outcome I was hoping for when I heard footsteps on the worn wood behind me.

I pretended I didn't hear, as though I hadn't been antici-pating this moment all morning, waiting for him to say something first. It wasn't until the footsteps stopped and no words came that I wondered if maybe this wasn't Gabriel. If maybe he was paranoid for a reason and their Big Bad was on the dock, watching me, seeing I had nothing to defend myself with and Gabriel was nowhere in sight. I was cursing myself for not bringing a knife or a baseball bat or anything useful, when I heard it.

It was someone clearing their throat, with a slight cough that would have chilled me to the core if I hadn't recognized it. I stopped pretending to read my book and turned around excitedly, finding Sam a few feet away from me, his goofy smile in place. He looked tired, and for the first time, I saw he was no longer the teenager I always pictured him as.

"Sam!" I exclaimed, jumping up to go and hug him, leaving my stuff abandoned on the dock.

"I thought you were supposed to be in the house," he chided, but the smile told me not to take it too seriously.

"I was going stir-crazy," I lied.

"Don't try to upset him, Luce. He has your best interest at heart, but I think he also has a dark side," he warned, knowing me better than I wanted him to.

"You have no idea how awkward it is. He doesn't have you to talk to while ignoring me, so he just doesn't talk. Asking questions annoys him, so I stopped, but I had no idea if you and Clara and Deanna were okay, I still don't know whether Embry is on his way or dead or..."

"Can't they not die?" he cut me off.

"They die and come back. But I don't think it's an exact science. And from what I gather, if the bad guy takes over, they'll be worse than dead. He can make them do whatever he wants. Even Embry wouldn't have second thoughts about ripping my throat out."

"Well, I can't vouch for Embry's well-being, but I think Deanna has Clara convinced this is a fun summer vacation at the beach. She doesn't understand why you can't be there, but I figure you'd rather she be mad at you than in danger."

"Of course," I assured him. "Now that you're here, I should go make those cookies."

"A double batch might be good." He smiled before helping me grab my stuff and walking back to the plantation house.

"Did he tell you any more than he told me?" I asked Sam once I had programmed him to be able to access the house. We were in the kitchen, with me gathering cookie-making ingredients and him pretending to help.

"Probably less. Before my mom died, she told me to listen to them, no matter how crazy it sounds, because they're keeping you alive. I do as I'm told, but they don't tell me more than 'there's danger, we're taking her,'" he explained.

"Gabriel didn't give you a time frame of how long he thought this would last?"

"He implied it was the biggest danger he has ever faced; the real one he's been waiting for all these years."

"Like their reason for being alive?" I asked, realizing this was bigger than I thought. I didn't know if I was more terrified because this guy was terrible enough to warrant making two men immortal in order to protect me, or because if they did somehow defeat him, they would both die.

"Protecting their descendants," Sam agreed.

"What do you mean?" I asked, confused.

"Isn't that why they care? You're either Gabriel's or Embry's great-great-great-great-granddaughter."

"No," I argued. "I think they both loved her, but I'm pretty sure someone would have mentioned it to me," I said, my certainty decreasing as I thought of all the secrets no one had bothered to tell me until a couple of weeks ago.

"One of them has to be." He stood his ground.

"No, I think they both loved and dated Annabelle, the first one, but she left town for years before she came back with a child. She died so they took care of her daughter. And then her daughter and so on." I pieced it from the memories and what Gabriel had said on prom night, but I only knew for sure that it wasn't Embry.

"That's a bit obsessive, no?" Sam asked.

"They loved her." It made sense in a tragic love story kind of way.

"But love isn't..."

"I'm not your daughter but you've been raising me and keeping me safe," I cut him off, knowing I had him. After losing all of my blood relatives before my sixth birthday, I had to rely on people loving me, or I would currently be being raised in an orphanage.

"That's for the money," he teased, which would have hurt if I hadn't known it absolutely wasn't true.

"You think that's funny, but it's just mean," I pointed out.

"Come on Luce, we grew up together. For all intents and purposes, you're my sister. I love you to death and would do almost anything to keep you safe. If you have kids I'll love them too, but I don't think I would spend lifetimes protecting your line," he argued as if just the idea of it were insane.

"I look like her," I reminded him. If ever I someday met someone who looked exactly like my mom, or Mrs. Boyd or anyone I had lost, even if I absolutely hated that person, I still couldn't watch them die. It would be like losing my person all over again. I couldn't imagine how hard it had been on Embry and Gabriel to keep having to watch Annabelle die over and over again. Plus, it wasn't like they could spend years protecting Beth, Cassie and Rosalind without caring about them as well.

"That's still weird," he acknowledged. "Especially if they both loved her. If she only loved one of them, the other is wasting his time, and if she loved them both, then she was playing them."

"I'm not saying it makes sense, it's just what they do," I defended, knowing from the memory that she had loved them both, and wasn't playing either of them.

"Well, I'll be happy when all of this is over, and this weird danger is no longer trying to find you," he said, sticking his finger into my mixing bowl to eat some of the cookie dough.

"When you said to make a double batch..."

"Yes, I want half of it raw," he agreed with a smile.

"It's not good for you. Raw eggs and all," I repeated what Deanna kept telling us, but I didn't believe a word of it.

"I've seen how much dough you leave in that mixing bowl when you make them. Deanna thinks it's sweet that you always offer to make the cookies and do the dishes after, but I know it's because you like eating the raw cookie dough and muffin mix and cake batter and..."

"Who doesn't?" I asked, taking a spoonful myself, before Gabriel came in and found us laughing and sticking our fingers into the mixing bowl.

"Is everything okay?" Gabriel asked Sam. He looked relieved that he wouldn't be forced to deal with me for a few hours.

"Yeah, we're all good. The beach house is great, Clara loves making sandcastles, and you know what they say, 'Happy Wife, Happy Life.'" Sam smiled as if Gabriel knew what he meant. Or even cared.

"Has there been any trouble? Anyone casing the house, approaching you, watching from afar?" he asked, implying this Big Bad might be going after them as well, or using them to get to me. I thought they went to the beach house to be safe, so I wasn't exactly thrilled.

"Are we worried about spies, or an attack?" Sam verified, but at least he seemed to have been expecting the second option. It was the spies that worried him.

"An attack. But he'll most likely send someone ahead to find out where she is," Gabriel explained.

"Unless he has Embry," I pointed out. I liked how Sam was getting him to talk, but Sam might not think to ask about Embry, and Gabriel wasn't being forthcoming.

"Embry is taking longer to get here because he thought he was being tailed and has to mislead and avoid them. He should be here within another week or so," Gabriel answered my question, but directed the answer to Sam.

"And why is this guy so interested in Lucy?" Sam asked like it was the millionth time and he still didn't understand. We were rich, so he understood the threat of kidnapping for ransom or blackmail, but he couldn't wrap his head around villains wasting their time to acquire me. Neither could I, to be honest.

"It's a long story," Gabriel said dismissively. "And you have to get back to your family."

"Lucy is my family too, remember?" Sam pointed out. He didn't appreciate being left out when I was in danger.

"I understand your concern," Gabriel agreed, his jaw set. "But this isn't about Lucy, this is about ancient history, which I see no benefit in sharing it with you. Why isn't important. All that matters is that he wants her, and we can't let that happen."

"Because he loves me so much, you know," I said sarcastically, reinserting myself into the conversation.

"If he gets you he wins. And that wouldn't be good for anyone," Gabriel spoke to me that time, but it did not make me happy, or feel like a victory. A chill ran down my spine and I was a little relieved when he went back outside.

"And you say he's always this fun and bubbly?" Sam gave me an apologetic smile.

"I think he might be friendlier when he doesn't talk and pretends I'm not there."

"If he keeps you safe, I can't complain," Sam said, kissing the top of my head before eating another scoop of dough. I laughed, because I knew it was what he was trying to do, to make me smile, but all I could think about were Gabriel's words, and how as soon as the cookies were done, Sam would be gone, and I'd be alone with Gabriel again.

We kept almost half of the dough, so while the cookies were baking in the oven, we took the bowl out to the porch swing and Sam dug in while I stared blankly off to the creek.

"Earth to Lucy," he said after a while, moving his spoon up and down in front of my face.

"I'm just thinking," I defended, curling up into a ball and leaning my head onto his shoulder.

"About what?" he asked with his mouth full, putting the spoon down to wrap an arm around me.

"I never wanted you guys to be in danger," I admitted. "If something happens to you or Deanna or...Clara." I had to swallow before the last name, and couldn't finish my sentence. The faceless danger hadn't been real to me the other night. At least not real enough to be able to hurt the ones I loved, but Sam looked worried.

"You never wanted any of this," he reminded me. "You were born into this messed-up world, just like I was. And contrary to what I said earlier, I am not here for the money."

"But you have a family."

"I do," he agreed. "And it includes you. When my dad died, they explained it all to me. I understood that they weren't exaggerating about your life being in danger and people wanting to kill you. I told Deanna she could leave with Clara. That I couldn't abandon you, but I couldn't stand putting them in danger either."

"Why didn't she go?" I asked.

"Well, aside from the fact that she loves me and doesn't want to live without me, she said that if I wanted her to leave, I shouldn't have made you part of her family too."

"Are you guys safe at the beach house?" I asked, looking up at his face, so I could see his eyes and know if he was lying to me.

"We are," he told me. "The house is almost like this one. As long as we don't go out, we're safe."

"But you do go out," I argued. He had mentioned sandcastles, and every time we went to the beach house before, Deanna and I spent half the time shopping at the outlets.

"But we're not the ones being hunted. You are." He tried to make it sound comforting as opposed to reminding me I was the root of all of this evil.

"They'll use you to get to me," I said, knowing it was true and hating myself for not realizing this earlier, when I was upset about missing orientation and having to defer university.

"Which is why keeping us safe keeps you safe. No matter how hard we try to stop you, if they got Clara, you would try to give yourself up," he said, looking at me like he was trying to convince me not to do that, although he was never going to ask. As much as he loved me, none of us were ready to sacrifice Clara for me. Except maybe Embry and Gabriel.

"Your point is that they won't hurt her or Deanna or you, they'll just dangle you in front of me to make me do whatever they want?" I summed it up.

"That is what I'm saying," he agreed, holding me close. "Smells like the cookies are ready." The smell was wafting outside, an overwhelming scent of home that reminded me of his mother more than anything else, but he was also trying to change the topic of our conversation.

"I could forget about them, so they burn, and you'll have to stay while I make more," I suggested.

"I have to get back to my daughter," he said, making no effort to get up, letting me decide if he would get his cookies or not.

"Well, I promised Clara," I said, sighing as I stood up.

"We'll be back at the manor before you know it." He stood up as well and wrapped his arm around me while we walked back to the kitchen. I didn't look into his eyes for that lie, deciding I'd rather not know the truth.

. . .

MY EGG TIMER went off as we walked into the kitchen, so I took the cookies out of the oven and prepared a basket while they cooled. I took my time lining the wicker basket with a checkered cloth, then some wax paper, before piling the cookies in.

"Do you want to keep some for you and Gabriel?" he offered.

"He doesn't deserve cookies," I said, realizing I sounded like a spoiled child. "I'll make more if he decides he wants some," I amended, hoping I wasn't coming off as bitter, considering what Sam was giving up, and the danger he was putting his own family in to keep me safe. I didn't have a right to complain or be upset that I had no one to talk to.

"Clara thanks you," he said, kissing the top of my head.

"Give her and Deanna a hug and a kiss for me," I said, so he held me tight one more time before leaving.

I WATCHED him go until his body melded with the trees and I could barely tell where he was. Gabriel came out of nowhere, silently and without showing any signs of hurrying. Still, he caught up with him effortlessly. He escorted him out, and I hoped Sam might remind him that I am a person in addition to being Annabelle reincarnate.

CHAPTER EIGHT

Two days after Sam left, Gabriel hadn't improved in the
talking department, but he was making a slight effort to
not roam the forest so often. He made it clear that he was not
interested in conversations, but he didn't object to my sitting
and reading in the same room as him.

We were both sitting quietly when I finished my chapter, my
arbitrary timer to go stir the spaghetti sauce I was making for
dinner. It was bubbling, so I lowered the heat, but not before it
sprayed onto my shirt. I put it on low, then headed upstairs to
change.

I was just going to put a different shirt on, but I had a closet
full of clothes I never wore, including a lot of pretty summer
dresses. I was going through some bright and vibrant ones
when I spotted my beige lace dress. When Embry saw me in it
last year, he stopped mid-sentence and said I looked like
Annabelle. At the time I thought he meant I looked like a doll,
but now I knew it was his first love he confused me for. I didn't
want to make Gabriel sad, but I decided it was time to try and
get some answers. I was going to put the dress on and hopefully
convince Gabriel to talk to me like he would her.

. . .

THE DRESS itself resembled a lot of my other summer dresses, but there was something about the lace detailing and the unassuming color that made words like romantic and vulnerable come to mind when I looked at myself in the mirror wearing it. I left my hair loose, like Annabelle did in her portrait, then walked slowly down the stairs, taking my time so that if Gabriel happened to look up, he would see me and get the full effect.

It took me until I was on the before last step to realize he was no longer in the library, so I gave up my slow, elegant walking and was going to grab my book and go read on the balcony when I felt it happening again. I barely had enough time to sit down on the couch before slipping into the seventeenth century...

"I'm glad you came," Annabelle said when she found Gabriel in the parlor, looking out to the grounds. There were men working the field, animals grazing and a million things he could be seeing through the window, but every time Annabelle looked out, all she saw was the past. Running through the tall grass with Embry and Gabriel while her mother called after them, warning that she'd be sorry if she ruined another dress in the mud. Annabelle had always pretended she couldn't hear her. More than anything, she could close her eyes and see the scene of years ago now, when Gabriel had brought her to the edge of the field, acutely aware of her parents watching them, and asked her to marry him. Her father had consented already, of course, but Gabriel had asked like her answer meant more to him. Like as long as she said that she did love him and wanted to spend the rest of her life with him, then nothing could ever be wrong in the world. It was because of that memory that she tried her best not to look out at the field, or to ever close her eyes.

"She was beside me when Embry extended your invitation, and she admitted she would love to meet you and take a walk in your gardens.

They're still the talk of the town, I'm afraid," Gabriel explained why he came, as well as why he brought his laughing lady-friend.

"You didn't want to come." She understood, of course she did, but that didn't make it hurt any less.

"Would you?" he asked instead of denying it.

"Gabriel..." she fumbled for words, but it was the hurt in his eyes that stopped her, not the anger his tone had implied.

"I am glad to see you're well and happy. Your daughter is beautiful and my condolences about your husband, but this is the last place I want to be right now." He was talking in a harsh whisper, each word cutting into her.

"I deserve that," she said, bowing her head before looking up into his eyes.

"Don't. Please," he told her, holding her gaze for a moment before turning away and avoiding her.

"You left. You were gone, and it took a year before I believed them that you weren't coming back. I would have waited until the end of time..."

"Then why didn't you?" he cut short her excuses.

"What you made me promise before you went. I told you I couldn't, that ours was the love stories were written about, that I would spend my life loving you whether you came back or not... but you made me promise that I would find someone else, get married and try my best to be happy, so I did."

"With my best friend?"

"With the only other person in the world who understood my pain. I made a promise I had to keep, and Embry was the only man I knew who would let me spend forever finding reasons to talk about you."

"You loved him." He wasn't buying her excuses.

"I did. I do. I've always loved Embry. You and he were like my brothers when I got here, you took me in as one of your own and I can't imagine my life without the two of you. But I fell in love with you and death wasn't going to change that. I would have married Embry and had a family and pretended to live happily ever

after, but I have never, not for a second, stopped being in love with you."

"I came back," he reminded her. "And you still left."

"Embry was like a brother to you, and I knew the only way to mend what I had broken was to leave."

"And what if I would have chosen you? Did I not have a say in deciding which relationship I needed to mend?"

"You loved me, which made it the hardest thing I have ever done to leave, but I knew you needed Embry. I was just going to go while you two forgave each other, but then..."

"You got married."

"No. When I left there was no room in my heart for any others. I met someone and discovered things about myself, things that make it better for everyone if I stay away."

"I can't imagine anything about you that would make me not want you here," he contradicted himself, but the way he reached for her, then had to remind himself not to, told her this most recent statement was the truth, not the first one.

"It was safer for you with me away."

"Then why did you come back, Belle? To drive me crazy, wanting someone I can't have, loving someone I can't even touch though every part of me is aching for it?" he asked, reaching out for her, then dropping his hand midway to her face, making her have to close her eyes and take a deep breath to regain her composure.

"It wasn't safe for us anymore, and I had nowhere else to go," she admitted, the tears filling her eyes this time.

Gabriel didn't even take a moment to determine whether or not it was proper, he bridged the distance between them and took her in his arms. "I won't let anything hurt you," he promised.

"I told Embry, but...I didn't come here to tear you apart, or start anything. It is going to take every ounce of willpower I have to stand back, but I need my best friends right now. I need to raise my daughter, to make sure she's safe and happy. This is the only place where I could think to do that."

"I'll do whatever you need me to." He kissed the top of her head, understanding there was a lot more to the story she wasn't sharing, but after waiting years, he figured he could wait and be there for her until she was ready...

I woke up in the library, expecting Gabriel to be there, kissing my forehead, but I found the sun had set and I was alone. I hugged myself and walked to the kitchen, where the spaghetti sauce was still in a pot on the stove. I turned the heat up again and boiled some water for the pasta, wondering if Embry knew Annabelle hadn't loved him. Or at least had chosen Gabriel. In a way, it made sense that I knew so little of this love triangle. Embry was the only one who answered my questions about his friendship with Gabriel, and he wouldn't want to admit he fell in love with his best friend's fiancée.

I set two places at the table and had just put the sauce on the noodles when I turned away from the stove and saw Gabriel in the doorway, staring at me. I was confused until I remembered I was wearing the dress.

"The spaghetti is ready," I said as if I hadn't noticed his gaze, bringing the plates to the table.

"I came back inside and you were asleep, so I made the rounds," he said, looking at me more than he had since we got here, purposely turning away before drifting back. "This sleeping in the middle of the day, are you having trouble sleeping at night or is this place boring to you, or..."

"I'm getting memories," I admitted.

"From your childhood?" he asked.

"From my ancestors."

"It could be dreams that you're making up," he dismissed me before hearing what I saw.

"The other day it was Annabelle coming back to town with a

baby. She wanted Father Brown to baptize Margaret," I said, getting a reaction from the priest's name.

"And this time?" he asked in a way that made me think he didn't want to know.

"Do you forgive Embry for being in love with Annabelle because you know you were the one she really loved, the one she would have chosen if she could?" I went where I definitely wasn't supposed to.

"This is not something I want to get into, Lucy." He looked down, but wasn't completely shutting me out. He stayed at the table.

"Okay, then tell me where you went? I've been going over everything I knew about Annabelle and I assumed you both loved her, she dated both of you, then there was a big fight and she left...but you left for a year to make her go to Embry."

"Does it matter?" he stalled.

"It might." After all, I wasn't asking for these dreams, so they had to have some purpose.

He sighed, and I thought he was going to tell me to eat quietly, or leave. Instead he answered my question, "My brother had left searching for an adventure. He was supposed to return by a specific date, but hadn't yet. My mother was terribly worried and begged me to find him and bring him home, so I went off to do so."

"I never knew you had a brother," I stated, realizing I didn't know much about him, or Embry, before they showed up. I was still surprised to have seen Embry with a family, and made a mental note to find out what happened to those descendants; whether he was looking after them as well.

"Patrick. He was three years younger than me. A dreamer, but also the nicest, most innocent kid you've ever met." He smiled, shaking his head and remembering him.

"Do I want to know why it took you two years and you never wrote home?"

"I found him, if that's what you're asking. He had settled with a small community in New York. He had a girl, Katherine, that he fancied…he promised me he would come home once he finished building the church. Then he wanted to bring the girl to meet my mother." I wanted to press him for more details, ask questions, but he had never shared a story about his past, and I was worried he might stop if I reminded him I was there. "I wrote home to let them know I found him and would bring him home soon, but letters took forever to get around back then, and it was common for them not to reach their destination. I figured I would help out with the church, so we could leave faster, but fate had other plans."

"You didn't finish it?" I asked, figuring the church was the part of the story he would be the least attached to.

"No, we finished it. You can still visit it if ever you find yourself in Sleepy Hollow…"

"With the headless horseman?" I couldn't help myself.

"That's a story, written in the 1900s, and set a hundred years after I was there," he argued.

"You're saying there is nothing supernatural about Sleepy Hollow, no headless horsemen?" I verified, slightly disappointed. I found it hard to believe The Gifted exist, but magic and fairy tales don't.

"I'm saying he wasn't in Sleepy Hollow when I was," he said, waiting for me to interrupt again, but I pressed my lips together. "The headless horseman is fiction, but Washington wasn't completely off in suggesting something supernatural was at work in Sleepy Hollow. Within a couple of weeks of the church's completion, all eight of us who had helped build it had died of seemingly natural causes and faultless accidents, without warning, after having been in perfect health."

"Patrick…" I asked, not sure I wanted to know.

"He drowned the day before we were supposed to leave. I

wouldn't have suspected anything if it weren't for all of the others."

"When you say all eight of 'us'..."

"I got sick. So sick that no one understood how I survived. I know some people are immune to certain viruses, but this wasn't an immunity. I got sick, I was fading away, and I slipped into a coma. Katherine, who was taking care of me, swore I died, but it was winter, there was a blizzard, and it was days until she managed to go and get the priest. By the time they found me, I had made a full recovery and was as good as new."

"That was the first time you died," I understood.

"I promised Annabelle I would come back to her," he said simply.

"Which is why you believe she'll come back to you?"

"I was brought back to life so I could be with her. It stands to reason that she will come back too," he agreed, implying he wasn't sticking around to keep me safe, but rather protecting me so he would have something to do while waiting for Annabelle's return.

He said it with a finality, letting me know it was not up for discussion, and he was done sharing. He got up and went outside, so I cleared up the table, did the dishes, and realized there were worlds of questions I needed to ask Embry that I had never even considered before.

CHAPTER NINE

I woke up and it was pitch black outside. Being in the middle of nowhere meant we had no streetlights and couldn't see any other houses. If we didn't count the stars, there was absolutely no light. I knew something had woken me, because it was not like me to be up before dawn. I quietly got out of bed and headed towards the door. I put my ear against it to see if I could hear Gabriel's footsteps in the hallway, but all I got was silence. I was working on convincing myself it had been him going out, but then I heard it. Or rather them. Muffled voices coming from outside, somewhere near the balcony. The hairs on the back of my neck stood up, and I brought my hand up to protectively rub the birthmark, before I recognized Gabriel's faint southern drawl.

I rushed to the other side of the room and put my ear to the patio door and strained to see out into the yard. I needed to figure out if he was talking to someone I knew, or if someone evil had managed to get in. Then I heard the hint of an Italian accent.

I slid open the balcony door and quietly walked down the

stone steps with my bare feet, not even bothering to put a robe over my nightgown. Gabriel saw me once I rounded the corner, but he rolled his eyes instead of letting Embry know, so I could jump from the bottom stair, onto Embry's back.

"Missed you, Bambolina," Embry called me one of his many Italian terms of endearment, like he had since I was a little girl. Bambolina, Principessa, Tesoro...each made me feel special and loved. He turned around so he could properly take me in his arms and give me a hug that felt like home. He sounded tired and worn out, but I couldn't tell if my arms encircled him easier because I was older and bigger, or because he was thinner.

"It has mostly been a borefest without you." I went along with the pleasantries, allowing myself to be happy he was finally here. I didn't want to complain about Gabriel being mean when he had been forthcoming yesterday, and there would be more than enough time to grill Embry on everything in the morning.

"I'm here now," he assured me, but he wasn't smiling and making everything okay like I had expected him to. "I'm sorry I missed your graduation. I hope someone took a lot of pictures?" he asked, so I nodded.

"Did you lose the people who were following you?" I fished for information.

"I did." Embry sat on the steps with me, while Gabriel disappeared into the darkness.

"I could have used you these past few weeks," I told him once we were alone.

"I think we all wish I was the one to tell you instead of him," he agreed.

"Why didn't you? You had a million opportunities over the past thirteen years..."

"You were a kid," he said simply, before noticing my reaction. "Not as in you were young or immature or couldn't handle it, but until the danger was concrete...I wanted to give you as much of a childhood as I could after everything you had already been through."

"I've been eighteen for months. Lots of them," I pointed out.

"I wasn't ruining your birthday with this, or Christmas. And Keisha and Clara are always there whenever I visit…" We both knew they were excuses.

"Maybe you should come more often then," I called him on it. He didn't tell me because he didn't want to tell me.

"I would give anything for your happiness Lucy, anything but your safety."

"Even the truth?" I asked, looking at him expectantly.

"I have been as honest with you as I could. There was no benefit to telling you all of this when you were younger."

"You could have trained me. Like John Connor." I tried to be serious, but we both laughed.

"What would be the point in saving you if I had turned you into a robot?" he asked.

"A badass, not a robot," I argued. "And I would have believed this a lot easier when I was five. The whole, we're Gifteds who don't stay dead while we wait for your dolls to come back to life."

"I wanted to tell you the supernatural parts when you were younger, so it wouldn't be so much of a shock all at once…"

"Then why didn't you?" I asked when he stopped himself.

"Your Grams," he said simply. "Evelyn knew everything and told you nothing about that stuff. She changed the stories to take out anything paranormal. She wanted you to be strong and confident, but she did not want you to be a part of our world."

"Did she know I was like Annabelle? That I would be hunted?"

"I think she suspected it," he gave me a sad smile. "But she didn't want you to know enough to be able to go looking. Neither did Martha."

"Will you answer everything I ask you now?" I verified.

"Anything I know the answer to," he agreed, looking worried, but I believed he meant it. He wouldn't volunteer anything, but he would answer whatever I thought to ask.

"J'ai trouvé un homme dans la forêt," Gabriel interrupted us, talking to Embry in a language I did not understand.

"Un des siens?" Embry answered with a question. My money was currently on French.

"Je pense. Il va à l'école avec elle, mais il a l'air louche."

"Louche comment?"

"The thing you're not telling me now is..." I knew I had a much better chance of getting information with Embry, especially after he told me he would answer all of my questions. Not only was Embry usually more likely to share, he was a terrible liar. Gabriel was already giving him an angry glare, knowing exactly what was coming.

"Gabriel found a guy in the woods," he told me in a tone that implied it was absolutely nothing to worry about. Just a precaution.

"Embry," Gabriel warned, nodding over to me. It was this that let me know there was danger coming, way more than Embry's slip.

"You realize I'm not a child anymore? You've already told me there's someone trying to find me whose main purpose in life is to kill me. Letting me know the details of how he's trying to accomplish this won't make much of a difference to my fear level. It just might let me prepare myself for what's coming, maybe see danger before it's right in front of me." I was mostly pretending to be so brave and unaffected. If I knew exactly what was going on, I could make a plan and figure things out. If they kept me in the dark, I not only had to fear the Big Bad that was after me, I also had to contend with everything my imagination was making up to fill in the blanks.

Gabriel shook his head before walking a few feet away, so Embry could fill me in. He knew exactly what was going on, but if he stayed away and wasn't a part of it, he could tell Embry 'I told you so' when things inevitably went wrong. It gave him plausible deniability.

"There was a guy creeping around in the woods. When Gabriel found him, he said he goes to school with you. We think he's harmless, regular townsfolk, but he might not have come of his own free will."

"Someone I know?" I asked, confused. No guy from school would come looking for me. Other than to do me harm.

"We think he's being possessed by the men who were following me," Embry admitted, exchanging a glance with Gabriel. I understood that was the secret part they didn't want me finding out.

"I don't really have friends who would come here otherwise," I confirmed their fear.

"He said his name was Tennison Montgomery."

"Then it isn't just people like you that he can..." I concluded, trying to find a nicer way of saying he takes over and makes you do what he wants you to, even if it hurts you or someone you love.

"It is. But there are more people like us than you realize. I don't know how he finds them, because most people..."

"Just die like they're supposed to," I finished for him, so he knew I was listening and understood the concept. It was an insurance policy, which most people didn't end up using, they were just nice to have, in case. "You think him being here means the Big Bad knows where I am, which is why you guys are talking French and Gabriel is angry." I was relieved it wasn't at me.

"We're trying to figure out our next move," Embry agreed. He made it sound like we were playing chess. The other team moved a pawn at the other side of the board and we were trying to decide if we wanted to jump two squares to meet it, or sneak over from the side. Gabriel's face, however, suggested we were in check and figuring out if we should take their bishop or move our king.

"Would it help if I talked to Tennison?" I offered. "He's the only guy in the world, other than Sam, who would possibly visit me."

"Really?" Embry got into overprotective parent mode.

"He's a friend," I argued.

Embry and Gabriel had a full-on conversation with nothing but shrugs, raised eyebrows and looks before Gabriel said, "He's in the shed.".

"Tied up?" I asked, knowing that even an innocent person left alone in our shed would take a pair of shears or something to defend themselves.

"Alive," Gabriel said like I should be grateful, before I followed Embry to the other side of the house.

"Lucy!" Tennison called out with relief when I got close.

"Tennison, are you okay?" I asked, seeing he was tied to a chair inside the shed. He didn't look roughed up, but he was terrified.

"What's going on? I came to see you and this guy knocks me out and locks me in this thing." He looked to Gabriel.

"I barely hit him," he defended himself.

"What are you doing here? Did you try my house first?" I asked, remembering that I wasn't staying at home, and this wasn't like peeking into the windows when someone doesn't answer the door. It was at least a forty-minute walk from the manor to the plantation. I don't even think Keisha had ever been before.

"You weren't there. No one was there, which was weird. You're always home." He had a point. "I got worried."

"Why were you coming to see her in the first place?" Embry asked, worried I wasn't being objective.

"You disappeared on prom night. I missed my sidekick. I missed you." He turned on the charm, but not in our usual banter way from when we crossed paths. This was how he talked to the girls that were all over him, the thing that annoyed Keisha. "I knew you had another property, so I figured I would look around and find my Buffy."

"Just friends?" Embry turned to me, not impressed with me lying to him. He looked like he was about to knock Tennison out like Gabriel had. I pointed my finger at him in warning, then walked away from the shed, knowing he would follow.

"That's not Tennison," I told him. "He must be skimming over the memories or they come in all messy because those googly eyes are not aimed at me. I was his sidekick when I helped him get Keisha to dance with him at prom. She's his Buffy," I stopped any further reproach.

"Our Keisha?" Embry asked, and even Gabriel perked up, though one was excited for her and the other worried.

"She left right after prom for a summer semester at MIT. Cops would be all over this place if she hadn't shown up; I'm the first person her mom would reach out to if she went missing," I warned Gabriel's look, not letting myself think that way. "And it was so cute," I told Embry.

"He knows you're here then," Gabriel stated.

"Maybe he sent him here to see? This could be one of many places he sent people," I suggested.

"You just said that isn't Tennison, so even if he is one of many, the person who is controlling him knows you're here," he argued.

"We knew this was going to happen. This is your home, he

was always going to come, we just needed a safe place for the two of you to wait for me," Embry assured me like it was nothing to worry about, all a part of the plan.

"If they know where we are, that means we're leaving, doesn't it?" Tactical plans and defensive plays were not my strengths, but it seemed logical and straightforward to me.

"Ultimately, yes, but I think they might try to stage an attack while they think we don't suspect it. You're safer in here than leaving when they could be watching." What Embry meant was that we had to leave, but he didn't know which way to go, in case we were surrounded. Or so said my paranoia, that I only got because Embry's eyes didn't participate in the comforting words that told me everything would be fine.

"We're just sitting here and waiting for them to try and attack us?" I asked in a way that hopefully told him I thought this was a terrible plan.

"I'm pretty sure he's still at least a day's travel away. They didn't know for sure where you were, so it'll only be the men he had following me who will come at first," Embry continued to act like it was no big deal, when I knew it was.

"And you can handle them?" I verified. They were staying alive so they could protect me, after all.

"We will try our best," he assured me with his confident smile, making an effort for the eyes to play along, so I momentarily believed we would win.

"Did your best work for the others?" I asked delicately.

"Rosie died of an illness, Cassandra was mugged, and Beth was in the wrong place at the wrong time when a theater caught fire," he let me know none of them were killed at the hands of the Big Bad, though they didn't tend to die peacefully in bed either.

"What do we do with Tennison?" I asked, looking back to the shed. I didn't feel like dwelling on how my doppelgangers died, so I elaborated. "When he's not possessed he's not evil. He's even friendly. Not to mention, he has apparently been in love with Keisha since the sixth grade, and I don't want to take that away from her."

"I'll take care of it," Gabriel said, exchanging a look with Embry.

"What is that supposed to mean?" I asked Gabriel, but quickly turned to Embry for backup.

"He'll be fine," Gabriel assured me.

"Because he'll come back to life?" I asked, not sure how far they would go to protect me...how far they would need to go to keep me alive.

"We don't know if he would," Gabriel reminded me, which did nothing to make me feel better. "I'll bring him to the highway and call him a taxi."

"My car's in the garage. The keys are...Where did he go?" I asked, looking around, but Gabriel and Tennison were gone.

"Gifteds often have a Gift," Embry explained.

"Hence the name?" I offered.

"Gabriel is a lot faster than your average human." He smiled at my smart-alecness.

"The Flash fast?" I questioned.

"He's not a superhero. It's just heightened speed, no stopping time or moving faster than speeding bullets," he explained.

"What's your gift?" I asked. Questions about them and their past was a lot less scary than our future at the moment.

"I can change the mood of people around me," he shared.

"That's a weird gift."

"I was good at talking my way out of situations, or convincing people to lay down their arms..."

"You were a charmer," I simplified.

"You could say that," he agreed with a sly smile. "When I was alive, I was good at negotiating and making people feel at ease, or safe, so that carried on."

"I would have found that made sense, but you're not helping much today." I wondered if he wasn't using it on me now that I knew about it.

"Your powers tend to grow stronger the longer you're alive, and it takes a while to come back in each new life."

"You died?" I asked, my heart beating fast again, the complete opposite of calming me down.

"It happens," he tried to dismiss it.

"That's why it took you so long to get to us. You were lying dead somewhere." I was horrified at the idea. I pictured him on the ground, dying alone, clutching his wound and feeling helpless.

"You're making it a lot more dramatic than it really is. I was injured and knew I wasn't going to recover so I got myself a nice hotel room, put up the 'Do Not Disturb' sign and got a nice long rest before heading here, with lots of detours, so I wouldn't be followed," he said simply.

"You said you wouldn't lie," I warned.

"You're not the one who is supposed to be worried, Tesoro. Especially not about me. I'm tougher than I look," he assured me.

"Why don't you two stay in the house with me? They can't get in and we can let the house protect us," I suggested. That was my Plan B to whatever their Plan A was. To bring everyone I cared about into one of these fortified houses, lock us all up in the bunker, then let the Big Bad grow bored and eventually give up.

"That can work for a little while, but then we're stuck. It's fire-resistant, but I don't know how long that would last. We don't want them to keep us in the house while they wait for reinforcements. We want to get rid of this search party and leave before the others get here."

"How long do we have?" I asked, looking around as if I

would be able to see them coming. This was why I wasn't the one making plans.

"I would say an hour if we're lucky, or a few minutes if we're not." At least he was honest this time.

"I need your blood then," I said before rushing inside to get the bloodsucking device from Control, so I could program him into the house.

I CAME BACK and pricked him, just as Gabriel hurried over in the dark, without making a sound.

"They're here," he said, all business. "Get inside," he added, turning to me when I took a deep breath to brace myself for their arrival.

I nodded before running back inside with the drop of Embry's blood. I knew Gabriel wanted me to run straight to the bunker and lock myself in, but I didn't see the point of that until someone defeated the two of them and managed to get inside the house. I still didn't know how the house would react to being breached by someone without access, but I felt certain it would put up a good fight. Otherwise I was poking everyone for a placebo effect.

I decided my time would be better utilized in Control, giving Embry access so he could rush inside if ever the fight wasn't going our way, which I hoped wouldn't happen.

I knew I would be a distraction and would get in trouble if I watched from a window, but I couldn't imagine not knowing what was going on. I was already in Control, so I played around with knobs and buttons until I managed to get the screens to show me the view from the cameras outside.

AT FIRST ALL I saw was Embry and Gabriel standing out in the open, no cover whatsoever, waiting for the others to show up. I switched to a few different camera views until I found the band of men that had been sent to spy on us and kill me. I watched them pass the gate at the end of the property and effortlessly go over the bridge that normally terrified people who hadn't crossed it before. Deanna had to watch me, Sam, and Mrs. Boyd cross it before she believed us that it was safe. The entire bridge looked like a well-placed gust of wind could make it crumble to the ground. Tonight, there were four of them, but only two of the strangers looked like they had any type of training and would know what they were doing in a fight. One of them had a leather jacket and combat boots, long greasy hair, and arms the size of my waist, while the other was basically a tattooed thug in a wife beater with a spiked-up Mohawk. Even in the dark, far past the point of accuracy for the camera, I could tell he had washboard abs, and arms that could lift cars. My money was on the other two being newly possessed, rather than voluntary recruits. They looked relatively tough, each one tall and wide, but their muscles were replaced by beer bellies. One had a red, plaid shirt on, like he was about to go out and work the fields, and the other had a really old, torn t-shirt. The type of guys who had wives at home who would wake up in the morning wondering where they were. Still, they definitely worried me when they finally fit onto the same screen with Embry and Gabriel.

For a few minutes, it looked like they were just talking, and after playing around with all of the buttons, I condemned the expensive system for not having something so pivotal as a microphone, to hear what they were saying. I considered going outside to figure out what was going on, but then the talking stopped and they drew their weapons.

I knew from experience that both of my protectors could shoot, as they'd used an old can as target practice once. I got to try a few rounds and had so much fun, as long as I was shooting at a cardboard box. I had no interest in hunting, or shooting people. Still, I was not surprised at all when it was knives and swords that everyone pulled out tonight. Now that I knew how old they were, it made sense. Big, heavy ancient weapons that were probably forged and blessed by priests, but looked so out of place with the modern day clothes. I would have found it funny if more than half of these medieval weapons weren't currently trying to chop my people into pieces. I was right in my original assumptions about the strangers. The main fight for Gabriel was with the biker, while the farmer occasionally butted in every couple of minutes, only to get pushed back with the handle of a sword, or a well-placed punch. The same was happening on the other side with Embry, the thug and the guy in the ratty t-shirt. They could tell the civilian types didn't know what they were doing, so the intent was to get rid of them, not to kill.

Embry and Gabriel were outnumbered, which terrified me, as proven by the nail marks in my palms, but they had also been training for this for hundreds of years. Their reflexes were outstanding, and I could barely keep up with them while watching, so it was hard to believe the other guys were still standing.

I would be able to breathe easier if Embry and Gabriel got rid of the farmer and the guy in the old t-shirt for once and for all. They were more than capable of it, but I understood why they weren't. Finally, Gabriel butted the handle of his sword into the head of the farmer, who had been rushing at him, effectively knocking him out. He then slid his sword into the biker's stomach, barely waiting for him to fall before he went over to help Embry. He put the guy in a ratty shirt in a chokehold and held him until he passed out. Gabriel was lowering his unconscious body to the ground when I saw the biker he had just stabbed getting back up.

· · ·

"GABRIEL!" I screamed as I rushed out of the Control room, down the hall and pulled open the heavy front door. "Gabriel!" I yelled again, this time with a chance of him hearing me, but the biker had already made his way to him and plunged a dagger into his back. Embry had finished his thug, slicing the guy's carotid artery by the looks of it, and hurried to take care of the dying biker. I decided it was safe enough for me to run out of the house now, not that I could have stayed back at this point, even if it wasn't. The fact that Gabriel wasn't yelling at me to stay inside scared me more than anything else.

"I need something to stop the blood," I told Embry once I got close, putting my hands over the wound and applying pressure like they show you in movies, everything from my textbooks and first aid classes completely forgotten. I could feel the warm tears falling down my face, mixing with the blood on my hands, but Embry watched on without moving. "Why aren't you helping me? He's hurt, we need to save him." He always had my back. Usually.

"He's not going to make it," Embry said, his face a mask of anger and fear and adrenaline.

"There has to be..."

"You have to let him go," he cut me off with authority, and the lack of emotion at losing his only friend of the past few centuries reminded me that unless these four attackers were the Big Bad Gabriel was protecting me from, he shouldn't really die. Or more specifically, he should come back.

"We can't leave him outside," I decided, wanting to get away from the two dead bodies, and to be far away when the other two woke up.

"I'll bring him inside." Embry handed me the weapons they had used before carrying Gabriel over to the house. I had watched Sam carry Clara like that hundreds of times, and could remember Embry doing it for me too when I was younger.

Watching Gabriel be the one who was limp in someone's arms made me have to struggle for air as I walked behind them.

Embry paused in the doorway, then cautiously stepped in when I nodded to let him know it was safe and the house wouldn't attack him. He put Gabriel down on the couch in the drawing room off the foyer, with his head on the pillow as if he was sleeping. It was then that Embry finally took me in his arms and let me cry.

CHAPTER TEN

E mbry insisted I go upstairs and wash the blood off of my hands and arms, so I took a long shower, trying to let the stream of hot water melt the chill in my bones. I nearly scalded myself the whole time, but I was still cold when I got out. I twisted my hair up into a bun, put on some leggings and a big cream-colored sweater before going back downstairs, ready to sit and wait.

Embry kissed the top of my head before going outside, most likely to take care of the bodies and leave the other men far away from us. I was more concerned with the body in my drawing room.

The wound had stopped bleeding, leaving sticky, red goop in place of the warm, flowing liquid I still felt on my hands, though I had scrubbed them clean. Gabriel's eyes were closed, and his skin was already taking on that sickly, bluish white color of corpses. I could see the veins sticking out of his pale skin when I sat on the floor beside him and held his lifeless hand in mine.

I understood that Embry and Gabriel were special, that he would most likely come back, but I had never seen anyone go through it. Gabriel's story from the other day implied it took days to wake up, although I couldn't imagine Embry wanted us to travel with him like this, and it wasn't like we could leave him behind.

It was nearly an hour later when Embry came back and found me still sitting on the floor, still holding Gabriel's hand, still far from being okay.

"It won't happen instantaneously," he shared. "You should go back to sleep."

"Would you be able to sleep now?" I shot back at him. Even with him telling me Gabriel would come back, even though I knew it should be true. Looking at his dead body, I couldn't imagine leaving him alone, or going on with my life as if he hadn't died on us.

"Then why don't you go make us something to eat while I get washed up?" Embry suggested. I knew it was mostly to distract me from Gabriel's corpse, but he had been travelling and must be starving, so I nodded before going to reheat the leftover spaghetti and put the kettle on.

By the time his food and my tea were ready, Embry was back in the drawing room. He didn't waste time standing under the water for ages like I did.

He grabbed his plate and I followed him over to the other, unoccupied couch in the room. I didn't drink the tea, but held it for warmth while watching Gabriel, waiting for him to wake up.

"You still have a few hours," Embry told me, shovelling the noodles into his mouth.

"How do you know?" I asked.

"It has been taking less and less time as we go along, and last time he died on me it took him about eight hours to come back," he said with his mouth full, swallowing when he finished.

"And how are we sure this time won't be permanent?" I voiced my fear and tried not to think about how many other times they had died on me, without my ever knowing it.

"We're never absolutely sure," he conceded. "But our job isn't done yet."

"How did you figure this out?" I asked, cuddling closer to him, keeping my eyes on Gabriel just in case.

"Didn't Gabriel explain it all to you?" he asked.

"We're talking about Gabriel," I reminded him.

Embry sighed, putting the plate down, and wrapped his arm around me. "We lived normal lives, with the usual attempts at happiness, until Annabelle was accused of witchcraft."

I debated calling him out on how he breezed over the love triangle that made them both so invested in my ancestry, but his last words shocked me. "Annabelle was a witch?"

"No. She was accused and found guilty of witchcraft, but she was innocent," he said with conviction, as if that made it better. "She was sentenced to burn at the stake for her supposed crimes. Once someone spoke up against you, guilt didn't matter so much. She knew that and accepted her fate to ensure they wouldn't come after Margaret."

"She sacrificed herself for her daughter," I understood.

"She made the most of a horrible situation she saw no way out of," he specified.

"And she left her daughter with you when they took her?" I asked.

"No. When the inquisition started, before anyone even suspected her, she and Gabriel went to New York, but came back without Margaret. They told everyone she died on the journey and was buried in New York."

"She wanted her to be safe from any accusations of witchcraft," I understood, suspecting that I knew who watched Margaret until Gabriel and Embry got her back.

"She was convincing," he agreed, mostly hiding it, but I could hear a hint of bitterness that Gabriel had been in on it while he had believed Margaret died.

"But she told you the truth," I ventured, convinced they

would never do that to him. I knew Annabelle chose Gabriel in the end, but I couldn't imagine anyone not turning to Embry if they were in trouble.

"Not at first, but when she realized she would be named, she came to Gabriel and I under the cover of darkness and confessed."

"To the witchcraft?" I asked. Magic was the next logical step in their fantasy world of people with powers.

"She confessed to hiding Maggie, but she also knew she would be accused and found guilty of witchcraft. We offered to prove her innocence, but she believed the outcome was inevitable. She told us she was going to die, and made each of us promise we would do everything in our power to keep her daughter safe. She suggested having my sister raise Maggie, as she was married and already had children of her own. She knew it was a big commitment, but she needed to make sure Margaret would be taken care of."

"And the promise bound your fate?" I asked, thinking of Gabriel's confession.

"I promised that her blood would be mine, and I would protect her child as if she were my own," he agreed, which explained why he would still be here, protecting me.

"What about Gabriel?" I asked, knowing he had already died and come back years before this promise.

"Gabriel was upset that she was accepting her fate instead of fighting so she wouldn't die in the first place. When she said that even if he didn't understand it, he had to accept it, for her, he reluctantly made the promise, and added that he would find her. Always."

"That sounds like a goodbye. Why is Gabriel convinced she's coming back?"

"She promised us she would. That night we made the promises, she said death was only temporary, and she would be back someday. That she would find us, and we would have the happily ever afters we all deserved."

"I know you loved her, but you didn't think she was crazy when she said that? Or you didn't suspect that maybe she really was a witch?"

"I would have, but you didn't see her. It wasn't the ranting of a mad woman, she wasn't trying to soften the blow of losing her by promising we would see each other in the afterlife. She looked us in the eyes, completely sane, and believed it when she told us she would be back. She promised, and if you knew Annabelle, you would know that she...a promise was a promise."

"You were going to say she would rather die than break a promise," I called him on it.

"And you would have thought that made it less powerful than it was. We both believed her without the shadow of a doubt."

"You were there when it happened?" I asked, not saying it, but he knew I meant when she burned. He got this faraway look, like he was seeing it, and made me regret asking.

"She didn't scream. The others all did, but she got this determined look on her face, and for a second I was convinced she truly was a witch and the flames weren't burning her, that she was going to wait for the ropes to burn, then she was going to walk over to us and we would run off, leaving the town stunned."

"But she didn't."

"No. She just didn't let them win. She bore the flames without making a sound, she closed her eyes and let them take her."

"Then you went to Sleepy Hollow, got Margaret from Katherine and gave her to your sister?" I asked without thinking.

"How do you know about Sleepy Hollow?" he asked instead of answering.

"I did manage to get one story out of him," I admitted, looking over to Gabriel and remembering when my biggest problem was him not talking to me.

"That was the plan," he agreed, still shocked that I got Gabriel to say anything about Sleepy Hollow. It definitely wasn't the kind of story Gabriel had ever shared with me before.

"What part didn't work out?" I asked.

"We didn't realize we were being followed. We didn't know what the men wanted from us, or if it even had anything to do with Annabelle, but it made us uneasy. We took detour after detour, finally losing them when we got to the hallowed ground of the cemetery where Patrick was buried."

"Gabriel's brother," I nodded to let him know I knew who Patrick was, which he had expected when I knew about Sleepy Hollow.

"You would think it would make us feel safe, finding out they couldn't follow us into the church, but what men can't walk on hallowed ground?"

"They were possessed?" I guessed.

"All but one. The man leading them was the same man we stay alive to protect you from."

"The Big Bad." I expected as much. "Did you know he wanted Margaret, or did you think he was after you?"

"We were convinced he was after us, so Gabriel sent word to Katherine through a priest, and she brought Margaret to my sister while we kept sanctuary."

"But he killed you, right? He killed both of you and that's how you found out the promise made you not able to stay dead?" I struggled for a word to describe what they were. They weren't immortal, and could be killed just as easily as anyone else. They simply didn't stay that way.

"A woman was a few feet beyond the gate, crying for help, so I went to her. I was unaware that she was possessed and put there solely to lure me out. Once I was far enough from the church, the man came and asked me where Margaret was. I told him I'd rather die than tell him, so he laughed and pushed his dagger into my heart. The pain didn't register so much as the fear when I saw Gabriel running towards me, knowing the man would kill him too. The next thing I knew I was waking up in Katherine's cabin with Gabriel."

"You had both been killed and come back."

"Katherine wasn't surprised, she said it was nothing she hadn't seen before. Although she confessed that the woman who had lured me out had given her bread and some honey for Margaret as they were setting off the week before. She worried the man got what he wanted and left."

"Did he?" I asked. No one had ever gone into what happened next, although I was under the impression that Embry and Gabriel raised Margaret together.

"He found my sister." Embry had that look on his face again, like he was seeing something terribly painful. "My niece, my nephews, my brother in law..."

"Is this why you never mentioned you had a sister, like Gabriel never mentioned his brother?" I asked, putting my hand on his arm.

"Time numbs and dulls pain, but it doesn't erase it. I have lived for centuries and can tell you that the pain of loss, it never goes away," he confided, then took a deep breath before continuing, stating the rest of the story like it was nothing but a bunch of facts. "Gabriel's mother had taken Maggie for the day. She was extremely devout, and happened to be in church when the man arrived in town. I don't know if he didn't go himself, or if he couldn't sense her because she was in the lord's house, but my niece was the same age as Maggie and looked quite similar, so they did their business and left town. We were long gone with the real Maggie by the time he realized his mistake and came back."

"Do you even know what he wants with me?" I kept asking this question, but never got a satisfying answer. "End of the world, apocalyptic things?" I volunteered when he stayed quiet.

"Which we won't let happen." He looked at me imperatively, like convincing me was the first step to making it be true.

"You know, when I think about everyone Gabriel told me is like you, the only conclusion I can reach is that you are good. It's like God put an insurance policy on some people who were supposed to do incredible things, to make sure they couldn't die for good before curing some disease or inventing something or painting the Sistine Chapel or winning a war...Even if they used terrible means to achieve their purpose. Everyone he mentioned has made incredible contributions to the world. Why him?"

"I don't know Tesoro. Maybe it's the balance of good and evil, maybe he's a fluke, maybe he isn't dying because there was something good he was supposed to do, and the evil is getting in the way of him doing it. I don't have all the answers."

"What if you can never kill him? And he keeps coming after me and everyone I love until we're all dead?" I asked, walking back over to Gabriel, not-so-living proof that my fear was rational.

"Luce..."

He was saved from answering when Gabriel woke with a start, like when you fall in a dream and it wakes you up.

"Morning sleepyhead," I said, the relief bringing back the tears as I smiled, unable to contain how relieved I was. "You're okay now. You're back," I said, getting him to calm down.

CHAPTER ELEVEN

R osalind went from bed to bed, offering water, offering her time, offering whatever it took for one of them to be Roger. Every once in a while, someone would tell her they had seen him. Weeks ago. Or was it months? Maybe a year. They all told her incredible stories in which Roger had been a hero and saved hundreds of lives, but still, none of them ended with him coming home.

It was a busy day at the plantation house she and her husband had shared, which had become a make-shift hospital. There wasn't much to set this day apart from every other day since she had offered her house up for the wounded soldiers. Not much, except for a man with a pair of the most intense eyes she had ever seen.

They had found him in the fields, badly injured, but not quite dead yet. He was placed with the others who had little to no chance of recovery, as nobody expected him to ever wake up. They were letting him die in peace in a bed, until he surprised them all. He had barely stayed awake a minute, just long enough to look up at her intently, as if he'd known her forever. He had said, "Annabelle?" questioningly before slipping back into the comatose state he had been in since his arrival. She knew it was more likely that it was a spasm, or a last moment of strength before he would die and hopefully be reunited with this

Annabelle. Still, the intensity with which he had spoken to her made her believe that maybe he was one of the miracles who was going to pull through.

It wasn't until late the following morning that he woke up and managed to take a small sip of water. When he kept down a few bites of porridge, they decided it was time to move him into another room, with other men who were not on their death beds. He wasn't entirely out of the woods yet, but they no longer expected to walk into the room and find him dead.

Once he was able to sit up in the bed, Gabriel took to watching her; the nurse who looked like Annabelle. He had been watching her for a couple of hours, without letting anyone know. She hadn't recognized him, so this couldn't be what Annabelle had meant when she promised to come back to him. But the women were practically identical, so he needed to find out everything he possibly could about her. So far, he had learnt that her name was Rosalind, this hospital was her house, and the little monster who kept trying to 'kiss people better' was her daughter.

The girl, for one, looked nothing like Annabelle, or Margaret, or even Margaret's daughter, Adaline. Her hair was a pale blond, the color of straw, and her eyes were a deep, dark grey. Gabriel found himself wondering what the father looked like, or if this Rosalind had simply taken in a stray. Although he had made sure that no one had seen him watching the woman, her daughter made no effort to hide that she was watching him. Ever since Rosalind rushed off to treat a new arrival, the girl had been sitting on a desk in the corner of the room, her eyes fixed on him.

He did the mistake of returning her stare, which got her giggling, and apparently implied that she was now allowed to walk over, sit on the edge of his bed and start a conversation.

. . .

"*W*HAT IS YOUR NAME?*" she asked, curiosity winning over her shyness.*

"*Gabriel," he shared, deliberately giving her a thorough once over. "And who might you be? You're much too young to be my doctor."*

"*I'm not a doctor." She laughed, one of those innocent, childish laughs that he hadn't witnessed in years. He had been traveling a lot, but always came back to Massachusetts to check on Annabelle's descendants. This was the first time he had been this close and interacting with them, rather than just making sure everyone was safe and happy from a distance. "I'm Molly," she told him, looking around. "This is my house."*

"*I appreciate you letting me stay," he told her, deciding that although her looks were nothing like Annabelle's, the way her boots were covered in mud and her fingernails caked with dirt hinted that she might enjoy the same pastimes at least.*

"*We let everybody stay," she told him. "At first it was just daddy's friends, but then they brought their friends and now we have all kinds of people. My mommy helps them," the little girl said before looking around again.*

"*Your mommy is..." he pretended he didn't know exactly who her mother was.*

"*Her name is Rosalind, but daddy always calls her Rosie. He says she's beautiful, like an angel. I think so too. Do you?" Talking about her mother gave him back her full attention.*

"*Maybe more so," he said, thinking of Annabelle. "I haven't met your daddy." He hoped the girl wouldn't realize he was prying for information.*

"*He's not here," the girl shared, her smile disappearing for the first time. "They lost him. But we're trying to find him. That's his picture. Have you seen him?" She pointed to the small lithograph on the desk she had been sitting on.*

"*I have not, but I can keep my eyes open for him."*

"*Do you normally keep them closed?" she inquired.*

He was about to explain that it was an expression when Annabelle walked back into the room and his heart stopped in his chest. Rosalind, he had to remind himself. This wasn't Annabelle, although he couldn't wait to get her alone to figure out what was going on.

"What is going on?" Rosalind asked her daughter. "I hope she isn't bothering you." When she turned to him, for a moment he couldn't speak.

"She's been lovely company," he assured her.

"The doctor tells me you're making an impressive recovery," she told him. He could tell the way he was looking at her now was making her nervous, but she was too polite to comment on it, and as hard as he tried, he couldn't help himself. "I was here when they brought you in. None of us thought you'd even last the night."

"Guess I had something to live for." He made sure to smile instead of sounding bitter. He had lived the first few years convinced Annabelle was coming back to him, but after he buried Margaret, and Margaret's grandchildren, he believed it less and less. He was still too good of a catholic to do the act of killing himself, but he didn't see the harm in joining the army and brazenly rushing into the thick of it. Unfortunately, his suicidal heroism only brought him trouble and pain. He kept waking up after the bullets ended his life, and then he would have to change towns. It got to the point where he couldn't tell if he had died and come back to life while he was there, or if he simply recovered. He had recently developed a phantom wound syndrome, where he could still feel the bullet holes and stab wounds, even after he came back. He would have to check under the bandages to be sure, but until he was ready to leave, he didn't want to reveal himself.

"Well, I'm glad you pulled through," she told him, and he was sure she didn't like people dying in general, but the way she looked at him made him think she had especially wanted him to make it.

"I had an excellent nurse," he smiled.

"You should get some rest," she suggested, beckoning for her daughter to leave his bedside.

She wasn't Annabelle, because there was no way she could have gone through that conversation without revealing herself. Still, it was incredible how much she looked like her. He had known Annabelle's *face better than he knew his own, as hers was the one he saw every night as he fell asleep, and Rosalind's face was an exact copy, without even a freckle out of place.*

That was the last time Gabriel had woken to the face of an angel and believed he would finally be with the woman he loved again. He had died many times and woken to many faces, both friends and foe, but it wasn't until he woke up in the dim light of the drawing room to Lucy saying "You're okay now. You're back." That he finally felt that relief again, that at least for a moment, he could believe her. That everything would be okay.

CHAPTER TWELVE

Gabriel wasted no time once he was back from being dead. Embry said they were always hungry when they came back, so I went to get him some food. By the time I brought his reheated pasta to the drawing room, he was sitting up and making plans with Embry like nothing had happened and he hadn't been dead less than twenty minutes ago.

"We have to go soon," Embry looked up to fill me in when I walked into the room.

"Now. Before they come back," Gabriel urged, taking the plate I was holding in front of him and putting it on the couch beside him without looking up. I saw a blood stain on the white material beside the plate and had to turn away from it. Blood didn't normally make me queasy. As a future doctor, I had trained myself to be used to it, but wounds that killed my family were not something I liked to look at.

"Where are we going?" I asked, sitting with Embry on the other couch.

"I have some friends in Asia," Embry suggested.

"What about your cousin in Italy?" Gabriel finally looked up and turned to Embry, back to acting like I wasn't in the room. Or maybe it took a while to adjust to coming back to life and me constantly staring at him wasn't helping.

"Won't he be expecting that?" I argued.

"No, he won't, because he knows we know he knows about him," Embry defended Gabriel's idea, which didn't make any sense.

"I can finally go to Italy," I looked on the bright side. I had been asking to go for ever. Sam and Deanna were going to take me a few years ago, before she found out she was pregnant with Clara. We were still going to go, with me tagging along for their babymoon, but the day after I told Embry about it, the trip fell through. At the time I didn't think anything, but looking back, Embry probably discussed it with Gabriel, decided it wouldn't be safe and told Sam I couldn't go. We spent nearly a month at the Beach House that summer, which was a lot of fun, but it wasn't Italy.

"Not for fun," Gabriel argued, finally acknowledging me and knowing exactly what I hoped to do in the land of pizza and tortellini.

"Oh, I'm assuming you won't let me see the light of day while we're there, but I'll still be in Italy. Psychologically, it'll make being locked up way more bearable," I explained, seeing him roll his eyes.

"I'll be sure to sneak you some gelato," Embry promised. He was born in Italy, before his family came to America, which I now understood to have been in the 1660s. He was only a little boy when he left, but he had been back enough times that he spent so much of my childhood raving about the food, the architecture, the paintings, the culture and the weather. It was in large part his fault I was so eager to go, and he knew it.

"And pasta," I said with a smile, getting Embry to smile as well, but Gabriel was impassive.

"Maybe Terrence's will be safer while we're both recovering," he suggested.

"It is closer," Embry supported the idea. The possibility of bringing me to his cousin wasn't so exciting when he knew I was a death magnet being hunted by the Big Bad.

"Who is Terrence?" I asked.

"A friend of Gabriel's," Embry filled me in.

"We would have to fly," Gabriel said it in a way that hinted he was okay with that, but Embry might not be.

"Whatever's best for her," he sighed.

"You need to pack," Gabriel turned to me, getting down to business.

"You need to eat," I countered.

"Go," he said, unimpressed with my attempt at making him do something, but he did at least pick up the plate and take a fork twirl of spaghetti.

"Clothes for a week or…" I tried to get an idea of how long we would be gone for.

"Light on clothes, they don't matter. Bring the Chronicles and shadow book," Gabriel requested.

"What?" I asked. These were not items I ever had in my possession.

"He means the Book of Shadows," Embry clarified, as if that was my issue with Gabriel's statement.

"Like in Charmed?" I asked.

"It is what witches call the book they put their spells in, but Annabelle's is mostly remedies and useful information about the Big Bad," Embry used my terminology.

"Then she really was a witch," I concluded. "I thought she was innocent?"

"She didn't do any of the crimes they accused her of," Gabriel said with finality.

"And remember, we're travelling light," Embry reminded me as I headed for the stairs.

"Like suitcase, carry-on and a purse, or fit as much as I can into my backpack?" I asked.

"Like riding in the back of a truck full of chickens and roosters through a countryside in the middle of nowhere," he shrugged. I smiled at him, until I realized he was serious.

I TRIED to make my backpack something we could grab and run if the situation called for it. I didn't know how computer-savvy the Big Bad and his army were, but I figured we were on the run from now on, so cash would be better than credit cards, and I shouldn't bring any electronics. Not that I'd ever gotten my cell phone back.

I was also getting the impression we would be using the sketchiest truckers and private planes to hitchhike from place to place. The stuff normal parents would warn their kids to never do.

I packed the essentials, like a toothbrush, underwear, a pair of shorts, some shirts, a dress…I hesitated at the photo album, knowing I wanted to bring it, but it was too heavy to be worth it if they made me walk for days, which sounded like a possibility. My blankie, however, I packed. It was the size of a scarf, so I could justify it as something to keep me warm in the cargo hold, or in case we had to sleep outside. The truth was that Deanna was right, and I couldn't bear to leave it behind when I had no clue where I was going or when I would be back.

ONCE I WAS DONE, I went back down to the drawing room, noting a pile of books on the ground, with Gabriel pouring over another one at the coffee table.

"These are them?" I asked, motioning to the pile.

"These are books we're not bringing, but that should not be left in the open," Embry came in and explained.

"Isn't the house just a bigger bunker?" I asked, finding it unnecessary.

"We can never be too careful," he shrugged. I understood these would be extremely dangerous in the wrong hands.

GABRIEL HEADED off to the garage, but Embry helped me bring the pile of books down to the basement. The bunker extended past the house, under the creek if my sense of navigation served me right, but the only entrance was through a small door along the steel wall in the basement.

"You realize this is insane," I said after having to try three times before getting the bunker open, then having to take the books from Embry and carry them over to put them in the chest by myself. I maybe understood why Gabriel was so insistent that I wouldn't have time to run into the bunker if I was out in the field when someone evil came. I still thought they went way overboard as far as security was concerned.

"After devoting my life to keeping girls like you safe, I can confidently say that you can never be too safe. We have to keep trying new ways to keep you away from him."

"Unless the real solution to all of this is to let him have me," I suggested.

"No." He looked as angry and severe as Gabriel got sometimes. "I don't presume to know everything, but I will never, ever let that man have you. And when I say I would give my life to keep you safe, I mean many lives. All of them."

"We're never going to win then. Eventually, if we can't defeat him somehow, he is going to get me, or the next version of me."

"Not if we can help it," Embry said, as if that were a valid answer. "Could you grab that case and the dagger please? We don't want to keep Gabriel waiting."

"What's in this?" I asked, lugging the extremely heavy case across the room to him.

"Guns," he said as easily as if it were socks.

"Neither of these are making it through security," I pointed out, picking up the sapphire-encrusted dagger that I assumed was to slit my wrists if I was in the bunker and the bad guys were making their way in.

"I'm sure you've figured out that we won't be flying first class." He let me climb the stairs first, staying behind to shut the lights. That way he was the one who had to find their way up in the dark.

"Even the passengers in coach have to go through security."

"I think you have a too fancy idea of the planes we use." I could hear the smile in his words and hoped he was teasing.

"But no boats, right? I hate boats," I warned, but this time I looked back at him and saw the smile that made absolutely no promises.

"Try crossing the Atlantic Ocean in a boat with hundreds of people, before indoor plumbing was a thing."

"Was it an experience you would like to recreate?" I asked.

"No," he agreed. "But if we have to..." he stopped talking when he bumped into me. I stopped before reaching the top of the stairs. *Something was wrong.* I couldn't see outside yet from where we were, but I could feel it. I faintly heard the birds flying off in the distance and knew they had breached the perimeter, even before all the little screens in every room of the house warned us.

"Get in the garage. Tell Gabriel," Embry warned, looking like he was ready to fight.

"You're not going out to them," I argued.

"I'll hold them back while you get away," he told me, determined, before softening. "Don't worry, I'll find you."

"You want to create a diversion, so we can drive away," I called him on it.

"I do," he agreed. "The faster you leave, the more of a head start I can give you."

"Or we can all go together. I have a better idea," I told him.

"WHAT ARE YOU DOING?" Embry followed me up to my bedroom, but couldn't come inside.

"Getting these." I came out with the box full of bottles I had carefully prepared for this moment.

"This is cute. But Molotov cocktails are not enough of a diversion for me to come with you. I need to stay behind," he was apologetic.

"These are filled with fuel. The shed had bags of old fertilizer that were recalled for dangerous levels of ammonium nitrate. I poured those along the perimeter Gabriel loves to patrol. As long as I shoot these far enough, the fertilizer will explode, and we will be cut off from anyone trying to get to us."

"How would we get through?" he asked, looking confused, impressed and a little uncertain about my logic.

"The meadow," I said simply. "You don't put these fires out with water, you need flooding. I didn't bother putting any there because it wouldn't catch, or would go out right away."

"Your car will make it?" he asked, putting the pressure on me.

"Or we make a swim for it," I teased, but neither of us was laughing. "It'll work," I told him.

"I'll throw," he decided, sounding worried, but at least he was giving it a shot. "Go to the garage and set the alarm. If I'm not with you by the time the beeping stops, you tell Gabriel to go," he said in a way that left no room for arguing.

"One good throw should set the whole thing off." I wanted to make sure he would have enough time to get to us, and not waste time throwing more bottles than he needed.

"Go," he told me.

. . .

As I RUSHED DOWN the stairs, there was a huge bang at the front door. By the time I ran past it, the person on the other side, a 7-foot-tall boulder of a man, had moved on and managed to plow through the unbreakable glass windows. For a moment we just stood there, staring at each other. My face probably reflected the fear that had me frozen in place, but he looked at me like I was his winning lottery ticket.

I tried to make my legs run, either to the garage or the bunker, anywhere, but before my brain even considered screaming for help, the boulder tried to climb through the window to get to me. As soon as his fingers moved past the point where the glass had once been, a grey dust appeared out of the cracks, coating both of his hands. The substance was either a very powerful glue, or paralyzing him, because his upper body was not moving.

"Is this a friend?" the house asked me as the screens began to count down from five.

"No," I managed, my voice sounding foreign. The boulder and I looked into each other's eyes one more time before the grey dust activated and his arms turned to ash in front of me. He was determined to keep coming, but it was like an invisible barrier had settled where the window once was, covering anything that touched it with the grey dust. He got more and more of the dust on him, until there was nothing left.

I REALIZED I was still standing in the living room, watching the spot where he had been, so I shook it off and went to the garage.

"What's wrong?" Gabriel asked, already sitting in the driver's seat. "Luce?" he asked when I put my backpack on the seat, but didn't go in.

"They're here," I admitted, hoping my altercation gave Embry enough time to come down before Gabriel made us leave. I also couldn't get my mind off the guy at the window. I now had my answer as to what the house would do, but I didn't know if he had been one of the evil ones, or simply possessed.

"Get in," Gabriel ordered, pulling me from my thoughts.

"I'm setting the alarm." I shut the door to the SUV and went to the pad near the wall. I didn't expect it to make a difference, now that the house was already on high alert and murdering intruders, but I didn't want to risk leaving without Embry.

"Warning!" the box yelled once I put in the code. "Fire hazards surrounding location. Follow current route," she said as Embry barged in.

"Come on Lucy," he told me, so I followed him into the SUV and let Gabriel drive us out of the garage.

"Go towards the lake," Embry and I both told him. It was a good thing Gabriel spent so much time patrolling the perimeter, because a circle of fire surrounded the yard, bringing a thick cloud of smoke that hopefully obscured us. We drove through the meadow, turning left before we hit the creek, following the beach to another tiny road in the forest.

"What the hell was that?" Gabriel asked once the smoke cleared.

"The kid used science to create a diversion," Embry told him, looking back at the fire and smoke through the tops of the trees. "I can't believe that worked."

"Of course it did. You added fuel to the fertilizer she lined the woods with?" Gabriel looked to the both of us, fuming.

"How did you…"

"I worked Oklahoma City," Gabriel cut me off, saying the place like I should know what it meant. "That was a risky move. There's a reason those aren't in circulation anymore."

"But you left the bags of dangerous explosives in the shed next to our safe house?" Embry gave him a look.

"I figured they might come in handy," Gabriel said sheepishly. "If they know what they're doing," he added.

"Not as dumb as I look." I gave a small smile, but the adrenaline hadn't worn off yet, so I was slightly shaking.

"No one ever thought you were dumb, Luce, we just want to protect you," Embry gave me an encouraging smile before we drove through the woods in silence.

CHAPTER THIRTEEN

"Nice wheels," Embry told me, looking around the inside of my SUV once we drove out of the small town I grew up in. He nodded appreciatively as he touched the leather and played with the settings for heated seats and sun roofs. We didn't usually leave the estate when he came over, and I would never be the one driving. "Way nicer than my first car," he added.

I could tell he was trying to get my mind off what we just escaped. "You mean your horse and buggy?" I teased, noting the tiniest of smiles on Gabriel's face before he suddenly had to adjust his side mirrors.

"You know, being cute will only get you so far until you have to start relying on your personality. And that was mean," Embry said, putting on his shades and placing his boots on the dash. When he leaned his chair back and folded his arms behind his head, he looked like the lead singer from a rock band of the 90s. He had the leather jacket, black t-shirt, blue jeans and Ray Bans. Looking at him you'd think he hadn't a care in the world, not that he was hundreds of years old and on the run for my life.

"Is it still mean if you really are as old as I'm implying?" I caught Gabriel's smile in the rear-view mirror before Embry turned back to me.

"For your information, I didn't say the first thing I drove, I said my first car. And either way, yours is still nicer."

"Sam chose it because it was the safest. If we crash, we have more of a chance of killing the passengers in the other car than of dying," I explained, cringing like I had when Sam excitedly told me that fact.

"Comforting." Embry's sarcasm and our back and forth made this finally start to feel more like old times, before dangerous people were looking for me. Embry would come in the summers to keep an eye on me, then Gabriel would show up and even he would be singing along with us to the radio...

WE DROVE FOR HOURS, with Gabriel eventually putting on the radio to drown out Embry and my singing a cappella. I think he was tempted to join in for our renditions of classic rock songs, so he switched it to some radio talk show. Embry and I had to find other ways to entertain ourselves, such as reading the car manual, to show Gabriel how even that was more interesting than discussing the lives of reality stars none of us knew.

AT SOME POINT, Embry and Gabriel switched drivers, but I was in that land between sleeping and being awake, where your eyes are closed but your ears are listening. When I woke up, it was light again and we were stopped in the middle of a corn field.

"I thought you said we had to fly to Terrence's?" All I could see for miles was a rickety old barn.

"We do," Embry agreed with a smile.

"This isn't an airport," I pointed out.

"No, it is not." His smile got bigger. "We can't risk you being on the manifest and in the system. He would know where we were going."

"Is it an invisible plane?" I asked, looking around and not seeing anything that could possibly take us up to the sky.

"It's right over here." He walked to the garage and pulled on a tarp to reveal what was once a bright yellow airplane circa Amelia Earhart, but now looked like a rusted pile of junk.

"That doesn't fly," I decided.

"Oh, but it does."

"Maybe a few lifetimes ago, but..."

"It's a cropduster, Luce. It goes out all the time."

"For short trips. Close to the ground. Because of the multiple times it crashes. It can't take us anywhere."

"It'll take us to Terrence," Embry was way too confident.

"Where's the pilot?" I asked. The barn looked as abandoned as the crop duster.

"Right here." Gabriel walked past us to the plane and stuffed his duffle bag into a compartment meant to hold the water. Or the seeds? Whatever you dust the crops with.

"Since when can he fly?" Even before I finished the question, I knew it was silly. All I knew for sure since Gabriel found me at prom was that I didn't know anything about him and Embry.

"The first world war? Maybe before, but we weren't always in touch," Embry said like trusting Gabriel to fly us was no big deal.

"Where's my seat?" I asked once we got close and I saw one seat in the first cockpit and another in the second cockpit, but nothing else.

"Do you want to go on an adventure or not?" Embry asked like this was a fun activity I had wanted to be a part of.

"I don't want to die, so this is the lesser of two evils," I corrected.

"Let's make the most of it." He took my arm and led me to the second cockpit. I couldn't tell if his constant smile was just him, or if it was all for my benefit, to keep me feeling safe and happy all these years. Either way, I followed suit.

"Is it a short flight?" I asked once I was as buckled in as I could be while sharing a seat with Embry. We were travelling so under the radar that Embry and Gabriel were more likely to kill me than the Big Bad was.

THE FLIGHT FELT like it lasted days. I was so cold by the end of it that even with Embry lending me his jacket and wrapping his arms around me, I couldn't feel any of my extremities. We landed on what looked like an old baseball diamond. I could make out the white bases, but the lines had long ago disappeared, possibly around the time the grass yellowed and browned. Our makeshift runway became a cloud of dust once we got close, but it soon cleared to reveal a ranch in the distance. Big, brown cows and horses were grazing, but I didn't see any fences or dogs to keep them shepherded.

"Are we sleeping in the barn?" I asked, judging by our method of transportation.

"I'm sure we can find you some room in the attic," Embry teased before helping me out of the cockpit. The ground felt weird after spending hours up in the air. It was like my legs were still vibrating.

"You're a sight for sore eyes," a man, most likely Terrence, said when we walked up to the house with a large, wraparound porch.

"And you're as charming as ever." Embry went to take him in for a hug.

"I was talking to Miss Owens. The two of you look like death." They did both look exhausted, but that expression meant something different now that I had seen one of them lifeless.

"This is Lucy." Gabriel went and got a hug as well, making

sure they both forcefully slapped the other's back as a cover for it lasting so long.

"Nice to meet you, Lucy. I'm Terrence," he told me, extending his hand once they pulled apart.

Terrence had maintained a thick Irish accent, but looked like a cowboy with his hat and boots, plaid shirt and jeans. I would put his age somewhere around thirty, but wouldn't be surprised if he popped up in a John Wayne setting.

"Thank you for letting us stay here," I said, not sure how much he knew. Neither of the guys had called to warn him we were coming, but he didn't look the least bit surprised to see us on his field in the middle of nowhere.

"Any time," he assured me.

"Five settings for dinner?" an older woman asked, coming out in fitted jeans and a cream-colored sweater with gold accents, her long white hair neatly braided.

"Thank you, Angela." Embry smiled, but she didn't return it.

"You're always welcome," she said with a slight reluctance.

"You three can go get cleaned up, then you can tell me about the new pickle over dinner," Terrence suggested.

I FOLLOWED the guys through the house, walking like they had been through this many times before and knew exactly where to go.

"What did you do to Terrence's mother?" I asked Embry, somehow making Gabriel smile.

"I didn't do anything to Angela," Embry said in a way that implied he was only right on a technicality.

"That's not the vibe she was giving," I argued.

"He's telling the truth," Gabriel told me before slipping into the second room on the right once we got up the stairs.

"Explain." I stepped ahead of Embry and blocked his way. He

had promised to tell me everything, and this didn't seem like something he would have to lie to me about.

"Angela was sixteen the first time I met her, and her father didn't explain it all to her until many years later."

"That's Terrence's daughter?" I cut him off.

"That's why it's a curse. We still look the same, so you see us as this age, but I've raised children who've had children who had children...I've loved generations of kids who have all grown up, gotten older than me and died," he said, putting a damper on what I thought was a teasing conversation.

"He's eventually going to watch his daughter die. He'll take care of her and do all the things parents shouldn't have to do," I understood.

"It's a fate I wouldn't wish on anyone," he agreed.

I nodded, feeling bad, before I realized what he was doing. "You're making me feel like a horrible person to deflect from whatever you did."

"I did nothing," he stood his ground before sighing. "She had a crush on me. I didn't see her that way. I talked to her, I paid attention to her, I asked her about her life..."

"You fed into her infatuation," I summarized.

"I did," he agreed. "But I didn't realize she saw me that way."

"Until..." I pressed, but his face had gone red, which I had never seen before.

"She...made a move." He was careful with his words, but the shade of his face told me her move was a lot bolder than simply telling him she liked him, and possibly involved minimal clothing. "I turned her down, she was deeply embarrassed and never forgave me, even after her father told her how old I was and how it was never even a possibility in my mind."

"Does that mean you see me as more of a granddaughter than a little sister?" I asked, because I thought of him sort of like Sam. A big brother who always had my back, but would also play with me and tease me and stuff.

"I would have to say a niece, or a daughter. A sibling bond is similar, but you're on a more even playing field, where you still fight. You shouldn't be expected to raise your siblings unless a tragedy occurs. Keeping you safe and happy has always been my priority."

"It's unbelievable what you guys go through," I shook my head at all of the realizations going through my mind.

"With great power comes great responsibility," he teased before we got to the end of the hall. "This is your room."

"Not the attic?" I asked.

"Even Gabriel isn't allowed in the attic," he hinted that it held Terrence's secrets and treasures.

COZY AND WELCOMING WOULD BE the best words to describe the room I walked into. There were throw pillows and blankets in warm colors of the softest materials. Most of it looked like it had been knit or crocheted by Angela, or maybe her mother. There was a pile of towels at the foot of the bed, and some simple toiletries in the en-suite bathroom. They either knew I was coming, or were used to people showing up unannounced and in need of assistance.

I showered less forcefully than I had when I was covered in blood, but took the same amount of time, enjoying the warm water after the freezing plane ride.

I put on some of the clothes I had brought, but appreciated the warm wool socks and flannel jacket that were left on the bed, hopefully for me.

WHEN I CAME BACK DOWNSTAIRS, Gabriel was talking to Angela while Terrence showed Embry something in a book. It was strange to see Embry be the unwanted one, while Angela's face lit up talking to Gabriel.

"Does it fit okay? I thought you might be cold, now the sun's gone." Angela was the first to notice me.

"It's perfect, thank you," I assured her. "Do you often take in strays?"

"It's my granddaughter's. That's the room she usually takes when we visit, but she didn't come this month."

"You don't live here?" I asked, realizing I had no idea where 'here' was.

"No, we live in South Carolina, but I try to come check on the old man every month or so. My husband's a pilot of real planes, so I flew in with him and he'll come get me in a few days."

"The Boeing-Stearman Model 75 is a real plane," Gabriel argued. This wasn't the first time they were having this conversation.

"You should have seen how beautiful she was when we first got her," Terrence agreed.

"It's both of your plane?" I asked.

"No, Gabe had his own." Terrence had a look that told me there was more to the story.

"Had?" I asked.

"There was maybe an incident," Terrence shrugged like it wasn't worth mentioning.

"I knew the plane wasn't safe," I shook my head at the guys for having taken me up for such a long flight in an unstable machine.

"Come and get it while it's hot," Angela called from the dining room as she brought dishes from the kitchen. I went over and helped her carry everything out.

"Did you know we were coming?" I asked. Even though my shower was long, she didn't have enough time to go get groceries, then prepare and cook everything for three extra people. Plus, Terrence called me Miss Owens when I arrived.

"Visitors are not unexpected here," she smiled. "But I always overdo it when I visit my father. I know he can take care of himself, but I don't think he ever learnt how to cook. If you're going to eat something frozen, it better be homemade."

"You remind me of the woman who raised me," I declared, seeing Mrs. Boyd in her.

"Is that a good thing?" she asked.

"The best," I assured her with a smile.

"Then I will take it."

WE PUT all of the dishes in the middle of the table and let everyone help themselves. I opted for the chili, then added some corn and shredded cheese to it.

"Have some corn bread. Angie makes the best I've ever had," Gabriel encouraged.

"That's saying something," I smiled at her while the others agreed.

"More likely they're going senile in their old age," Angela dismissed the compliment.

"She's modest," Terrence told me. "And mean."

It was interesting watching the two of them interact. Angela still teased her father about being old and behind on the times, but she was the one who was older-looking and getting frail. I couldn't imagine what it would be like to stay young and healthy while watching your child eventually wither and die. I could understand why Embry never had kids, and Gabriel always tried to avoid attachment.

WHEN THE MEAL was done the men offered to do the dishes, so Angela took me out onto the front porch.

"How are you holding up?" she asked me, like she understood a lot more than she let on, and infinitely more than anyone told her.

"I'm okay," I told her. "How are you?"

"I'm old, but I'm not daft yet," she told me. "Uncle Gabe comes by pretty often, and as far as I knew, you were unawares of any of it and he wanted to keep it that way," she told me.

"Uncle Gabe?" I asked. This could explain how Terrence knew who I was earlier, but I couldn't picture Gabriel taking my picture from his wallet to show all his friends.

"He's my godfather. The only family my father has ever had, and the reason I got to have one," she shared.

"A family?" I asked.

"I didn't know any of this until I was in my twenties or so, but my father and Gabriel got close during the war, even before they found out my dad was like Uncle Gabe."

"They met before your dad first died," I understood.

"They fought battles, saved lives and my father spent 99 percent of the time he wasn't listening to other people's problems talking about how much he loved my mother and couldn't wait to get back to her. When he got shot in the head and woke up unscathed a few days later, he left his dog tags and helmet on another fallen soldier. He knew they would assume it was him, notify my mother and give her his last letter and her picture."

"It would be hard to explain surviving something like that," I ventured.

"True, but he could have been MIA rather than dead." I could sense some bitterness.

"He waited until the war was over to find her?" I asked.

"No, he meant it when he said goodbye to her in that letter. The war ended and he came to America, bought a piece of land and planned to live out his days as a hermit. Uncle Gabe confronted him as soon as he found out, and my dad told him that he had to leave her because he loved her, and knew this was no life for a mere mortal, and he didn't think his heart could take losing her later. He felt she was better off moving on with her life and finding someone new."

"The Gabriel way of no attachments," I agreed.

"No, Uncle Gabe talked sense into him. Told him there's no use in living forever if you never go after the things your heart wants. If you don't have someone to share it with, you're not dying, but you're not living either. He said he would take any kind of torture if it meant he could have a lifetime with the one he loved. His Annabelle," she rolled her eyes like she'd heard enough about this character. "My dad came back to Ireland, hoping to woo back my mum and found out he had a daughter. She'd only found out she was pregnant after he went to England and he supposedly died before she could tell him. He never would have known about me and I never would have met him if Uncle Gabe hadn't interfered."

"He always seems so distant and disconnected." I tried to picture Gabriel waxing poetic about true love.

"I'd be slow to grow attached if I lost everyone I ever cared about," she defended him.

"If you keep letting more people in, you can't lose everyone," I argued, thinking how I frequently lost people, but was never alone because I kept letting new people in.

"I didn't mean...of course I know you've had a hard go of it as well," she assured me. I couldn't help wondering what Gabriel had told her about me. Was he complaining about me trying to be friends with him? Feeling sorry for me because I only had Keisha?

"I'm used to it now," I assured her, sort of answering her initial question.

"It's incredible what humans can get used to," she sighed. "But it doesn't mean we should," she added before the others finished in the kitchen.

TERRENCE AND GABRIEL had a night cap while the rest of us enjoyed a tea Angela made from leaves Terrence grew and dried himself. It had hints of lemon and honey and berries and I couldn't tell you what was in it, but the first sip warmed me to the bone.

"We should get an early night if we want to be out by sunrise," Gabriel told Embry once he was done his whiskey.

"Where are we heading now?" I asked.

"You're staying here," Embry corrected.

"What do you mean? I thought you were supposed to protect me?" I did not like this new plan at all.

"We'll be gone a couple of days, a week tops."

"Where are you going?" I asked.

"We need supplies and information."

"On what? From who? You said we were travelling light, but we had tons of supplies at the plantation. And at the manor."

"You'll be safe with Terrence. I promise," Gabriel told me, so I understood this was one of those things they weren't going to tell me. I wanted to remind them I was an adult now and keeping secrets wasn't cool, but that would have been the perfect ammunition to prove they were right and I was too young to understand.

CHAPTER FOURTEEN

When I woke up the next morning, Embry and Gabriel were gone, but Angela made toast with eggs, bacon and hash browns.

"They left that," Terrence said as I came and sat beside him at the table.

"The Chronicles?" I recognized the leather-bound book my grandmother used to find my bedtime stories in.

"Thought you should know where you come from." He gave me a smile before we ate.

AFTER BREAKFAST, I set myself up in the living room and read some of Annabelle's entries. The first was from 1671, when a seven-year-old Annabelle took the Arabella to America with her parents. You could tell it was a child writing from the way she mentioned dolls and her pet cat, but I knew I was going to like her. She mentioned her fears, and all of the unknowns she was facing, but she carried on as if she didn't have any.

. . .

"ARE you sure they wanted me to read this?" I asked Terrence when he came and sat in his armchair the following day. Annabelle was quite the writer. So far, the book was her diary, recounting her school, her family, her friendship with Embry and her love for Gabriel. He had just proposed to her in her father's garden.

"It's your history, isn't it?" he pointed out, but I got the feeling he was purposely ignoring my question.

"I don't think Gabriel would want me to see him like this," I argued, coming to sit on the end of the loveseat beside him.

"How is that?" he asked.

"Sweet and romantic."

"It doesn't show anymore, but back in the day, I believe Embry was a player and Gabriel was the hopeless romantic."

"Player?" I asked.

"My great-granddaughter teaches me the lingo," he explained.

"That's nice." I could picture Mr. Boyd using a phrase Clara taught him in the same way, had he still been around. "It's hard to picture either of them like that."

"You should have known them when they were younger," he told me with a winking smile.

"Did you know them back then?" I wondered if Angela didn't know the whole story about her father's origins.

"No, I met Gabriel on the battlefields of the Second World War. But I have heard stories. From both of them, about themselves and about the other. It's a shame they haven't figured out that they've forgiven each other yet."

"You mean it's a shame that they haven't forgiven each other."

"No, I meant what I said," he assured me. "They think it's easier to pretend to hate each other. Old habits die hard."

"They're both still in love with the same woman. That they

think is coming back to them. If she does, them being friends would make it awkward all over again," I pointed out.

"Nonsense. People don't come back to life after being burnt at the stake centuries before. And if she did, she would be with Gabriel."

"How do you know if you've never met her?" I was intrigued by his convictions.

"They talk a lot when they're drunk," he said simply before deciding I needed more information. "If she comes back, hypothetically speaking, Gabriel will let her go with whomever she chooses. He loves her in that way where he wants her to be happy above all, even if it isn't with him," he shared, letting me know he did not see this ever happening. "Embry, on the other hand, will tell her to go with Gabriel. He knows that she loved him first, and was only ever with him because she thought Gabriel was dead. If she hadn't left town, he would have told her it was okay."

"You're all assuming she would choose Gabriel."

"They both say he's the one she's in love with. Majority rules," he told me.

"Have you tried explaining this to them?" I asked.

"They're stubborn as mules." He shook his head at what he saw as their stupidity, before changing the subject. "You just graduated from high school, right? Valedictorian?" he asked.

"Second in class," I corrected him. "My best friend was valedictorian." I thought of Keisha in her dorm room, completely oblivious to all the madness going on in my once semi-normal world. She always told me the others were crazy to think I was weird. How wrong she was.

"What are your plans now that school's done?" he asked.

"Not dying?" I shrugged.

"Not dying doesn't matter if you're not living," he told me. "My granddaughter went to art school. She paints like Van

Gogh." He said it proudly, but I cocked my head, wondering…
"Way before my time," he answered.

"I'll leave the painting to her and Embry," I turned down his art school suggestion. "Are you all artistic?"

They'd mentioned Da Vinci and Hitler as examples, and I knew Embry painted. I was also pretty sure Gabriel drew the portraits he had of Annabelle in the East Wing…it explained calling them Gifted.

"I can play the fiddle if need be," he smiled. "My grand-daughter says it's amazing what you can see in the most mundane objects when you try to paint them."

"I'll take her word for it."

"Before all hell broke loose, what were you going to study in the fall?"

"I was going into pre-med," I admitted.

"After my own heart." He brought his hand to his chest. "I was miserable at it. Hated the sight of blood, but couldn't stand the thought of carrying a weapon," he shuddered.

"Still?" I asked.

"Nah, I got better," he assured me. "At both."

I lost him for a moment before he shook it off. "Gabriel was better. He took me under his wing. Even talked me through stitching him up once. When I said I had no idea what I was doing, he said it was fine as long as it lasted until he found a better place to die."

"Was that when you already knew?" I asked.

"That he was going to come back to life and give me a heart attack?" he answered my question. "No, that's when I found out. Saw him die half a dozen times before I found out I was like him, then I understood that the stitching doesn't matter."

"Wounds disappear when you come back?"

"From the outside, yes," he agreed.

"What did you study outside of the army?" I asked.

"I wasn't one for books. I've taken a few classes here and

there if I find them interesting. Lots of history ones, to hear all the facts they get wrong." He smiled, and I could picture him sitting in the back of the class, getting into debates with teachers who couldn't compete with someone who lived through it. "I'm not one for the college experience."

"Me neither," I smiled, knowing there was little chance I would be going to parties and drinking kegs if ever I made it to college.

"So doctor is your dream? Saving lives or prestige?" he asked.

"Saving lives," I answered like the question should have been rhetorical, but he caught on to my slight hesitation.

"But doctor isn't your dream." He saw right through me.

"It's my dream career," I amended.

"Is it something embarrassing or are you afraid talking about it will stop it from coming true?" He wasn't letting me off easy.

"It's just silly," I tried to dismiss him, but he kept his eyes on me, knowing me better than he should for a stranger. "I love school. And learning. I am so excited for all the classes I'll take and things I will learn in med school..."

"But..." he pressed.

"But more than anything, what I want when I finish school, all of it, is to fall in love with an amazing guy, get married and have a bunch of kids. I want them to go to school and make friends and be confident and never be afraid and not lose everyone they care about," I said it quickly, like he wouldn't understand as long as I spoke fast enough.

"You want to give your children the childhood you never had," he finished for me.

"It's terrible, and I hate myself for it, but I am so jealous of Clara. She's like a sister to me, because her dad is my guardian, but she has her mom and her dad and a grandfather on her mom's side and she goes to the park and makes friends with complete strangers and...I want that," I admitted.

"Someday you'll have it," he told me.

"I'm hiding out at your ranch in the middle of God-knows-where because there's a guy, who basically can't be killed, who is hell-bent on killing me," I reminded him.

"You also have two men who will fight to their last breaths to make sure you get your happy ending. And many more of us who will do everything in our power to help."

"I wasn't complaining. I don't want to sound ungrateful, I just..."

"You don't want to get your hopes up because the most likely scenario is that it never happens," he understood. "You should try knitting."

"To defeat the Big Bad?" I asked, confused. He said it so seamlessly with the rest of our conversation.

"You're nervous and you're picking at your nail polish because you need something to do with your hands. Knitting gives you something to do and you get something cozy out of it."

"Is that what your wife did whenever Gabriel brought you into something?" I asked, looking around at all the knit blankets and pillows.

"She did," he agreed. "But I did as well. She made socks and sweaters, but all the pillows and blankets are my handiwork," he shared.

"You're full of surprises, Mr. Terrence."

"Most people spend their time showing you who they are, we're just too busy to pay attention."

THE NEXT MORNING when I came down for breakfast, Angela was knitting on the couch, what looked like a sweater dress in beautiful rust color. A pair of knitting needles and a ball of yarn sat on top of the Chronicles, waiting for me.

"I can teach you if you'd like," Angela offered without looking up.

"He likes solving problems," I said of her father, coming to sit beside her.

"He likes helping people," she corrected.

"He's good at it."

"My dad and Uncle Gabe stayed close for a reason," she told me with a smile, that I returned, but I couldn't wrap my head around her calling him 'Uncle Gabe', or how smiley he was with her.

"What's your dad's...um...gift?" I asked, not finding a better way to say it.

"You tell him the truth," she said simply.

"Like a lie detector?"

"No, it just comes spewing out, which was not cool when I was a teenager and didn't know it was basically magic," she said like she could name many instances where it got her in trouble and she shared way more than she wanted to with him. "He'll tell you he was bad at the medicine, but he was an incredible medic. People tell their secrets on their death bed, and he went from soldier to soldier, listening to their biggest confessions, aspirations and regrets. He listened and gave them peace."

"Like a priest," I ventured.

"No, my family stopped believing in God a long time ago," she said like she had no interest in a false savior.

"Was your mom like them?" I pried.

"Nothing like it," she shook her head with a smile. "She made the rule that us kids were not to know. I think she only agreed to tell us the truth because my brother had no tact and pointed out that she was getting old while dad looked as good as ever."

"Do you have a lot of siblings?" I asked, fascinated with the idea of someone like them having kids. It either had to be a family secret or you would have to keep abandoning them.

"My parents adopted twins when I was ten. My sister died when she was little..."

"I'm so sorry," I gave her my sympathy, but she waved it off, like old wounds you don't want to think about.

"And my brother was in Africa last I checked, taking pictures of lions or giraffes or something."

"That sounds like an incredible adventure." Africa was high on my list of places to visit. Everywhere was, but I wanted to work for Doctors Without Borders and take safaris on my days off.

"He bought into all of my father's adventures and still hasn't figured out that dad spread his experiences over multiple lifetimes with the knowledge that he wasn't going to die if his parachute didn't open when it was supposed to."

"He's given you a lot of heart attacks," I understood.

"Don't be the oldest," she told me.

"How come?" I asked, thinking how Clara basically made me an older sister, though I was the younger sister to Sam.

"You worry. So much. And you put this burden on yourself, like you're responsible for anything that goes wrong. All the pain, all the tears, as if you could prevent it." I got the feeling it was her sister's pain that kept her up at night.

"Isn't that where you try your best and that has to be good enough?" I said it more because it was what I was told than because I believed I would be able to tell myself that if something happened to Clara.

"But how much of yourself can you lose before your best becomes more than you had to begin with?"

CHAPTER FIFTEEN

The Chronicles turned out to be an excellent insight into the lives of my ancestors. After Angela left the ranch, I took it out with me to the barn and read on the upper level, that someone had converted into a tree house type of reading nook. Annabelle used the Chronicles as a diary, with near-daily entries up until she left town. She left the book behind, along with her heart.

To sum up the years she spent away, as well as the short time she was back for, someone had written a single paragraph:

"Annabelle married Henry Hathorne on January 8th 1690 in Salem, Massachusetts. Margaret Hathorne was born to them on December 22nd 1690. Annabelle returned to Boston in June 1691 and was burnt at the stake on July 19th 1692. Margaret Owens was then raised by Embry Dante and Gabriel Black."

Rosalind had a few entries after Embry explained everything, but she clearly wasn't inspired and didn't see the point to the Chronicles. She shared a couple of stories from encounters she had with soldiers during the war, and took down pages of remedies and medical procedures. Every page had a child's drawings in the margins. From what I could tell, she lived a mostly quiet life and died of consumption shortly after America won its independence.

Things got interesting again when I got to Cassandra's stories. I gathered that Embry and Gabriel kept her in the dark about her ancestry. She was many adventures in by the time they told her the truth. The first dozen pages were her trying to remember incidents that happened years before, when she had no idea about Gifteds, or Annabelle. It wasn't until Embry and Gabriel came clean to her that they became friends rather than distant relatives.

I had taken my time with Annabelle's entries. Each page felt like I was spying into the private lives of men who might not appreciate it. Cassandra's, on the other hand, was incredibly easy to pour through, like a novel. She had double the entries Annabelle did, but I was getting through them twice as fast. She made the most fantastic stories of guts and courage sound like run of the mill, everyday occurrences. She had a group of friends who kept popping into her adventures, especially Teddy, Lorie and Gen. I was surprised that a lot of her crusades weren't supernatural at all. She fought for labor laws and against abuse. I was reading about her arrival at Seneca Falls for the first gathering of the Women's Rights Movement when I flipped the page and felt myself going again…

"What do you mean, he found us?" Cassandra asked, the terror apparent in my voice. I knew I was her because Rosalind would never have worn such a beautiful dress in this vibrant yellow. Cassie was the ancestor who married into the money that bought us all of the cars and houses and most of my inheritance. Based on her doll, I always pictured her as the type of woman who walked around with an umbrella in the sun, smiling and making sweet tea. The Chronicles had since proven that she was a lot tougher than I gave her credit for.

"Gabriel saw him in town this morning. He's trying to get us *passage on one of the ships, but we don't have a lot of time,"* Embry *told her in that calm, soothing voice I mostly loved. Except when I had a valid reason to be upset and didn't want to be told everything would be okay. Especially now that I knew it was his Gift.*

"I can't leave Corinne. Alan already doesn't understand why we keep leaving without notice and I can't go without them," she argued, *and I reminded myself that Corinne was her daughter, and Alan was her husband. So far, she was the first of my ancestors who looked like me to never love Gabriel or Embry. Her heart always belonged to the man she married.*

"We can send for them once we are somewhere safe, but for now, you're the only one who is in danger," he was apologetic, and she knew *it wasn't his fault, but she was still upset.*

"Because I look like Annabelle," she said, exasperated, as if she had *been told many times but still didn't quite understand. I got the feeling that if she ever found herself face to face with the Big Bad, she would tell him to just get over it.*

"He wants you, and I made a promise that he would not get you," Embry *said in a way that made you believe him, even if you knew he had no way of keeping his word.*

"I think your promise ended a century ago," she argued before *everything got foggy.*

WHEN THE FOG CLEARED, *it was nighttime. Neither Gabriel, nor Embry were anywhere near. I could feel Cassie's fear. Although I wasn't in any real danger, I knew she was, and my heart was pounding in her chest. I was convinced you could hear it from miles away, which was probably how the man found us. He wore a nice, dark grey suit and looked like a proper gentleman, except for the murderous look on his face, and his eyes. Embry and Gabriel's eyes were black, which I had frequently pointed out when I was younger, but this man's eyes were so dark that I wasn't even sure if they were eyes at all, or if they were just dark holes.*

"*Run and catch, run and catch, the lamb is caught in the black-berry patch,*" *he said, taunting her with a smile. He enjoyed seeing her like this, terrified, and knowing nothing she could do would stop it. "No bodyguards tonight?" he asked, tilting his head and coming closer, dangerously close, so I could smell his breath. A mixture of pipe tobacco and strong alcohol.*

"*If you have me, you stop? No more coming after my family?" The words shocked me, but they were the first she said with purpose.*

"*Of course, love. Once we get you, there's no more family for us to come after," he said with a laugh that curdled my blood.*

"*What do you mean? What do you want with me?" she asked, having not accounted for this. She came out in the middle of the night, alone, knowing he would find her, because she thought it would be the end of their hunt for the women of her family.*

"*You don't only carry your essence in that lovely little shell of yours. You carry the essence of your entire line. Past, present and future." The joy in his laugh would haunt me, as it would have haunted her, if she hadn't taken off, running surprisingly fast for the high heeled shoes she had us wearing.*

She ran through streets she knew well, turning before I even real-ized there was another street, or alley. We were getting away, and she became more and more confident as we got closer and closer to where I could only assume Embry and Gabriel were.

I recognized the cliff from one of the paintings in the manor. You could see a lighthouse in the distance, and I remembered noticing a cottage at the base of the cliff, when a searing pain shot through my side.

I had never expected the men who hunt us to use guns, and I doubt Cassandra had either. We stopped for a second, for her to put her hand to the wound and see from the crimson on it that she had effectively been shot in the back, through her lower abdomen, and the warm blood was pouring out, running down to her leg.

She looked back and saw that he was gaining on her, so close now and so sure of himself, of his win. She had to know there was no way she could outrun him like this, but she kept going, slower than before, and in excruciating pain, as he laughed, no longer worried because he knew he had her. She stumbled, and his laughter grew louder, until she got to the side of the cliff. She inched away from the wooden railing that hid a staircase, closer to the jagged rocks you could hear the waves crashing into.

"What..." I heard him start, afraid for the first time, before I felt us jump. I was falling, the air like ice against my face, but a calm rushed over me, like I was finally at peace. He wasn't going to get me. We were safe.

I WOKE up with a start on the edge of the upper level of Terrence's barn, confused as to why a pair of strong arms encircled me. I tried to break free at first, terrified that the man had found some way to follow us off the cliff and get us. Then I saw that it was Gabriel's arms, and they were the only thing that kept me from jumping off the second floor of the barn.

I looked up to him, trying to catch my breath, aware that tears were running down my face. He was breathing heavily, like he'd had to run around before finding me up on the landing, about to jump to my death. While I was terrified, he looked furious. As soon as he gave me a once-over to make sure I hadn't been harmed, he released me to the side of the room that didn't have a twenty-foot drop.

"What the hell do you think you're doing?" he asked. I thought he was using this fury to disguise how he was just as scared as I was.

"Cassie wasn't shot in a robbery. She jumped," I said, trying to process the lie I had been told when I asked about the others. Burned at the stake, consumption, robbery, fire. That was what I had been told. He looked at me, shocked, before spotting the Chronicles on the floor by the couch. He looked at me with a mixture of anger and guilt, but also like I was the one who had done something despicable, before walking off without another word.

I brought my arms around myself in a hug, and looked over the edge, wondering for the first time if the dreams might not be a warning from my ancestors, like I had thought, but a game of this evil person's, to see if he could get to me without even lifting a finger.

CHAPTER SIXTEEN

I brought the Chronicles with me back to the house, where Embry was waiting on the porch. "What happened?" he asked.

"You lied to me," I said, torn between wanting to let him take me in his arms and comfort me, and being mad at him for yet another lie after he promised it would be the truth from now on.

"I can count on one hand how many times I've seen Gabriel that upset, and I wouldn't need three of my fingers," he implied Gabriel was the more pressing matter.

"Cassie was shot in the stomach and jumped off a cliff so the Big Bad wouldn't get her," I stood my ground.

"You read it," he understood, seeing the leather-bound volume in my arms. His body language immediately changed, going from being tense and upset to guilty and defeated.

"I started to. Did you put the truth in the book, or did you lie in the Chronicles as well?"

"Saying she was shot in a mugging isn't entirely a lie—"

"That isn't the point," I cut him off even as he tried to diffuse the situation. "Was Cassandra shot in a mugging or did she jump off a cliff so the Big Bad couldn't have her?"

"Getting shot would have killed her. She just sped up the process by jumping," he said as if it was a technicality issue, as opposed to him lying to me about why she died. "It's all in the Chronicles that you somehow felt you had the right to read."

"It's my history," I defended myself, deciding not to incriminate Terrence.

"And their diaries," he reminded me. "You can't just read the Chronicles and assume you know everything. They're one-sided and..."

"I didn't," I argued. "I mean, I did read them, but I didn't get to the part where Cassie dies yet. I lived it."

"What do you mean?"

"I was inside her while it happened. I felt her heart pound against my chest, the bullet pierced my back...I was her." I kept bringing my hand to my stomach, expecting it to come back bloody like hers had, but I was fine.

"Has this happened before?" he asked, concerned rather than defensive.

I nodded before admitting, "I used to think they were dreams, but then I realized they weren't. I was sure it was them, my ancestors, giving me clues or warning me. Now I think it might be the Big Bad attempting to kill me from a distance." A shiver ran through me.

"How?"

"I woke up in Gabriel's arms, because he caught me when I jumped off the cliff," I explained.

"He was controlling you?" Embry looked horrified.

"No, I was Cassie. She jumped, and I was inside her, so I tried to do the same."

"Did that happen the other times too?" he asked.

"No, but I haven't died as the others yet." When he looked at me, he could tell I was shaken, but it was dying as Cassie and almost dying as me that bothered me more than the lie at the moment. Although that wasn't cool either.

"It's okay," he told me, coming close.

"I don't want you to calm me down now," I argued. "I want answers."

He sighed before admitting, "She left while we were recovering. There was a confrontation and we managed to get the upper hand, but I died and Gabriel got hurt. He was holding on until I came back, so she wouldn't be completely exposed, but we were in no condition to protect her." I could hear all of his guilt for not being with her when it happened.

"You were waiting in the cottage at the bottom of the cliff." I had figured as much, from how fiercely she tried to get to it.

"She could see we were no match for him, even when we weren't lying half-dead in her Summer house, so she got the idea that giving herself up would somehow protect Cory."

"It wouldn't," I shared. "If they'd gotten her, she and Cory would have died."

The confirmation of his suspicions, or the fact that I knew this information, surprised him for a moment. That part wouldn't have been in the Chronicles, as he was never privy to her final conversation. "Almost losing you, then reminding him of how we lost her..." he tried to defend Gabriel's reaction.

"He needs to grow up."

"He was never great at dealing with emotions," he agreed. I gave him the tiniest of smiles, because I knew it was what he was trying for.

"If he doesn't want anything to happen to me, you guys shouldn't leave me like that."

"We needed information and Terrence would have defended you as fiercely as we would," he stood by their decision. "But we're going together this time."

What information?" I asked, but he got a look that raised another question. "We're leaving?"

"They found us," he admitted.

"They're coming here?" My heart beat faster and I suddenly felt sweaty.

"I don't think they know where the ranch is, but they landed at Houston Intercontinental." He used what must have been the old name for the George Bush airport, but at least it gave me a better idea of where we were.

"Where are we going?"

"An old friend's."

"You have a lot of those," I pointed out.

"I'm very old," he conceded with a smile.

"If you can't defeat him, what are we even doing?" I brought it up even though I knew he didn't want me to. I assumed that as my protectors, they could protect me, but if the bad guy won every time... "What's the point?"

"We are keeping you alive," he said like it was the only justification needed.

"We spend the rest of my life hiding, running away every time he finds us, hoping we never have to go up against him? That doesn't sound worth it," I pointed out.

"Your life is always worth it," he told me. "And we can't let the alternative happen."

"What happens if he gets me?" I pressed. "The guy with Cassie said something about my essence?"

"I don't know exactly what he wants with you Tesoro, I just know it's bad and that Annabelle let them burn her alive to prevent it," he said with finality, so even though I had more questions, I went upstairs to put everything I brought into my backpack. I also found room for a misshapen pair of socks I spent an embarrassing amount of time on.

When I got downstairs, the guys were waiting for me in the kitchen.

"You have been a wonderful, yet nervous house guest and it was a pleasure having you." Terrence got up from his chair to take me in for a hug.

"Thank you, so much. For everything," I said, trying to let him squeeze the fear and nervousness out of me.

"Don't forget this." He picked up the knitting needles and ball of yarn I had been working on.

"I don't have room for it," I argued.

"Taking care of great adventures is perfectly fine, but you need to take care of yourself as well," he insisted.

"Thank you," I said again, hoping he knew how much I meant it.

"You can come back anytime. We will always have a room for you."

"Same goes for you at my place, once it isn't so dangerous," I assured him.

"You take care of yourself now."

"You too." I gave him another hug before going outside and waiting for the guys to join me.

"WHERE TO?" I asked, looking at the expanse of land with only the crop duster and Terrence's truck to get around.

"The River," Embry told me, while Gabriel was quiet. Silent was his default setting, but today he was doing it on purpose.

"I don't see a river," I pointed out, looking around. I also didn't remember seeing one from above.

"Didn't you say you wished we could do more hiking?" Embry smiled, trying to pretend this morning hadn't happened, as we followed Gabriel to the wooded part of Terrence's land.

"When I was eleven and we played the survival game in the woods," I agreed, realizing as I said it that some of the 'games' Embry did with me when I was growing up were more like training for this eventuality.

"It'll be fun," he said with a smile that told me it would not be fun, but we would get through it and have stories to tell someday.

"What happens to Terrence when they show up looking for me?" I asked, taking a look back at the ranch that was as peaceful and quiet as when we arrived.

"He'll talk his way out of it," Embry told me confidently.

"You don't believe that," I argued.

"I do," he said naively. "If he doesn't, then he'll wake up in six to twelve hours and we will make it up to him," he assured me.

"Will he try to get information from them?" I asked.

"I don't think he has the upper hand against..."

"Not like that, but with his power."

"Oh...he told you?" Embry was surprised, and I could tell that Gabriel was listening in, even as he walked ahead.

"Angela did. Although I'm pretty sure he used it on me."

"It's not like that. A Gift like Terrence's is always running in the background, whether he wants it to or not. If he encounters someone with mental defenses, he might have to concentrate and work at it, but otherwise it just happens."

"And you're sure he hasn't done whatever he was supposed to?"

"Unless his purpose was to harbor you. We never would have gone to him if he had," he assured me.

CHAPTER SEVENTEEN

We spent the rest of the day in the woods, not exactly hiking, but walking through sometimes treacherous paths to get to this river they implied was out there. I usually lived in flip flops all summer long, so I was happy I opted for hiking boots instead. Not so thrilled we hadn't taken any of Terrence's horses.

"Are we there yet?" I asked Embry expectantly, getting him to laugh.

"Soon," he assured me.

"Is it really this far or are we lost? Or is this our new technique, where we wander the woods, lost, and hope they can't find us because we can't find us either?" I asked, more to make conversation than because I thought it was true, but I could see the back of Gabriel's shoulders tense up with his annoyance.

"We know where we're going," Embry assured me without any hint as to how far it was, or if we were taking a roundabout route to get people off our tracks.

"Should we play I Spy or…"

"This isn't a game." Gabriel stopped and turned to face me,

unable to contain what I thought was annoyance, but could now see was anger.

"Wandering through the woods, or the adventure you've taken me on?" I asked. He didn't know it yet, but I knew exactly what was going on.

"Both! We took you away from the manor and are trekking through the woods right now because someone evil is after you. They want to kill you, or worse." He tried to scare me into seeing the seriousness of my situation.

"Gabriel," Embry tried to warn him.

"I know," I said simply, with a heaviness I hadn't used for the banter with Embry.

"Then why are you acting like a child?" Gabriel brought his hand to the pulsing vein in his forehead, which I usually found funny, but not today.

"Because you're treating me like one. I just felt Cassie's last moments. I didn't see them, I felt them. Then I woke up and I was hanging over a ledge. I would be dead if you hadn't caught me. And that's not even the bad guy you're warning me about, that's just me. So yes, I get it. This isn't a game. But I'm not a child. And lying to me won't make this easier. Tell me where we're going and tell me what I'm up against, but don't leave me somewhere for a week with the promise that I'll be safe when no one can promise that." I blew up at him, cursing the tears that made me feel weak and vulnerable when I wanted to convey how wrong it was to keep lying to protect me.

My words gave Gabriel pause, but his anger was ever-present.

"None of the others had the dreams," Embry filled me in. "It's new for us too."

"Do you think it's from him? Or from them?" I asked of the Big Bad and of my ancestors.

"I hope it's from them, but I don't like how far you went, or how close you came to…"

"She was off the ledge," Gabriel shared through gritted teeth. I got the feeling he believed the memories had less friendly origins.

"Any of the others jump to their deaths?" I asked, a terrible attempt to lighten the mood, but it did the trick.

"No," Embry gave me a desolate smile.

"Can we stop being mad at me and hiding things from me now?" I asked.

"We will try to include you." Embry looked pointedly to Gabriel for confirmation.

"If there's a benefit to you knowing it," he reluctantly agreed.

"What about the location of the river?" I got a small smile.

"We're not walking in circles, we're avoiding a canyon, which is why you didn't see the river from the plane," Gabriel shared. I was starting to understand that Embry didn't know where we were going either.

"Will we get there before it gets dark?" I asked.

"You'll have a roof over your head to sleep," Gabriel assured me, kinder than he had been all day, but I still wasn't sure what that meant.

It was nearly 9 o'clock by the time we got to what I would call a mudslide. Branch-like-roots grew from the ground, which was slanted in a way that would be dangerous to climb, even in the best of conditions, but especially today, when everything was slippery.

"Can we get around it?" I asked as the sun began to set, leaving us more and more in the dark.

"Nope."

"We have to go through it," Embry shrugged.

"Not through it, into it. This hill..."

"Landslide," I corrected.

"...takes us down into the ravine, which we can follow to the river," Gabriel continued like I hadn't said a thing, though I did get a stern look.

"Where we have…" I asked, dreading the answer, but anything else would be worse.

"A boat. It's much too far to swim," Gabriel told me.

"I did tell you guys I hate boats, right?" Both of them had gone back to the mudslide. "Rowboats and canoes on the creek are fine, but anything else is…" I didn't want to go into details about the time my class took a tour of the Boston Harbor, but it was far from being pretty, and not an experience I ever wanted to repeat.

"It won't be like your field trip," Gabriel assured me, so I turned to Embry, knowing I hadn't told Gabriel about it.

"You'll be fine," Embry assured me before we got down to the muddy ravine floor, with the tiniest of streams, and followed it to the bed of the river.

"How far is your friend?" I asked Embry, seeing nothing but a single kayak on the smooth rocks surrounded by trees.

"We wouldn't make it in that," he told me, shaking his head.

"Do I get to spend lots of time on your big ship?" I asked with fake enthusiasm, remembering how horrible I felt on the rough waters of the Harbor.

"I would call it lots of things, but big isn't one of them," Gabriel said, moving some branches and moss off an old tarp, to reveal a tiny fishing boat, about half the size of the one from Jaws. All I could remember was that line…

"We're going to need a bigger boat," I said to myself.

"It's perfect," Gabriel argued. "Small enough to stay under the radar of anyone looking for people travelling long distances, but big and powerful enough to get us to our destination."

"Which is how far, exactly?" I asked, not a fan of our means of transportation.

"A night or two, depending on if the current cooperates."

"There's no motor?" I asked, shocked.

"There is, but it's small. A strong current would tire it out, but we should be fine," he assured me. Embry didn't look any happier than I was, but he wasn't complaining.

The boat consisted of a tiny glass cabin from which Gabriel could steer the boat, and what I might call a 'crevice' below deck. The deck itself had to be walked by one person at a time and even then, Embry's football player frame found it tight. Gabriel offered me his hand to get on board, where I immediately went below deck with my blanket, hoping it would be better if I couldn't see the water.

I GOT LULLED into a false sense of security, thinking I had been wrong and boats weren't all as terrible as the one from my class trip, until the calm, stream-like river turned into River Rapids leading us to the ocean. The boat rocked so violently I was convinced we were going to tip over and be lost at sea.

"We're fine," Embry assured me, sensing my fear.

"It feels like we're tipping," I argued.

"You'll be better up on deck," he suggested, as I gripped the sides to brace myself and closed my eyes in an attempt to not throw up.

"Seeing it won't help," I argued.

"It does," he promised. "When we came to America, it was terrible. Our boat was bigger, but there were so many people and the stench made me feel like I couldn't breathe," he reminded me of his past experience with ships.

"Didn't half the passengers die during those crossings?"

"Not half, but a fair amount," he agreed.

"I think the only reason I'm not sick is because I would die if I had to spend the rest of the trip in a closed space with vomit all over me."

"That's smart," he humored me. "But I've always felt it's better out than in."

"Not helping," I warned him.

"Do you want me to distract you?" he offered.

"Yes please." I closed my eyes tighter. "Tell me about you."

"You know all about me," he argued.

"I know the lies of omission," I corrected.

"I know we kept things from you, and you have every right to be upset, but that doesn't mean that what I told you before was a lie," he got defensive.

"But it wasn't the truth," I called him on it.

"You didn't find it strange that we never got older?" he tried to put the blame on me for not noticing on my own. Deanna had also pointed out their youthful looks, but people in my world tended to leave before getting noticeably older.

"Neither did Sam," I argued. It took me until this summer to realize my big brother wasn't fifteen anymore. "And I trusted you. I had no reason to doubt you."

"Without fail, every single one of you has been way too trusting," he sounded exasperated.

"If I couldn't trust you and the Boyds, I had no one," I defended myself.

"I'm not saying you shouldn't...I'm saying you should question things, no matter who tells them to you."

"Do you plan on lying again?"

"I want you to know the difference and catch me on it if I do." His words stopped the rest of my rant.

"You might want to brace yourselves," Gabriel poked his head down.

"Why aren't you driving?" I asked, not appreciating the sight of our captain in a place where he had zero visibility of where we were going.

"The boat can't be steered right now, the storm is going to take us wherever it wants to," Gabriel said calmly.

"Why am I the only one panicking?" I asked, looking to the two of them. Embry was bracing himself for something unpleasant, but Gabriel was entirely unconcerned.

"We aren't going to crash or sink, but it might take us a little longer to get where we're going," Gabriel shrugged before going above deck. Before he closed the latch, I could see the sky was a ghastly shade of black, with lines of white when lightning tore through it. This was not the time to be on a boat.

"Why don't you try to get some sleep?" Embry suggested.

"Sure, we're about to be torn apart by the ocean, so why don't I go take a nap." I looked at him like he was crazy.

"You've been hiking all day, it's nighttime, and there is absolutely nothing you can do. Might as well get some rest rather than stay up worrying about it so you're tired and useless to us tomorrow."

"Could you sleep?" I turned it on him.

"I could if you did," he shrugged. "Come on." He motioned for me to come over, so I reluctantly let go of the side of the boat and sat beside him. He immediately wrapped an arm around me so I had something anchoring me down.

"I don't think this is going to work," I warned even as I yawned.

"At least your eyes are closed," he pointed out.

"That's not the same thing," I argued, cuddling closer.

"Rest your eyes then. I've got you," he told me, and even with his warning about not trusting people, I somehow believed him and managed to fall asleep.

CHAPTER EIGHTEEN

When I woke up, I could hear the storm still raging outside, but the water felt calmer. Embry was asleep with a tiny pool of my drool on his shoulder. I would have been embarrassed, but the more awake I got, the more I felt sick. I decided to try Embry's advice and went onto the deck.

The sky was still dark, with grey clouds and rain, but it looked bluer. It was like this rain was trying to wash us clean while the other had been trying to drown us.

"Everything okay?" Gabriel asked, putting away a telescope as he came over to me in his bright yellow raincoat. He opened the door, so I could follow him into the glass shelter.

"Are you using the stars to navigate?" I asked. "We have GPS and satellites now."

"I'm making sure we're going the right way." He rolled his eyes at me.

"Where are we going?" I asked.

"It's a safe house for people like us."

"Whereas that was Terrence's house-house," I understood, having stayed in the room his great-granddaughter usually sleeps in.

"If the safe house gets compromised we just find a new one. No one gets discovered or is in danger."

"Do you think he'll find us there as well?" I asked.

"Eventually," he admitted, causing a shiver to run down my spine. "But we will hopefully have moved on by then. We'll try it for a couple of weeks. If everything is safe and quiet we will stay longer. If we hear whispers or rumors about you, we'll find somewhere else."

"And that's our game plan?" I asked, not very reassured. "Keep running, making sure we're one step ahead so we can leave by the back door when he knocks in front?"

"You don't want to be lied to anymore, right?" he verified before answering.

"Right," I agreed. I was certain that I wanted to know what was going on instead of the lies they had been giving me, but I was also aware that I would regret the decision.

"Right now, it's all we can do. We can protect you and keep you safe, but hiding and running are our main defenses. In open battle, against him and his army all together, we don't stand a chance."

"So we always need to escape before he reunites with his army," I said like it was simple rather than terrifying.

"Exactly," he agreed.

"Forever?" I asked.

"From my experience, he usually gives it his all for a few months, then leaves us alone for a while."

"How long is a while?" I asked. I could deal with this for a few months, but I wasn't sure I trusted the possible calm before what would definitely be the storm.

"Months, years…it depends. I'm just saying this isn't what the rest of your life will look like."

"We just need to keep me alive long enough for him to give up for a few months," I summed it up.

"Exactly." Compared to the alternative it was good news, but it still painted a pretty bleak picture.

I STAYED in the cabin until it stopped raining, right before the sun peeked through the clouds to light the horizon. It would have been absolutely beautiful if the waves hadn't threatened to pull us to the ocean floor. I went out onto the deck at that point, holding on to the rail for dear life. Embry was right that being outside helped. He joined me not long after the sun claimed its spot in the sky, then took over in the glass cabin so Gabriel could get some sleep.

BY THE TIME Gabriel woke up from his nap, I was starving, and my empty stomach liked the rocking of the waves even less than my fed stomach had.

"Perfect timing," Embry said when he saw him.

"Why?" I asked, spotting what looked like a shipwreck graveyard in the distance. Some of them looked like old pirate ships, some were fishing boats, and there was even a rowboat by an orange buoy. I told myself its occupants had jumped ship, rather than imagining that something from the water came out and got them.

"We're here," Gabriel explained.

"I think I'm safer with the minions," I voiced my concern.

"You're better at this part," Embry told Gabriel, leaving him the wheel in the glass cabin so he could maneuver us through jagged rocks, coral and ship carcasses. I spotted an eel and possibly a crocodile, but refrained from asking them if the kraken and inferi were real, deciding I would rather not know until we were out of this particular area.

· · ·

"WHAT WAS THAT?" I asked, bracing myself when the entire boat shook. It felt like we hit an iceberg.

"Not what, who," Embry said with a smile.

"Caleb," Gabriel explained like he'd had the same reaction once upon a time.

"I was worried you wouldn't make it." The voice belonged to nearly 7 feet of pure muscle, but he had the kindest face when he smiled over to Embry. Caleb steadied our boat on the shore with one hand, helping us disembark with the other.

"How does everyone know we're coming?" I asked, figuring the Big Bad would find us as easily.

"I heard what happened at Terrence's. You were either heading to me, or to Rosenberg, and he's better at confrontation." They exchanged a look that made me feel like I didn't ever want to meet Rosenberg.

"Is Terrence okay?" I asked of our last host.

"They were using Silas, so they didn't even bother sending him into his next life." Caleb didn't sound happy about it.

"Really?" I was relieved Terence was okay, but it did not make sense to me that this evil person who was hell-bent on killing me would get their hands on someone who harbored me, and let me escape, but just let him go.

"Silas is similar to the man who's hunting you. He won't control you, but if he touches you, he can read your mind. Even after he's gone, that touch is a bond and it's like he's right in front of you," Embry explained as if he'd experienced it before.

"If Terence eventually found out where I was, Silas would just have to check in sporadically so the Big Bad would know as well?"

"Yes. Which is why Terence is now persona non grata and won't be checking his messages until The Big Bad or Silas enter the next life," Caleb assured me, adopting my name for him.

"We don't always come back and we're not always the same

when we do. It's a last resort," Gabriel answered the question I didn't ask.

"I wasn't..."

"It's a valid question," he assured me. "If you get hurt, why not finish the job and be good as new? Eli lost an ear during a drunken duel in Marrakesh and stayed half-deaf for three decades because he lost half his powers in a previous life and didn't want to risk it." I was equally fascinated by their stories as the fact that they had friends and lives outside of protecting me and mourning Annabelle.

"You must be starving," Caleb broke from the conversation he was having with Embry to address everyone. He was looking at me like Sam did sometimes.

"Food would be welcome," Gabriel agreed.

"Etta here?" Embry asked, looking over to a lighthouse, the only building on the island. The remnants of ships in the peninsula told me it wasn't doing its job.

"She likes to come a week or so when I'm stationed at the safe house, but I think she enjoys running things when I'm gone," Caleb smiled.

"She runs things when you're home as well," Embry pointed out with another smile.

"100 percent. But this is when she gets to remodel and throw away the stuff I never use."

"Didn't she already enact the Two Lifetimes rule?"

"I think that's more for hats and shoes she swears will be making a comeback." He even smiled while he rolled his eyes at her.

"You don't live here?" I asked of the island while Caleb crouched down beneath a row of bushes. There had been a faint humming, but then I heard a click and it went silent. He emerged with a pebble, but Gabriel beat him to it and threw a rock at the wooden fence ahead of us. When it hit the wood and fell without getting electrocuted, Caleb went ahead and opened the gate for us all to go through.

"This is a refuge for The Gifted," Caleb answered my earlier question. "If you get discovered, if you're on the run, if something terrible is going to happen and you need to contact someone...We each do our time."

"Even you?" I asked Embry. Gabriel had some extended absences, but Embry always came by.

"You can trade if you find someone who is willing, or who loses a bet," Caleb shared.

"But the last time I was the guardian was 1841, back when it was in Argentina, and I'm not supposed to be back until 2086," Embry told me, explaining why Gabriel was the one who knew how to get to the island.

"How can you plan that far ahead?"

"People move on, others step forward...Corbett will step in for any no-shows because he enjoys being here all by himself," Caleb shrugged.

"How do people find you?"

"It's not like all The Gifted are enrolled or on a mailing list. We don't advertise, so a lot of them will never know we exist. Most of them fly under the radar so we don't know about them. Lola can track Gifteds once they're in their second life, but no one is ever forced to be a part of our club."

"We need a treehouse," Embry teased.

"DOES EVERYONE LIKE FISH?" Caleb polled when we got to the back of the lighthouse. Spears of fish were roasting atop a tiny campfire, surrounded by wooden logs and Adirondack chairs. An interesting setup for a mostly deserted island.

"It smells delicious," was my answer.

"Then dig in," he invited us.

Caleb handed us all a plate and fork, then brought the spear around so we could each take a fish. Once the first spear was empty, he scooped some sauce from a pot in the fire onto our plates and gave us each a tin foil-wrapped potato.

"No electricity on the island?" I asked of his primitive cooking practices.

"I like a little outdoors every once in a while," he corrected me with a knowing glance at the guys, before going inside.

THE FOOD WAS DELICIOUS, and Caleb re-emerged with a stick of butter and a bag of shredded cheese.

"No onions?" Embry asked.

"Or sour cream?" Gabriel looked around.

"This is perfect," I voiced.

"The garden has some onions you can dig up, but I don't even know what sour cream is made of." Caleb shrugged his shoulders apologetically.

While I dressed and ate my baked potato, I took the time to look around and explore the island, and the lighthouse. In addition to the fire pit and garden, there was a potato field, a forest and a lake. Unfortunately, the lighthouse, however beautiful, didn't look like it could fit even one person comfortably.

"Are we camping?" I asked.

"Because of the campfire?" Embry asked me.

"And you're taller than the lighthouse is wide," I explained.

"It has a basement," Caleb shrugged.

WE STAYED at the fire until it got dark, with Caleb offering everyone coffee from an iron pot, which only Gabriel accepted.

"You caught me on a cowboy day, but I can Martha Stewart like nobody's business," he let me know.

"No judgment," I assured him.

"Ready to call it a night?" Embry turned to me in a way that told me the others would be staying up. I wanted to say no and be a part of whatever conversation they were about to have, but a yawn escaped. I felt exhausted.

"Sure," I agreed instead.

I FOLLOWED Caleb inside the lighthouse, which looked as rustic as I had expected, but with a shiny fridge in the corner that looked out of place.

"Etta?" Embry asked.

"If the water isn't ice cold, she won't drink it. She forgets that she used to drink from a well, but it's either this or she leaves me for Clyde." He winked at me before lifting up the rug in the middle of the room to reveal a latch.

"A basement?" I asked. The lighthouse might be like the manor, that held more secret passageways than I could count.

"Isn't that what you call the town-like tunnels under your house?"

THE 'BASEMENT' was like a submarine with huge iron doors that could lock off sections.

"Is the new plan to lock me up in here until he gets tired or I run out of food?" I asked, thinking it might be their endgame.

"This has been the Safe House since 1918. That's when we made a sturdier version of the tunnels. Bringing trench warfare home," Gabriel explained the décor.

"Your very own bunker tomb," I commented.

"Not everyone gets a head start like you," Caleb pointed out. "Some locations have been exposed, but others were destroyed when their Big Bads caught up with them...it's only a safe haven for as long as it's safe."

"I appreciate it," I said, feeling the guilt. I wasn't a fan of my situation, but I was incredibly grateful everyone I cared about was okay.

"It's what I'm here for," Caleb assured me before explaining the system. "Pick a room and write your name on the chalkboard, so people know it's yours. Erase it when you leave."

"Thank you," I told him before going off and doing as I was told.

From what I could tell, all of the rooms were identical, with a bunk bed, a desk and a small wardrobe. There were communal washrooms at the end of the hall, but I had no idea how many rooms this place held. The first chalkboards had names on them, but we were the only ones on the island at the moment. Delia had a heart beside her name, someone else drew a top hat on Jacob's and there was a note that read 'food stays in the kitchen!' on another one. I chose the first empty room on my right, not wanting to venture too far into the maze and get lost. The guys went off, either to explore or to reclaim their own rooms. I put my bag inside the wardrobe and sat on the bed. At first, I was just going to look around and organize my thoughts, but then I got so tired that I fell asleep on the bed, without even bothering to get under the covers.

CHAPTER NINETEEN

I woke up without knowing which rooms everyone else took, so I couldn't tell if the guys were up yet. I went to the underground kitchen and found Caleb making what looked like a dozen-egg-omelette.

"They're bigger here," he defended himself.

"Does living on this island make you part-farmer?" I asked.

"We have essentials delivered every month or so, but there's a chicken coop on the other side of the woods and some animals I try to tend to," he said, putting his omelette on a plate and cracking more eggs into a bowl. He was right, they were much bigger than the ones we got back home. "Mushrooms, peppers and any cheese that isn't blue or from a goat, right?" he asked me.

"Which one did you know?" I understood exactly how he knew, and what some of last night's looks meant.

"Cassie," he said with a warm smile. "I met Beth a couple of times as well, but Cass was family."

"As in..." I wondered if the men in my family hadn't died so much as become Gifted.

"Some ties are stronger than blood," he shook his head.

"Embry introduced you?" I guessed.

"No, Etta did."

"She's your wife?" I assumed.

"My heart and soul," he agreed.

"Did Etta help them protect her?" I asked, trying to remember if anyone else had popped up in my dreams of Cassie.

"No, but Cass tried to protect Etta. In her first life," he said pointedly.

"I know that's supposed to mean something, but..." I raised my shoulders to let him know I had no idea what he was getting at.

"Your first life is before the first time you die and come back. Most of us don't know we're Gifted until that happens, so knowing someone before their second life is a big deal."

"It makes you family?" I asked.

"In some cases," he agreed.

"Is Etta short for something?" I asked, the wheels turning in my brain.

"Loretta," he shared.

"You're Teddy and Lorie," I clued in. He definitely fit the description of 'a mountain of a man with a heart of gold who reminds me of a giant teddy bear'.

"We are," he smiled. "If Etta were here right now, she would have smothered you in hugs the second you arrived."

"You wanted to," I called him on it, remembering the look.

"I did," he agreed. "But I held myself back when it was Cassie as well. Back in the 1800s, it was considered improper to sweep a woman up in your arms if she wasn't your wife."

"If history serves, that wasn't common either," I pointed out.

"No, it wasn't," he agreed with a laughing smile. "Etta was extremely proper, so it drove her mad, but she also loved it."

"What was Cassie like?" I asked, having nothing more than her accounts and a couple of dreams.

"According to society, she was the perfect, docile woman every mother-in-law dreamed of."

"A bore," I smiled to show I got his meaning.

"She knew how to fit in," he defended her.

"Did Alan know the truth?" I asked, ever curious about my ancestors. I was fascinated by the women who came before me, but so intrigued by the men that I never had the chance to encounter. Grams had explained that the women in our family were simply stronger, but it seemed more like the men were cursed.

"By the time I met her, he knew everything. He was the most progressive and supportive husband I had ever seen. He traveled for business and he would bring back elaborate protective devices from Asia and Africa for her, because she always insisted on getting into trouble."

"He was the Lucius Fox to her Bruce Wayne," I smiled.

"Batman references?" he sounded surprised.

"I grew up with an older brother."

He was mid-nod when he decided my answer made even less sense than the reference. "A full-brother?" he asked.

"All my 'full' relatives died when I was little, but the couple that raised me had a son who was a few years older. He's my guardian now." I was aware that as an eighteen-year-old I didn't legally need a guardian anymore, but Sam liked to say parents didn't stop being parents when the kid turned eighteen, it was a lifelong adventure.

"I'm sorry."

"It was a long time ago," I said awkwardly. I didn't often meet new people, so it rarely came up.

"Still hurts," he told me.

"Why were you shocked at the idea of me having a brother?" I asked.

"Cassie had three brothers who all died in infancy, and she

suffered miscarriages before Corrie," he looked uncomfortable, like he wasn't sure he should be telling me.

"Could the protective devices help against this man who is hunting me?" I changed the subject for him, figuring I would ask Embry about it later.

"The ones from Africa might have. They had voodoo or shaman powers or something, but most of them were leather gauntlets or spiked purses, heels with blades that sprung out…"

"That sounds like super cool spy stuff," I pointed out, impressed.

"It was. I think she freaked out with excitement when he brought them home to her, but we never saw that. By the time she used them with us, she acted like it was completely natural for a woman to shoot spikes from her umbrella."

"Seriously?" I was in awe.

"She was the coolest," he told me, placing the second omelette in front of me.

"I have none of that," I shared, accepting the fork he handed me.

"The gadgets?" he asked with his mouth full.

"The confidence, the skills. All I can do to defend myself at this point is run and hide."

"Do you want to change that?" he asked instead of the reassurances Sam would have given me.

"Is that your magic power?" I asked.

"My Gift is my strength," he filled me in. "I can teach you how to box. I mostly do it for fun now, but there was a time when I was training or sparring against the best the field had to offer."

"I would love that." I didn't realize how much I meant it until I said it.

"Then finish your breakfast and meet me in the gym," he smiled.

"Where is that?" I asked. This place was huge, but it didn't have any signs.

"Take a left out of here, right at the theatre and straight down to the end," he told me like it was the simplest thing ever. "We keep meaning to put signs, but we don't usually get visitors who don't already know their way around," he explained.

"I'm sure I'll figure it out."

I FINISHED my breakfast and went to the room where I had left my bag to change into shorts and a t-shirt. I tied my hair up into a ponytail and tried to retrace my steps back to the kitchen, then from there to the gym. The 'theatre' looked like the inside of a movie theatre, with about fifty seats. I was surprised to find the gym had at least a dozen exercise machines, and a section with every weight imaginable. The machines looked like they had never been used before, while the heavier weights had the most wear and tear on them.

"Over here." Caleb poked his head through a door behind the row of treadmills.

The room he was in had a boxing ring and punching bags, but it looked like everything came from the 1920s, when you would sew your bag back together rather than using duct tape.

"This came with the building?" I teased.

"It used to have mats for wrestling, which was pointless because we were never two people. A week into my first time as Guardian I had Etta come join me with my stuff."

"And it stays here?"

"Etta was more than happy to get rid of the dusty old bags."

"She sounds…"

"She's amazing. I just like to pretend complain about her," he assured me. "You can take Etta's wraps and gloves." He nodded to a pile of thick strings and well-worn pink gloves.

"Wraps?" I asked, totally clueless.

"Let me help you." He smiled to himself before coming over and taking one of the thick strings. He put a tiny loop from the end of it onto one of my thumbs, then proceeded to wrap the rest of the material around my hand and wrist.

"Wraps. I get it," I told him.

"Everyone has to start somewhere. You're way ahead of everyone who sits on their couch and doesn't try anything," he pointed out.

"You're very glass half-full, aren't you?"

"Eternal optimist," he agreed. "I know that bad stuff happens, but I've been lucky overall. And Dale had a point. When you act enthusiastic, or happy, you can't help but be."

"I like it," I assured him, wondering if he had only read the book, or had actual conversations with Dale Carnegie.

HIS FIRST LESSON consisted of showing me the proper stance for boxing. He placed my feet shoulder width apart, then had me jump a few times to figure out my left is my dominant side. At least for balance and boxing. I brought my right leg back, then Caleb nudged me a few times, with increasing strength, to make sure my base was strong. It was only then that we moved on to my arms, which needed to be high enough to defend my face, but not close enough to get punched into it…it was a lot to remember just to be able to look the part.

"Your feet," Caleb called me on my stance while he taught me how to jab.

"I seriously doubt my footwork will give him pause," I argued.

"You won't knock him out with it," he agreed. "But the stance was made for a reason. It's to help you move and pivot and…" as he spoke, he gave a demonstration, punching into thin air, but he looked fierce and powerful doing it. Graceful even, when he pivoted on the right hook.

"Don't worry, Cash didn't get it the first time either."

"You taught her too?" I asked.

"Her?" he was confused. "Oh, Cassie."

"Who were you talking about?"

"Cassius."

"Clay?" I knew enough about boxing to know Muhammad Ali's real name.

"He was a sweet kid," he agreed.

"You trained him?" It made sense that if you lived for centuries you met a lot of cool people, but there was a lot of subtle name dropping going on.

"Of course not. I trained at his gym for a couple of years when we settled down in Louisville. He would use me as a training partner sometimes."

"You guys should all write books about all of your adventures."

"No one would believe it," he waved me off.

"Fiction, obviously."

"Fiction has to make sense. Reality is the one that doesn't," he told me.

"I'm thinking you don't read a lot of fiction," I argued.

"I'm thinking you're stalling," he called me on it.

WE STAYED in the boxing room until 2 o'clock, when the watch on his wrist flashed with a fireworks display. He went off to his room and I went upstairs to the outside world.

It was weird being on an island with no one else, especially when it didn't look abandoned. I figured I would rather get lost looking for them up here where I could always find the lighthouse, than down below where I could wander for days before being found.

I spotted the chicken coop Caleb mentioned, as well as some cows grazing by the woods, before finally encountering another human being. Embry was jogging on the sandy beach at the other end of the island.

"Have a good lesson?" he took out an earbud and asked me.

"It was practically a two-hour lunge, so my legs will hate me tomorrow, but it was a lot of fun," I agreed.

"It's hard not to follow along whenever he gets excited about something," he understood.

"Did you meet him through Cassie?" I asked.

"No, I fought with him in the Texas Revolution. But she introduced me to Etta," he shared.

"Do you box?" I asked. I knew he could shoot, play sports and run a lot faster than me, though nowhere near as fast as Gabriel, but I didn't know what his other skills were.

"Caleb taught me, so we do spar sometimes, for fun, but I prefer kickboxing and he gets insulted by that."

"Can you teach me the kicking part once I figure out the boxing?"

"I'm not a teacher but we can take a class sometime," he smiled, as if my new interest in martial arts confused him.

"I'm not gifted, so I need to have something to not feel so useless," I explained.

"Luce," he reproached me for being hard on myself.

"No, Embry, I have lots of talents. I know I'm book smart. But if this big scary guy shows up, I have nothing. I either run and hide or stand frozen like a deer in headlights and neither of those sound appealing." I thought of the plantation and what would have happened if the house hadn't attacked.

"It's not like you can defeat him in a boxing match," he said delicately.

"I said I didn't want to *feel* useless," I got him to laugh. "And I know we don't stand a chance against him, but maybe I can defend myself from someone he takes over to try and get to me."

"I'll see what I can do," he assured me.

· · ·

189

THAT NIGHT, Embry made us Spaghetti e Olio to go with the seared scallops Caleb prepared. The guys paired it with a nice wine, but I didn't join them, although I doubt any of them would have stopped me for being underage. I figured one of us should be sober and alert if ever the Big Bad managed to find us.

WE GOT into a new pattern on Caleb's island, where I would spend my morning boxing with Caleb, then have a quick lunch before Embry or Gabriel, or both of them, would teach me simple self-defense.

"What about S.I.N.G.?" I asked Gabriel during his first solo lesson.

"I don't think your singing is terrible enough to send him away," he teased, so I pretended to be offended.

"I mean from Miss Congeniality."

"I have no idea what that is."

"Here, try to grab me from behind," I told him.

"I haven't taught you how to defend yourself from that."

"I won't hurt you for real, I promise," I said, which he possibly felt attacked by, because he obliged.

"I grab you from behind and..."

"Solar plexus, instep, nose, groin!" I showed him the steps and yelled them out at the same time. "Would that work in real life?" I asked, smiling at the absolute shock on his face.

"That's from a beauty pageant?" he asked.

"A movie about a beauty pageant," I agreed.

"Life isn't a movie Lucy. The force you would need to elbow me with, the chances of you inflicting any pain in my foot through my boots..." he shook his head. "If you manage to break my nose you'd have a tiny window to maybe get the groin, but..."

"I'm sorry. It was just an idea."

"It's great that you want to defend yourself. I'm glad you're taking this seriously. But he isn't a drunk guy at a bar who won't take no for an answer," he said more gently.

"I get that," I assured him. "Are you saying it's pointless and I shouldn't do anything?"

"No, you should never be complacent, or powerless in your own life. I want you to be confident and know how to defend yourself. But I never want you to argue when we tell you to run, or to hide. No matter how well-trained you are, these aren't fair fights and I can't lose you." His eyes were as intense as I had ever seen them.

"I'm not delusional."

"Okay." He picked up one of the pads Caleb had lent us. "Let's try some krav maga."

CHAPTER TWENTY

On the fourth day, after Caleb's boxing workout, he brought me to the kitchen for a cooking lesson.

"Croque-Monsieur?" I verified after he told me what we were going to make.

"The key to a man's heart is through his stomach. This gives you the stomach," he agreed.

"Maybe a man should be cooking his way into *my* heart." I resented the implication that my goal in life should be to find a man to marry me, then remembered that he was from that time period, even if he didn't look it.

"Etta loves fancy French things. Or simple things that are fancy because they're French. She grew up with a bit of Paris-envy." I thought he was ignoring my comment, but then he said, "And he does need to woo you, and be worthy, and you should have an equal partnership, but on his birthday, or times when he's amazing and you want to let him know you appreciate him, this is a meal that can do that."

"I was mostly teasing. You're incredibly old, so you can't help it," I assured him with a smile.

"You're right, I am very old," he agreed. "But I have also been a huge feminist for over a century."

"To impress Etta?" I asked, sensing a trend.

"Because society was implying that she didn't have the same rights as me. That she was somehow less than human," he said like he found the entire concept unfathomable.

"I'm sorry," I apologized for my assumptions.

"It wasn't just my size that got me the giant teddy bear nickname. I'm strong, but I'm a bleeding heart. We went to marches and demonstrations, but if we weren't Gifted, she never would have lived to see any of the things we fought for come true."

"She sounds incredible," I gave him a smile.

"You think I'm biased, but she's amazing. She's stronger than me in every way but physical. She's fierce and vulnerable and caring...she's perfect."

"Why do you come here to be the guardian then?" I asked.

"I figure a year every couple of centuries is enough to make her miss me," he smiled.

"I hope I get what you have someday," I told him.

"I hope everyone does," he agreed. "Now are you ready to learn?"

"Yes, chef." I gave him a salute and got a nod in return.

"Two pieces of bread, ham, butter and cheese," he told me the ingredients while whisking away in a frying pan.

"What are you making?" I asked.

"Béchamel sauce. It's butter and flour, a little milk, then some mustard and nutmeg to be fancy," he said while combining the ingredients.

"Is this a ploy so I can make it for you every day as a thank you for the boxing lessons?"

"This is out of the kindness of my heart. If you feel so inclined to practice on the daily, that's your prerogative," he played innocent.

"I see." I looked at him skeptically while he finished making his sauce.

WE PUT the béchamel sauce on the first slice of bread, then we layered it with cheese, ham, cheese, another slice of bread, more cheese, ham and topped with cheese.

"This is really decadent," I said while he put them in the oven for all the cheese to melt.

"I told you. Simple, fancy, French," he put words together that didn't form a sentence, but I completely understood.

WE STAYED in the kitchen to make sure we didn't burn them, then went outside to eat them on the Adirondack chairs out front.

"The view is gorgeous," I said of the island, biting into my Croque-Monsieur. "And this is delicious."

"Why thank you," he said with a head tilt and a smile.

"You guys lived in Paris?" I asked.

"We've lived all over."

"What's your favorite place in the entire world?" I thought of all the magical places he could name.

"Wherever Etta is," he smiled. I should have expected it.

"If she was with you wherever you went," I amended.

"Texas," he said after a while.

"Really? I've heard Europe is gorgeous, Iceland looks amazing...what does Texas have?" I asked.

"Nothing anymore." He took a bite that encompassed at least half of his sandwich. "It's where I'm from. They say home is where the heart is, and Etta is my heart, but Texas is my home. If I go back, I know none of them are there anymore, but it's where I feel closest to my mom and my sisters and my brothers..."

"I get it," I assured him. My whole life, I wanted to travel and see the world, especially since I was always confined to the manor, but the more time I was spending away from it, the more I missed the rooms and hallways that smelled like home.

"What are we talking about?" Embry asked, coming out with one of the Croque-Monsieurs we had left on the counter for him and Gabriel.

"Home," I shared. "Yours would be Italy?" I guessed.

"Italy is home," he agreed.

"But that wasn't your first thought," I called him on it. "Boston?" I asked.

"That is where you are," he smiled.

"Where is your favorite place in the world?" I asked, rolling my eyes at his answer.

"Anywhere can feel like home, depending on who is with you," he gave a cop out. "I spent so long speaking of Italy like it was the home I lost, that I didn't realize home had changed until it was the Boston from my childhood, or a villa in New Orleans that I missed."

"You don't realize what you have until it's gone." Gabriel stepped out as well, so the four of us sat in Adirondack chairs eating fancy grilled cheeses.

"I know exactly what I have," Caleb assured them.

"Not if you're sitting here with us you don't," Embry argued.

"Or I also know what's at stake."

"Are there a lot of Gifted who are hunting other Gifted?" I asked, figuring my life wasn't the only thing at stake.

"Not a lot, considering how many of us there are, but enough to warrant places like this," Caleb told me.

"Not all of them are hunted by other Gifted. When you look twenty-three and your driver's license says you should be eighty-six, people start by assuming it's a forgery, but eventually they take notice," Embry added.

"This is like an FBI/CIA hideout too?" I asked.

"Law enforcement have been an issue," Caleb glanced at Gabriel, who did not look happy.

"But scientists and armies are usually the bigger concern. Subjects that don't die are exactly what mad scientists and ruthless generals want to study and replicate," Embry sent a shiver down my spine.

"Have any of you been caught?"

"I have my doubts about Area 51." I could tell Caleb was teasing to lighten the mood, because he smiled instead of looking worried.

"No one I've known has been caught and tested against their will for longer than a night or two, but we've had doctors we trust run every test in the book and medically, there is nothing wrong with us," Embry told me.

"It's like we're frozen in time," Gabriel shrugged. "We don't age, and we heal back to however we were before we first died."

"What happens if you accomplish your—"

Before I finished my question, an alarm went off inside the lighthouse, as well as on Caleb's watch. "What does red mean?" I changed my question, knowing red lights weren't good.

"This doesn't make sense." Caleb stood and looked around as if he expected and army to rush at us from every direction.

"Which part?" I asked.

"We have different colors for different warnings. Blue when someone enters the airspace, green if a boat is nearby. Yellow means a threat is attempting to breach, like when we were coming through the rocks and the coral with the abandoned ships," Embry explained to me while we went underneath the lighthouse.

"Red means they're already here?" I guessed.

"It means they've made it past all of the defenses and breached the final perimeter," Caleb explained.

"The electric wooden fence?" I asked, remembering how he had to turn it off for us to come in.

"Exactly."

"What happened to the other alarms?" I asked, thinking we missed a few.

"They can be turned off, like if I know a cruise ship is going by or an air show is coming up and I don't want to be bothered. They were on when I checked last night, but lower level alarms are something you could disable by hacking into the computer system."

"He hacked us?" I asked.

"It's a high-level encryption, especially remotely. I assume he got someone who knew the codes."

"You don't change them?"

"We do, but the Gifted can always find them so they can get help," they implied that the Big Bad was using one of the people who knew the access codes. Or that someone switched sides.

"Red can't be disabled though. Every time a new person sets foot on the island you need to manually turn it off with the current guardian's fingerprint, or the alarms go off," Caleb explained why we got at least that much warning.

"How long will this hold?" I asked of our underground haven.

"Against nuclear attacks or human enemies, we can stay months or even years until we run out of food and water," Caleb said proudly.

"But against a Gifted who knows how to get in?" I asked of our current situation and got nothing in return. "How long do we have?" I asked again, knowing that them not answering meant things were bad.

"It depends on what they want and who they have with them. We have six sections down here and each one has reinforced steel doors. They can withstand an explosion, so we can hide you at least three doors deep and—"

"If the Big Bad is up on the island with his magic and an army of Gifteds, and what he wants is me?" I cut him off.

"We're not going to wait here long enough to find out how long we have," Embry told me. "We're leaving."

"How do we do that?" I asked as the alarms got louder. As far as I could tell, the only entrance on the island to get down here was in the lighthouse, which wouldn't take long to breach.

"There's an escape in the theater. The tunnels are tight, but it will bring you to the buoy," Caleb shared.

"The one with the rowboat?" I asked.

"Exactly," Embry tried to be reassuring, which worked as long as his attention was on me, rather than figuring out our next move with Gabriel.

No one but me seemed concerned with us escaping via rowboat after we barely survived coming here with a much sturdier vessel. "Won't they know about the escape? Or see us rowing away?"

"Only guardians know about the escape and only people who have used it would know where the escape ends up. A lot of tunnels leave from different rooms and let out at different locations," Caleb sounded sure of himself, but it had to be for my benefit. "And we can use a distraction to make sure they're not looking at the water while you row away."

"Any more fertilizer?" Embry turned to me with a smile.

"I happen to be a life-size distraction, so I'll go give them the guardian schpeel while you leave by the theater. Hopefully I can give you enough time that they won't be able to catch up," Caleb decided.

"I don't like this plan," I voiced.

"You don't have a choice," he told me.

"They'll kill you," I pointed out. They kept saying I wasn't taking this seriously, but Caleb was about to face them on his own to cause a diversion.

"I have a few tricks up my sleeve," he winked at me before turning to Embry. "I've got this," he assured him, leading to a long look between the two, which ended with Embry nodding.

"Have you accomplished your purpose?" I asked Caleb. It might be naïve, but with my limited knowledge of the Gifted, as long as he hadn't done what he was meant to do, he could lose his powers or gain new ones, but he wouldn't die.

"I don't think so." He was honest, but it didn't reassure me.

"You heard him, let's go," Embry ordered before I could comment on the admission. I looked to Caleb, horrified, but he nodded in a way that told me to leave, so I did.

AT FIRST, I thought Caleb was exaggerating. The tunnels behind the screen of the movie theater were big enough for the three of us to crawl through comfortably, with Gabriel leading and Embry tying the rear. Eventually though, they got smaller. Much smaller. I took off my backpack and had to keep my body flat and pull myself along, wiggling through, but unable to stay on my knees. I was having trouble, so I could only imagine how hard it was for them.

The alarms turned off suddenly, which I feared meant we lost Caleb. It took what felt like hours after that before I saw the light at the end of the tunnel. The buoy was hollow, and while it looked like it was floating from the outside, it was held in place by the tunnel it was attached to. I had to roll my body onto my back so that I could hoist my upper body through, then stand inside the buoy, which was wider than usual. I put my hands on the top of the rim and jumped up, like you do on a pool ledge. Gabriel was on the other side, in the rowboat, to help me over.

I could see the island off in the distance, but we were on the other side of the forest. Other than the lookouts, who were facing away from us, no one could see our tiny boat. They had me lie down on the bottom and covered me with a blanket before Embry rowed us further and further away from what was supposed to be a safe haven.

CHAPTER TWENTY-ONE

W e took the rowboat in the opposite direction we had come from, and I completely rethought my theory about being more comfortable in smaller boats. The open air was nice, but the small boat rocked and added a deep element of fear to the queasiness I felt on our first ship. Once they let me out from the blanket, Gabriel suggested I focus on a point in the distance that wasn't moving. Unfortunately, watching the island go up in flames brought on a lot more uneasiness than relief. Can a Gifted come back to life after their body is eaten by fire?

By NIGHTFALL, all I could see was a tiny speck in the distance, that I assumed was the island in flames, but it could have been anything. I gave up on asking the guys where we were going, or if Caleb was okay. The consensus was that they knew absolutely nothing about our next move. We traveled mostly in silence, with directions the only thing that broke it. Gabriel took over rowing for a while, then they switched a few times before we let ourselves float. I felt like this was a terrible idea, letting the water take us wherever it wanted to, but they both pretended they had a plan and knew what they were doing.

IT WAS dawn by the time our rowboat hit sand, waking me with a tiny thud.

"Where are we?" I asked, trying to get my bearings.

"I was aiming for Mexico, but it could also be Cuba," Embry shrugged. It didn't matter where we were, as long as it wasn't where the Big Bad was.

"And where do we go from Mexico-slash-Cuba?"

"We need to keep moving," Gabriel said simply. I hoped he was right about the Big Bad giving up after a few months. For many other reasons, but I would not be able to spend the rest of my life on boats.

"Towards Italy? Or towards a cave in the middle of the amazon?" I tried to figure out what my life was going to look like for the next little while.

"Off the grid, but safe," Embry told me. "We will stay in remote places and travel under the radar, but we will also try to bring you to friends and find bunkers where we can keep you safe."

"Until they burn the island to the ground," I pointed out.

"You're the only person who didn't have an opportunity to not be a part of this," Gabriel reminded me.

"What happens if Sam and Deanna need help? How can they contact us if we're off the grid?"

"You're forgetting that we were around long before cell phones and the internet. If Sam needs our help, we've taught him ways that he can reach out. Even if we're off the grid and don't see it, someone will, and someone will help him," Embry reassured me, either through his confidence, or his Gift.

"Today is a beach day then?" I made an attempt to lighten the mood, to show him I was okay.

"No, today is a hiking adventure through beautiful scenery with wildlife all around us," Embry sold it like a super fun excursion to unsuspecting tourists.

"Let's go," Gabe was all business, heading straight for the line of trees that bordered the beautiful, abandoned beach we shipwrecked onto.

"Aye, aye, captain," I sighed before following him. Embry was right about it being absolutely beautiful. I would have loved to go on an adventure vacation last year, but now that it was a rushed and intense trek through wilderness to hopefully avoid the army that was trying to kill me, it wasn't all it was cracked up to be.

For the first hour, we had no trail to speak of. It took forever to advance even a little bit, because Gabriel and Embry had to move the overrun vines or help me climb over fallen trees. Eventually we came across an abandoned hiking trail that hadn't been cleared in a while, but at least I could tell where we were going. Fallen trees became an obstacle to get over, rather than the norm.

"I don't want to ask how much longer, but..." I asked after my stomach made a growl that could rival a lion's roar.

"But we haven't eaten since the grilled cheese yesterday," Embry let me know he understood.

"Normally when people say something was so good that they don't have to eat for the rest of the week, they don't mean it literally."

"You can eat the nuts," Gabriel said of one of the trees we had passed.

"How many lives would you bet on that?" I asked. The tiniest of smiles cracked through Gabriel's serious façade.

"If memory serves we're an hour from a little farming town. We can get something there," he softened.

"You've been here before?" I asked before the trees opened up to reveal a gigantic waterfall.

"One of Caleb and Etta's many weddings," Embry smiled at my expression.

"It's beautiful," I remarked, taking it all in.

"Beautiful enough to make you forget—"

"Still hungry," I cut him off without taking my eyes off the view. "But if we're going to take a break, this place is perfect."

"Maybe a few minutes to get organized," Gabriel gave in, removing his backpack and pulling out something thin and pointy.

"Do you think someone will be waiting in the small farming town?" A shiver ran through me.

"Of course not, they would have no way of knowing where we ended up."

"So that's just in case?" I asked, nodding my head to his weapon.

"In case someone happens to be in town on vacation, or the villagers don't take too kindly to strangers, or if there's a wild animal. Lots of variables." Gabriel was either trying to reassure me, or to remind me that the world at large could be dangerous even if you weren't on the run.

"It's just a precaution, but it's better to be safe than sorry." Embry put his hand on my arm and I couldn't help but relax.

"I hate that you can do that," I said, smiling in spite of myself.

"Even if I tried not to use my Gift, I would still be trying to make you smile," he explained why it was nearly impossible for him to turn it off with me.

"I guess there are worse things than having someone who wants to see you happy," I conceded.

. . .

WE WERE able to stay a few more minutes at the waterfall before we continued our hike, encountering some monkeys along the way, before finally meeting our first human.

"Hola," I told the little boy from behind Embry and Gabriel, who each had their arms out to protect me from the child. "Estas solo?" I had been waiting years to put what I learnt in Spanish class to good use.

The boy, who looked to be about six, stared at me, making no effort to communicate, or to get back to whatever it was he was doing on the path.

"Do you know another dialect he might understand?" I asked Embry.

"He understood," Embry assured me, looking distrustfully at the boy, who pulled out what I thought was a toy, but saw was a gun just before Gabriel pounced.

He used his speed rather than force, removing the bullets and emptying the chamber while the boy looked on in wonder.

"Superman?" he asked with a heavy accent.

"Not even close," Gabriel said before carrying the boy over to one of the thicker trees and tying him to it.

"I'm sensing this isn't a quiet, friendly, farming town," I confronted them.

"It is. But there's also a cocaine farm on its outskirts, the kind that is heavily guarded, illegal, and will shoot witnesses rather than finding out why you're on their property."

"Even little kids?" I asked. The boy was barely older than Clara.

"Sometimes," he said simply before we kept moving.

EVENTUALLY WE MADE it to a clearing with tall grass and tiny houses in the distance. At least a dozen men worked the field, but not a single one of them approached us or reacted in any way when we walked past them to get to the closest house. We stayed along the forest line, in case we had to retreat.

"You've got this?" Gabriel asked Embry once we found cover.

"You know the drill," he agreed, giving me a smile before walking off, as Gabriel put out his arm to hold me back.

"What's the drill?" I asked him.

"He's going to ask if we can borrow a truck or buy passage to the border."

"And if he says no?"

"We run."

"Gabriel." I didn't find it funny, but he wasn't laughing.

"Embry is highly trained, and he knows how to control the room."

"I'm not sure how helpful it'll be to make them happy and calm," I argued.

"People don't usually want to shoot you when they're calm and happy, but those aren't the only emotions he can summon."

"Is he going to make them love him?" I realized that would be a way to buy him time to escape, but it also made me rethink my relationship with Embry.

"Love doesn't work like that. We can't make someone feel it, or take it away. Even Etta can heal anything, but she can't mend a broken heart."

"Interesting." I liked the idea that the Gifted had limits to what they could do.

"Embry uses his Gift to make people happier whenever he can, but he can also use it to make them feel small, helpless, depressed, suicidal...you can fight it if you know it's coming, but if you suspect nothing..." he let the thought linger, but shook himself out of it when he saw my face. "He usually convinces people with words and a smile," he assured me.

. . .

I WAS STRESSED out and staring at the house for another five minutes before Embry came out with a smile on his face, giving us the thumbs up.

"A car?" Gabriel asked.

"Horses?" I saw a bunch of them galloping in the distance.

Embry shook his head for both of our guesses. "Oscar can take us as far as Albuquerque, but if we get stopped at the border, he'll pretend he doesn't know us."

"I have my passport." I reached into my backpack to try and find it. This would be my first chance to use it since I convinced Sam to let me have one. And to renew it when it expired. All without ever leaving Massachusetts.

"We won't be needing it," Embry shook his head. "And if we did, we wouldn't use yours."

"Right. Under the radar."

"Way under," he agreed.

"I THOUGHT YOU WERE JOKING," I looked over to Embry, involuntarily jumping when the rooster beside me pecked at my head. Embry had talked our way onto the back of an old pick-up truck, filled with hay and poultry, covered with a grey tarp.

"I thought they'd be in cages," Embry apologized. "You get used to it."

"Do you do this often?" I leaned as far away from the rooster as I could without exposing myself to the chicken on my other side.

"Once with Cassie," Gabriel surprised me when he spoke up, a fond smile on his face.

"And once before it all began," Embry added.

"Before what began?" I asked.

"Before she left," Embry said simply. "When my biggest concern was finding someone my father approved of, and we all knew Gabe and Annabelle were going to get married and live happily ever after."

"My bachelor party," Gabriel said like he had completely forgotten up to that point.

"You guys traveled like this voluntarily?" I raised an eyebrow at them.

"We mistakenly trusted John, my older brother, to be the sober and responsible one," Embry explained. "Halfway through the night he decided we were having a lot more fun than he was, so he joined in."

"And the chicken truck came in..."

"We left the local watering hole and each stumbled towards home, but Embry and I took a nap on the way. We hit the hay," Gabe recalled. I couldn't help but smile at the way they were both remembering a time when they were happy and the best of friends.

"We woke up in a neighboring town, to a surprisingly unhappy friend of my father's," Embry shared.

"He was friendly when I offered him the rest of my ale," Gabe shrugged with the hint of a smile.

"I'm sure," I smiled, picturing it with difficulty. Gabe never let loose, so I couldn't imagine him pass-out drunk and making a joke.

"How did you get back?"

"We helped him deliver the rest of his eggs, then we convinced him to drop us off at home."

"Embry was the best at getting you out of trouble," Gabriel smiled. "I wish you'd been at dinner when I explained to Belle what happened."

"She was upset?" I asked.

"We'd had plans for the afternoon and I showed up smelling like chicken and manure," Gabriel said before he caught himself, realizing he'd shared too much.

"I bet she forgave you." I wasn't sure where it came from. I didn't know much about her, but I could see Gabriel pulling away, and I wanted him to talk about her. About a time when no one was special or in danger and they were just young and in love. Or, in Embry's case, trying to find love.

"It took tea with her aunt as well as letting her father give me a tour of the gardens," Gabriel confirmed my suspicions.

"I thought her gardens were the talk of the town?" I asked, remembering her memory.

"They were, the first hundred times we saw them. After growing up in them and having to give the tour a million times, to every new person who came to see them, we sort of got tired of them," Embry explained.

"Mr. Owens never tired of them. He loved explaining how the garden was enough to sustain them, and it represented his family, and they brought some of the plants with them from England… Annabelle usually saved me from the tour, but that night she did not."

"Well, you deserved it," I sided with her.

"I deserved a lot worse," he agreed.

"At least you got a couple of decades of fun before thirty-five or so miserable ones."

"They weren't all miserable," Embry argued, looking to Gabriel to back him up.

"We had a few good ones," he agreed, somewhat reluctantly.

"A year every other decade?" I asked.

"Most people are miserable," Gabriel shrugged.

"So being semi-immortal is more of a curse than a gift?" I asked.

"Yes," Gabriel agreed while Embry said, "No."

"Sometimes," Embry relented.

"No one wants to live forever alone," Gabriel said simply.

"I'm sorry," I apologized.

"It's not your fault," Embry assured me.

"Some things are worth it," Gabriel added.

"Like getting to meet you," Embry teased.

"That's really sad if I'm the highlight of your last three centuries," I laughed at how pathetic that would be, which got Embry to join in, and Gabriel, after trying to get us to quiet down.

"I'm glad I met you too," I said. "Not only because I'd be dead without you, but I'm glad we were friends before all of this happened."

"Me too," Embry agreed.

CHAPTER TWENTY-TWO

After long days that felt like weeks in the chicken coop, driving through the middle of nowhere, we made it to Albuquerque. The most eventful part of our border crossing was when the immigration officer asked Oscar if he was okay. He was sweating bullets, so the officer proceeded to offer him some water instead of investigating the back. I suspected it had more to do with Embry's Gift than the officer's good-heartedness, but Oscar was impressed. He let us off at a truck stop where we got ourselves some food, then continued our journey on foot.

WHEN IT GOT DARK, we stopped at the most rundown, disgusting, rent-by-the-hour motel I had ever seen. If this were a movie, I would be yelling at the screen for the characters to get back in their cars and turn around. It was the kind of place only serial killers and psychopaths would stay at. On second thought, the psycho would probably kill their victims, dissolve the bodies in the bathtub and then drive off to sleep somewhere more inviting.

The three of us went together to the front desk to check in, but it would have been safer for me to wait outside, alone. If I still had hopes of it having cable or a swimming pool, they vanished when I saw that the front desk hadn't been touched by anything but dust since the eighties. The carpet was orange shag, the walls had lime green wallpaper, and there was even a lava lamp in the corner.

"Can we have a room please?" Embry asked the old woman who was sitting behind the counter on a Chesterfield. She was about 300 pounds, noisily chewing her pink bubble gum, and looked about as happy to be there as Gabriel did.

She gave us a once over before asking, "King bed?"

The way she raised her eyebrow with the hint of a smile almost made me sick.

"Two beds and a cot," Embry specified, as pleasant as ever, while Gabriel inched closer to me.

"If you say so," she lost all interest in us. "No cots, so one of you can take the floor."

We got an actual key for the door, and wouldn't have been able to pay with a credit card even if we had wanted to. Her registry was paper, and she saw nothing wrong with Embry saying his name was Cesare Borgia.

"Do you think the Big Bad is busy checking hotel registries and credit card statements? Would he ever know if we paid cash to stay at a hotel that didn't have bed bugs?" I imagined the Big Bad as an ancient, demon-like guy in a travelling cloak who was baffled by computers and possibly even electricity. If he could rule ancient magic, I was going to remove his current technology, at least in my mind.

"We might be old, but we still adapt. If the two of us have been able to figure it out, he will too," Embry warned, not wanting me to underestimate my foe. We unlocked the door and got into the musty room that while relatively clean, hadn't been used in the past ten years or so. I would be amazed if the television even turned on. It was one of those huge boxes with a tiny screen, and a knob that you had to get up and physically turn in order to change the channel. Even Embry, who had been around long before the invention of television, was eying it with apprehension.

"Rock, paper, scissors?" I suggested as a way of determining who would get a bed and who had to sleep on the floor. I wasn't sure which option was preferable.

"Are we vying for the bed bugs or the blood-stained carpet?" Embry was hopefully just trying to get a rise out of me, but it worked as I rushed over and turned on the lamp to see if the ground truly had blood stains.

"Maybe we can pitch a tent in the parking lot. If anybody miraculously figures out that we're here, they'll barge into the motel room and we can drive off in their car. Safe and sound with clean seats and air fresheners," I offered. Embry nodded, still looking to the stained carpet between the two beds, but Gabriel had a horrible look on his face.

"Gabe?" I asked, wondering if he had discovered a dead body. It wouldn't surprise me at this point.

"I'm with her." Embry turned to face Gabriel and realized, like I had, that it was something outside the window that was troubling him. Not like the stains were troubling us; he looked scared. Unless it was regret I saw etched onto his face. Either way, I didn't like it.

"They're here," Gabriel told us, remaining calm, but I could see the electricity coursing through his body as he prepared himself for what was to come.

I had less than a second to react before the door behind me burst open, with a man entirely dressed in black barging through it. I was closest, and my hand was still beside the lamp, so I picked it up and smashed it on the top of the intruder's head with all my might. He fell to the floor immediately. I looked over to the guys, childishly expecting praise, but he hadn't been alone.

"Behind us, now," Gabriel yelled as Embry took my arm and placed me in the corner of the room, so anyone would have to go through them to get to me. It also meant that I had nowhere to go if ever that happened.

LUCKILY, the men and women who barged in had no weapons, or at least they didn't have time to take them out before Embry or Gabriel overpowered them. They were all dressed like civilians, and their hand to hand combat was mediocre at best, which made me think they were being controlled rather than voluntarily trying to kill me. I knew it was an arbitrary system, that evil people could be dressed like normal people, but it was reassuring for me to think that the majority of the Big Bad's army would disappear if someone managed to kill him. One person was easier to fight than an entire army.

I was inching closer to the fighting, wanting to help as I saw my guys growing tired and making mistakes. The steady stream of assailants was never-ending. Before I could attempt to make a difference, a chilling voice called out from the middle of the parking lot.

"Stop!" it called, making the hairs on the back of my neck rise. Even scarier than his voice was how every single member of his army froze without question. Whether they were hunting me by choice or being controlled, they were terrifying.

CHAPTER TWENTY-THREE

Embry and Gabriel waited expectantly for the fight to resume, but when it didn't they turned to the window, to see where the voice came from. They both looked straight at me, horrified.

I made my way over to see what they were seeing, then ran for the door half a second after Gabriel's arms wrapped around me. He held me back so that all I could do was scream "Sam!" over and over again, as I tried to fight my way free from Gabriel, as if I could do anything to help Sam.

"Let go of me Gabriel, I have to help him," I argued, fighting and twisting to try and shake him off.

"Do you promise not to go out to him?" he asked, holding on to me as if I weren't moving at all.

"He has Sam." He knew there was no way I would stay in the room while Sam was being held by a man with a knife to his throat.

"Sam's dead if they get you," Embry was delicate, but I wanted them to stop focusing on me and start helping Sam.

"It's Sam," I repeated, giving up the fight. I looked at them pleadingly, so they finally agreed.

"Stay behind us. If you have a chance, run, then find a car and drive," Gabriel let me know not to stay and wait for them if anything happened. His eyes were as intense as I had ever seen them, letting me know that there would be hell to pay if I didn't listen.

"Okay," I said, knowing I could never leave the 3 of them behind. I didn't mind staying out of sight as long as I could listen. I went to get my backpack from the corner and slipped the dagger into my boot.

"I know you're inside, and you see I'm alone. You have no reason not to come out," the man called.

"Lucine Suzanne Owens you stay inside!" I heard Sam use my full name, to show me he was serious. The man chuckled, not at all concerned by his outburst, knowing it wouldn't deter me in the slightest.

Embry and Gabriel looked at me like they would rather I listen to Sam as well, but I stood my ground. Gabriel opened the door and stepped out first, followed by Embry, then me.

The man who held Sam was a couple of inches shorter than my brother's 6 foot 3, with blonde hair slicked down to his head. His eyes were the same color as the men in front of me, but while theirs came off as intense, his were dark and scary hellholes. He smiled at us, making him even more ominous, but it was the knife to Sam's throat that solidified him as a horrible, evil person in my book.

He kept his smile while Embry and Gabriel came into his view, but the look he gave me made my blood curl. I had been the victim of catcalling, and guys looking at me like they wanted to do ungodly things to me, but he looked at me like I was a piece of meat, something to be butchered for the parts and then discarded.

"You must be Lucy," he said, bowing to me. Sam had to go down as well, to prevent his neck getting sliced by the ever-present blade. If his goal had been to show me deference and respect, he failed. All I did was cringe until I saw Sam come back up, unharmed.

"What do you want, Donovan?" Gabriel asked as if he was completely unfazed by the way he was handling Sam. I had hoped knowing the Big Bad's name would make him less scary, but so far it did not help.

"Bypassing the formalities?" Donovan's amused smile made me want to punch him, had I been able to reach him. "You both know what I want. It has been the same for centuries. I want the girl." His look told me that if I gave myself up, I would not be making it out alive, and they would never find what was left of my body. Still, I wouldn't be able to not go to him if the price of keeping me safe was someone I loved.

"Our answer has been the same since you came after Margaret. We will die before we let you have her, and even then, we still won't let that happen," Gabriel said.

"I expected as much. But you brought the girl out with you. Do you think that she will stand back and watch as I slice into her big brother, the man who has been raising her?" Donovan moved the knife so it glistened in the moonlight. Embry took a step back to put his arm on my shoulder, ensuring I wouldn't fall for it and run to my death. "Will you still be able to hold her back when it is his daughter I eviscerate? When I cut every freckle off of that fire-kissed little girl?" Sam's hands were balled into fists, and if the knife hadn't been so close to his jugular, he would have used them.

"I'll lock her in a cell and throw away the key if it means you can't have her." I had expected it to sound like a lie coming from Embry, but he was just as convincing as if Gabriel had been the one saying it. He meant it.

"Will you drain her blood and incinerate her to keep her from me? That is what you did to Cassandra, right? She thought that if she could just get to you, she would be safe. Do you still value the mission more than their lives?" Donovan was playing with the knife, making me incredibly nervous. I wanted to yell at him to stop when I saw a speck of red on Sam's neck, but I also didn't want to remind anyone that I hadn't made a mad dash for the highway yet.

"If necessary." Gabriel's face was stone, and it shocked me that I believed him. I knew Cassandra would have been dead before they did anything to her, but the conviction in his eyes made me realize for the first time that I wasn't their mission. Sure, I was the promise they made, but protecting me might not mean my life so much as whatever it was of mine that this man wanted. I loved them like family and I knew they loved me too...but if I ran out and let the man take me, would they be fighting to save me, or to stop him?

WHETHER BECAUSE HE saw what I was thinking, or to keep me in place, Embry gave my shoulder a squeeze. My first instinct was to shake him off, but I knew that even if they would sacrifice me to stop him, they were still all I had.

"See dear, you think they care about you, but they would slaughter you faster than I would. Come to me so I don't have to kill the boy," Donovan addressed me. I got his logic, but loving and caring about someone wasn't something you could turn off. Which was why I tried to go for Sam, causing both Embry and Gabriel to put themselves in front of me.

"If I can't go to him, what is our plan for saving Sam?" I asked without taking my eyes off of my big brother.

They exchanged a look that implied they had no intentions of letting me turn myself in, or of putting me at risk while they saved Sam.

"We either come up with a plan or you will have to carry me over your shoulder for the rest of this trip," I warned, letting them know that I wasn't kidding either. I just didn't have the same bargaining chips that they did.

"Luce, he knew what he was getting into. We all signed up for this," Embry tried to talk me out of it.

"He didn't. He maybe knew that this was a possibility, but I was dropped into his lap when his parents died. You two chose to love Annabelle, and to dedicate your lives to this, but Sam just feels like he has to take care of the girl he grew up with."

"He made his choice when he agreed to take you," Gabriel said calmly, but I could see the vein pulsing in his forehead.

"If I'm going to die either way, I'd rather it be saving Sam than whatever else you have planned."

"We don't plan on you dying at all," Embry assured me, sensing a slight edge to my voice.

"Feel free to continue talking as if I don't have a knife to his throat, but if the girl isn't walking towards me within the next five minutes, I am slicing until I reach the bone," Donovan sounded more annoyed at the prospect of having to slit Sam's throat than anything that would imply he had some humanity left in him. Assuming he had any to begin with.

"We have five minutes to come up with a plan," I turned to Embry and Gabriel expectantly.

"We have five minutes to get you as far away from here as possible," Embry argued.

"Or we could waste it all debating," Gabriel was exasperated.

"Have the two of you ever taken him on alone? Is it a possibility that while I walk over and he releases Sam, you could fight him and win?" I asked, looking from one to the other. "Wouldn't it keep me safe if while he was dead, we locked him up in a steel box and tossed him to the bottom of the ocean?"

They looked at each other, weighing the situation and deciding whether or not they had a chance of managing that. Two of his men still hovered a few feet away from us, but I felt like it would be easy enough to get past them. Then it would be my two guys against Donovan, but I got the feeling Donovan was older and more powerful somehow, especially with all of the freaky magic stuff. I took it as a good sign that he hadn't used any of it against us, but the guys were not as optimistic.

"This isn't the entire army. This is just Donovan's scouting crew," Embry said before a bunch of men and women dressed in black showed up. They came from every possible hiding place, surrounding us so that other than barricading ourselves back in the motel room, there was absolutely nowhere we could go. Any hope I'd had of being able to fight Donovan to get Sam back disappeared. We would be lucky if any of us made it out alive, which was an issue, because once I was gone, I was not coming back.

Sam was mouthing for me to run, resigned to his fate, but not only could I not leave him, I didn't have anywhere to go.

"Like Prom," Gabriel told me, reaching for his bag.

I barely had a moment to realize he meant escaping through the bathroom window before they all pulled swords and guns out of nowhere, prepared to fight to the death. I stayed there, frozen in place, before making eye contact with Sam, who once again mouthed that I should run. I reluctantly rushed back into the motel room and locked the door. I was shocked when no one followed me, but one look back through the window showed me Embry and Gabriel wouldn't let them. I grabbed my bag and locked myself in the bathroom, which was a bright pink I attributed to the seventies. The lock on the door might hold if you tried to turn the handle, but one good push or some jiggling would get you in.

The window was right on top of the toilet, so I was able to stand on that to pry it open. It was harder than I expected, due to a layer of rust and mildew, but my arms were used to lifting Clara and had spent hours boxing with Caleb. I threw my bag out into a bush, then hoisted myself through the opening, trying my best not to get tetanus or some other infection from the ledge.

I expected an army in black to be there waiting for me. They were everywhere on the other side, but the woods were completely deserted. I could hear the busy highway, with its constant flow of cars that could take me away. It was what the guys wanted me to do, but I had nowhere to go, and I wouldn't last long without Embry and Gabriel. So, instead of doing the smart thing like I had promised, I spotted a tree I could climb and found cover, just as a woman poked her head out of the bathroom window. I tried to convince myself that she got past Embry and Gabriel because they calculated how much time I needed and knew I would be safe, but I saw how many people they were up against. It was more likely that my line of defense was lying dead in the motel parking lot.

CHAPTER TWENTY-FOUR

Luckily, the woman who came looking for me thought I would have done the smart thing and gone to get help, as opposed to making myself a sitting duck, just waiting to be found. A couple of the guys who followed her walked around the edge of the tree line, but the forest wasn't dense, and the trees weren't thick enough for me to hide behind. I would have been discovered if they had bothered to look up, but they were satisfied that I was gone when they couldn't see me running off in the distance.

I tried to get settled into the branch I was on, wondering how long I should wait before going to check on the guys, when I felt my eyes drooping. All I could think was that this was the worst possible time for this to be happening, before the forest disappeared, and I was someone else...

"I love you truly, truly dear, life with it's sorrow, life with it's tear, fades into dreams when I feel you are near, for I love you truly, truly dear! Ah, love 'tis something, to feel your kind hand..."

Beth sang to the great bulge of her stomach, one hand rubbing it while the other flipped through the pages of an incredibly old volume. Even older than the Chronicles. The pages had turned brown and looked frail, which she reflected by carefully bringing up each page and gently putting it down on the other side. The right pages held incredible amounts of text, the fancy kind that makes it hard to understand with all of the extra legs, but the left had beautiful pictures of people, places and things. There were happy families, smiling men and women, lakes, small towns, great towers... all of them warm and bright.

She was more focused on the child in her womb, that I could feel moving and pressing on my organs, especially my bladder, than on the happy pictures.

"Ah yes, 'tis something, by your side to stand, gone is the sorrow, gone doubt and fear, for you love me truly, truly dear!"

Her singing became distracted when she got into darker images of two towers with smoke billowing out, a giant wave taking over buildings, a forest on fire...

She stopped suddenly when the page revealed nothing more than a crescent moon on the back of a woman's neck. It was completely harmless, but I would have stopped even if she hadn't.

I could feel the words and hear them coming out of my mouth, but I would not have been able to decipher what was written on the page otherwise. "Prophecy of the Crescent Moon," she said before looking around, as if to make sure no one was there.

"The earliest historical account of the Crescent Moon Prophecy was in the fevered rantings of Saint Malachy, shortly before his death in 1148. 'She who is marked by the Crescent Moon brought forth the Coalescence, and the world was bathed in light. It was miraculous to behold such a blessed sight of angels in white.'
The next was from the accounts of Ioanit, trusted historian of Talina and Zeke, who ruled the earthly realm from 1385 to 1460. Though he

*did not bear witness to the ritual, he recorded part of the incantation
here:*
'From the kindling of Emmanuel's Betrayal
burns the soul of his untouched child.
Let the tears of Isis fuel the flames
in the arms of Yggdrasil.
As the blood of the incumbent quells the fire,
may the heart of the Bearer of the Crescent Moon
originate the Coalescence.'
*Without the completion of the ritual, the powers granted through the
Coalescence could not be passed on, so shortly after 1460, they
returned to the source. It is said they lie in wait for the Bearer of the
Crescent Moon, so they may be claimed."*

Beth flipped through more pages, then found another book and
looked up 'Bearer of the Crescent Moon'.

"Little is known of the origins of the Bearer of the Crescent Moon in
regard to the Prophecy. Most historians agree that it refers to the line
of Talina and Zeke, who ruled over many tribes for nearly a century,
though some have attempted to create her."

The page was covered in drawings of these attempts, including
knives, fire, actual crescents...The next page was even worse, with an
amateur surgeon listing the steps to remove a heart from someone's
chest while it is still beating. I wanted to turn away, but Beth kept
reading.

"Mommy?" A tiny voice came from outside the room, making us
jump. A girl, maybe three-years-old, cautiously walked in.

"Helen." Beth's face lit up as she gently closed the book she had been
reading from. I had assumed Beth was pregnant with her daughter,
Helen. As far as I knew, my great-grandmother didn't have any
siblings.

"What are you reading?" the little girl asked, coming close.

"Just some nonsense, love. What have you been up to?"

Helen tried to look at the book once more before giving up and answering the question, "Daddy's making dinner."

"Pasta again?" Beth asked with a smile, like she wanted nothing more.

"The baby's favorite!" Helen said excitedly, putting her hands on our stomach. The baby kicked, and I swore it was like it recognized its big sister and was saying hello.

"You know what the baby really wants right now?" We got up from the chair and brought the little girl out of the room, leaving the old book behind.

"Ice cream?" Helen asked with a smile, sharing what she wanted.

"Maybe after dinner," Beth humored her. "Right now, he would love for you to play the piano and sing for him. Mummies lullabies aren't doing the trick and his soccer match is all over my organs." The way she referred to the baby as a 'he', after my conversation with Caleb, made me think I might know exactly why I never heard about this child, and I felt sick. Part of it was Beth's morning sickness, but a huge part of it was feeling this baby inside me, feeling how much she loved him, and knowing he was never going to grow up.

"Do you know what song he wants?" Helen asked as she took her seat in front of the piano. "Clair de Lune?"

"That would be perfect." Beth took a seat beside the piano and the little girl played and sang us the French folk song. "Au Clair de la Lune, mon ami Pierrot..."

We rubbed the stomach and smiled for the girl, but while this should have been a perfect, happy little moment in time for Beth, who might not know she was cursed, but all I could feel inside her was dread...

I WAS BARELY HANGING on to the tree when I woke up, so opening my eyes gave me the tiniest of jolts and I fell, trying my best to spread out the impact like Sam had instructed when he caught me jumping off the boat shed when I was little.

Hitting the ground knocked the wind out of me, but I was still reeling from the shock of what I had seen.

I was trying to figure out a different way the prophecy could be interpreted when two men, dressed all in black, with eyes as dark as coal, came and stood on either side above me.

"Well, well. Look what we have here. Not so great at hiding, are we?" They both leered down at me.

This was not good.

CHAPTER TWENTY-FIVE

The two men each grabbed one of my arms and half-dragged, half-carried me around to the front of the rundown motel, to where their boss was waiting. As soon as we rounded the corner, I saw that Sam was now being held by a few of Donovan's henchmen. He looked like they might have beat him to find out where I had gone, but I breathed a sigh of relief. He was alive. I took it as an excellent sign that he was standing on his own, even if they had him restrained.

It wasn't until we were about twenty feet away from Sam and Donovan that I had my suspicions about Gabriel and Embry confirmed. To make sure I had no doubts about it, Embry was in a pool of blood. I would have told myself it was someone else's, but I could see that it was coming from the large gash on the side of his head. Gabriel, my last defense before the woman managed to come after me, was lying in the doorway of our motel room. There was an axe on the ground next to his chest, which was covered in red. I had to turn away so I could catch my breath.

"Miss Owens, I am so glad that you finally decided to join

us." Donovan came over as his minions let go of me. They stayed on either side, and more of them were all around us, so I knew I had no chance of escaping, even if I had known how to hotwire a car.

"That is the last thing I would ever want to do." I made sure I was standing straight, looking right into the dark holes he used as eyes while I said it. I was doing my best to appear confident, and in control, even though it couldn't be farther from the truth.

"Lost your nerve?" Donovan asked with a smile. "No longer rushing to save poor Sam now that you don't have your lap dogs to keep you safe?"

"I stayed, didn't I?" I pointed out through gritted teeth. His relishing of Embry and Gabriel's deaths upset me more than the way he mocked me.

"That, you did. I am still trying to decide if that was out of bravery or stupidity." He looked me up and down, sizing me up in a way that made my skin crawl. Unlike prom night with Danny Kinks, Donovan didn't have any desire in his eyes.

"You had my people," I explained. As soon as I saw Sam through the window, there was no way I was leaving.

"Stupidity then." My answer bored him. He was talking slow and walking around as if he had all of the time in the world. True, it did look like he had won and no longer had anything to worry about, but I still had a dagger strapped to my ankle, and my guys were going to wake up eventually.

"Or decency," I said it under my breath, but with conviction. He heard, but instead of being offended, he looked back at me with the tiniest of smiles.

"But I digress; I have not called you here to taunt or insult you, my dear. I apologize if I have made you uncomfortable or scared. You'll find I can be a very accommodating host." He was still gauging my personality, figuring out which buttons to press to get what he wanted. Was I hot-tempered? Would threatening me work? Or was his original assumption right, that the easiest way to get me to do what he wanted was to threaten to hurt my family? I had made the answer clear, but he wasn't accepting it.

"Why? Are you planning on entertaining my heartless body after you bleed it dry?" I knew he needed my heart, and chanced a guess at the rest. I got the feeling that my death wouldn't interfere with his plans, but Cassie had thrown herself off a cliff so he wouldn't have access to her dead body. That the guys then burnt. Blood seemed like an ominous equivalent to my 'essence' for an occult ritual.

"Your friends should have told you that vampires don't exist," he smiled at me.

"Then what is it you want to do with me?" I asked. "What do I have to do for you to let Sam go? To leave him and his family alone?" I chanced a glance in Sam's direction. He looked disappointed that I had come back rather than running off to ensure my own safety.

"That's quite simple Lucy; all you have to do is join us."

"Join you?" I knew this was a trap, but him killing me would probably be better than what would happen if I joined him.

"I want you to decide, of your own free will, that you wish to be a part of our organization." He raised his arms and looked around at his followers, who all stood at the ready. I wondered how many of them were here of their own free will.

"I have a lot of trouble believing that all you want is for me to be one of your minions," I argued.

"You would not be a minion. You would have an honored spot at the side of the king," he said as if this were a seductive idea I should be tempted by.

"I would rather die," I said with a courage I was only pretending to feel.

"Of course. Your death would be the first step, but eventually, it would be an incredible reward."

"I would be dead," I reminded him. I had seen horror films with necromancy, and it churned my stomach.

"You are so blinded by your ideals of good and evil that you're not even considering the whole picture," he sighed.

"Then enlighten me. Tell me exactly what I would be getting myself into, so I can make an informed decision as to whether or not I want to willingly join you," I said, partially because I did want to know what he planned to do with me, but also because the more time he spent talking, the closer we got to Embry and Gabriel waking up, and the longer Sam stayed alive. I wasn't naïve enough to think we could talk for the eight hours Gabriel and Embry would need, and I knew help wasn't coming, but I needed to keep him talking long enough to come up with a plan.

"For centuries we have been collecting a variety of items for a ritual. There have been many attempts since the beginning of time, but few of us are still searching. Most of them gave up when they kept trying and failing." He had a gleam in his dark eyes when he mentioned the ritual, and pride when he spoke of the others who gave up while he forged on.

"What makes you think yours will work?" I stalled him.

"We have yet to attempt the ritual, because we are missing a pivotal ingredient." The way he looked at me made me feel extremely uneasy. "You see, over a few centuries, you can collect most of the essential ingredients. Splinters from the cross Jesus of Nazareth was nailed to, soul of a virgin...a lot of religious or supernatural paraphernalia I won't bore you with. The issue comes with the heart of the Bearer of the Crescent Moon," he gave weight to each word, waiting for me to understand his implications.

"You want my heart," I stated. It was the one thing I knew for sure from Beth's memory. He waited, possibly for a reaction, but I didn't know what he wanted me to say. At this point it wasn't my life I was going to plead for. If I died, Donovan's quest ended, and everyone else would be okay. I didn't have a daughter to worry about like Cassandra had.

"Precisely. For centuries, men like us have been branding their slaves, their wives and their children with crescent moons. Some believed it had to be the virgin, some thought an innocent child. Hundreds tried, but none ever succeeded. It was not up to us to brand someone with the Crescent Moon, we had to find the women who already had it."

"Annabelle had it, so you've been tracking her descendants, waiting to get your hands on another one who has her birth-mark," I concluded.

"We have everything else," he agreed. It bothered me how he spoke of himself as a collective.

"Then why am I still standing? Shouldn't you be slicing into me and letting Sam go?" I asked. It was cruel to torture me if he was ultimately going to rip my heart out.

"You need to give it willingly," he reminded me.

"Did the virgin willingly give you her soul?" I shot at him. I normally only talked back to Embry and Sam, sometimes Gabriel, because they felt more like friends or older siblings than parents or elders. With Donovan, I figured he was going to kill me anyway, although I didn't like how much he was enjoying it.

"She did, believe it or not. Magic, whether dark or light, has precise nuances. One virgin's soul over another's can make a world of difference in a spell. Combining powerful elements such as those required for this ritual...it takes more than finesse, it can go terribly wrong. A heart given willingly will always be more powerful, and easier to control than one taken by force." His eyes lit up as he spoke, which was extremely hard for them to do. This was his life's work. I was the final element to his masterpiece.

I was going to tell him he could have my heart if he let everyone else go, but I was still hoping we could hold out until Embry and Gabriel came back to life. Then we could defeat the monster and all live to see another day.

"You want me to rule, metaphorically, because my heart will be...what? Your source of power? What does the spell do?" I pressed to keep him talking.

"Everything." The holes he had as eyes grew wide with excitement. "The one who succeeds in completing the ritual will be powerful above all others. You have seen how easily we control those who are like us, those who do not die until their business is done. Once the ritual is completed, we will be able to control the entire planet in that way. Kings, presidents, armies... no one would be immune to obeying our commands. Our power would be unimaginable. We would rule the world."

"And everybody wants to rule the world." I rolled my eyes at how cliché it was. I knew the song and could hypothetically see the attraction, but I would wish for a million other things before ruling the world ever crossed my mind.

"You don't agree?"

"Do you realize how crazy it is that you basically can't die, and instead of taking advantage of the past...I don't know how many hundreds of years, you have been tracking down a line of women and trying to kill them? You could have travelled the world for pleasure, gone to every church and museum in Europe, learnt every language, painted, written novels, read every book ever published...you could have accomplished so much."

"I stay alive so the ritual can be completed. If all I wanted was to write a few poems, I would have died."

"It's not just culture. You could have found someone to love and be happy with, raise a family, instead of becoming this monster hell-bent on killing my family. Isn't it lonely knowing you're killing the only person who isn't under your control?" I knew it was pointless, but if he did have a heart somewhere deep down, it couldn't hurt to try and reach it.

"You're not controlled, but you aren't a willing participant either. That's why I want you to see that we are not entirely evil. When we take over the world, we will have order, and go back to a simpler, less forgiving way of life. Society has become much too tolerant of late. And best of all, we can bring you back, Lucy. True, we need your heart in order to complete the ritual, and you will die. But once it is done and we have all the power, we will be able to bring you back to life. You will be able to rule at our side, a coveted position," he offered as if he were doing me a favor.

Something in the dark way he smiled had me worried. "What exactly is your plan for the rest of the population, once you can control everyone?"

"Those who are useful can join our society and contribute. The weak and the poor, who exist solely as leeches or parasites will be eliminated, as was suggested millenniums ago. We haven't worked out all the details yet, but the gist of it is… anything we want."

I knew better than to expect his new world would be a utopia, even a dysfunctional one. Judging by how he treated me, Sam, and even his minions, I got the impression that not many people would survive his reign, especially not caring, selfless people like Deanna and Sam, or sweet little girls like Clara. I looked to Sam, who was still standing about ten feet from me, with tape on his mouth and his hands tied behind his back. It was determination and irrepressible sadness that he found in my eyes once we made contact. I saw the same emotions in his as he nodded. He knew what I had to do. Even if I willingly gave up my heart, he would still meet the same fate.

"I would be glad to enlighten you further on the ride, but we must get going. We have a long drive ahead of us." Donovan extended his hand, still expecting me to follow and willingly let him murder me to protect the ones I loved. I would have, if there was even a possibility it would work, and they would get to live happily ever after. But we all knew they wouldn't.

I looked back to Sam and mouthed "I love you," which got a tiny nod, before I used my fingers to count down.

Three...

Two...

One.

CHAPTER TWENTY-SIX

W hen all of my fingers were gone and my hand was in a fist, Sam bopped his head back to knock out the man behind him, who had loosened his grip on the knife. I grabbed my dagger from my boot and planted it a few inches to the right of Donovan's heart. The element of surprise was the only way I managed to get that close. He was fast, and strong, and threw me to the ground with a force that knocked my breath out.

Sam managed to incapacitate two of the men charged with holding him, but more of them took their place. One of them now had his knife dangerously close to Sam's jugular, as Donovan used his boot on my windpipe to pin me to the ground. I tried to push it off, but gravity and biology were on his side.

"I take it this means you won't be coming willingly," Donovan concluded. "That is a shame. For you, at least. The challenge of an uncooperative heart is one we have been expecting since that slut got away," Donovan's voice had taken back its bored quality, except when he referred to Annabelle, my ancestor, as 'that slut'. Pure hatred laced those words, and I feared what he might do to someone who looked exactly like her.

My refusal of his offer and trying to escape disappointed him. Any victory I might have felt from learning that he could still be hurt, that I had hurt him vanished the instant he nodded to the men holding Sam. I barely had time to turn my head before the blood was pouring from Sam's neck and he slowly fell to the ground.

"Sam!" I screamed, rushing to him as soon as Donovan let me go. He knew he had me now, so it didn't matter if I cried from a distance, or leaning over Sam's lifeless body.

I CRUMPLED onto the ground next to my big brother, taking his head into my lap, running my fingers through his carrot top head. He hated the color of it when I was younger, until he met Deanna and found out she liked it. All I had known growing up was my mom, Grams, Mr. & Mrs. Boyd, and Sam. As the warm blood continued to flow from the wound on Sam's neck, onto my jeans, all I could think was that every single one of them was gone now.

The tears poured freely, which blurred my vision, so I didn't notice that the army of men and women that made up Donovan's army had diminished. I looked to Donovan, waiting for him to mock me for crying, or to taunt Sam for being dead, but he was on the ground, right next to where he had been crushing my windpipe.

I couldn't even summon any excitement over my stab costing Donovan one of his unlimited lives. All I wanted to do was lie down beside Sam until he woke up and told me it was all a horrible nightmare and we could go home now. Sam's death would be in vain if I didn't figure out a way to escape before Donovan came back to life, but I didn't have any fight left in me.

. . .

ALTHOUGH MOST OF the people who followed Donovan had been under his control, some of them did so by choice. These were the men who now recovered Donovan's body and put it into the large Hummer they had found us with. They could see from my catatonic state that I wasn't going to run or put up a fight, so they let me be. Even if I had tried to escape, it wasn't like I could reach anywhere before the dozen or so of them that remained caught up to me.

I knew I didn't have long, that they weren't forgetting about me, just dealing with more pressing things, but it took everything in me to focus on a plan rather than the crushing pain around my heart. It was like I couldn't breathe, and I was breathing too much, all at the same time.

I needed something to make sure Embry and Gabriel would find me, so they could stop Donovan from using my heart to end the world as we know it. I was relatively certain no one would make an executive decision to kill me until Donovan woke up, so I had a bit of time. Unfortunately, I had no more weapons, and everything I brought was in the backpack Donovan's minions took when they found me at the foot of the tree. Not that I could think of anything in my backpack that could help me. I could see Sam's car keys sticking out of his pocket, but I didn't see the mini-van anywhere. Unless I could find it, get in, start it and drive off before one of the minions could get to me, the keys weren't going to help. The key wasn't even the type that you could use to scratch someone's eyes out or stab them. It was a small, rounded, rectangular shape that you just needed to have in your pocket for the vehicle to let you in. I was reproaching us for buying fancy cars instead of the ones with weapon-like keys, when it hit me.

I made sure no one was watching me, then reached into Sam's pocket to release the standard dealership keychain, the one where he put our Onstar stickers, so we would always have our numbers. I looked around again and saw that they were still huddled around Donovan's body, doing god-knows-what. I threw Sam's keychain as far as I could in Embry's direction, slipping the actual key into my pocket. I breathed a sigh of relief when the keychain landed on Embry's stomach, his shirt muffling the sound. Hopefully, Embry would see it when he woke up and remember how to work the Onstar.

THE MINIONS FINISHED their task and remembered me, so two of them came over and lifted me by the arms when I refused to leave Sam. They pulled me towards the side of the vehicle, both of them dressed like they were in special ops, all in black, with matching cargo pants and side arms. The taller of the two was the muscle, not saying much other than occasional grunts, but the shorter one kept barking orders when the others looked to him for confirmation. He had his brown hair slicked back with way too much gel and was clearly in charge now that Donovan was out of commission. He was about to open the door for me when one of the other men called him over.

"Tie her up while I teach Miguel how to discard," Slick commanded Muscles, who was still holding on to me.

"You could have had it all," Muscles told me, shaking his head like I had torn up the winning lottery ticket. His knots weren't stellar, but they were too tight for me to be able to do anything. He helped me into the backseat, then let me sit alone and wait for another fifteen minutes while they figured out what they were going to do. Or maybe they talked about the weather, because they still didn't know what they were doing when they got into the car. They had me move to the middle seat, with a minion on each side. Muscles took the passenger seat while Slick had the wheel. I saw the other guys following us in another car as we turned to get out of the motel parking lot. All I could do was hope Embry and Gabriel had time to wake up and find me before Donovan came back to life and killed me.

. . .

PERHAPS I HAD SEEN TOO many movies, but I was fully prepared to get a burlap sack put on my head and spend the next few hours counting turns and how long we drove so I would be able to escape and find my way back, or help someone find me if I got my hands on a phone. The fact that none of that happened, that they let me know exactly where we were, told me they were either terrible kidnappers, or that no one expected me to be rescued, so they didn't care what I saw or heard.

We drove for hours, making lots of elaborate detours, and sometimes driving in circles. I didn't know if they were worried someone would come and save me, or if they had other enemies they were trying to avoid, but either of those options would give me a chance to escape. The first hour was in almost complete silence, and I would have sworn we had been driving at least three hours if the dashboard clock hadn't let me keep track of time. It wasn't until Muscles turned the radio on that they all loosened up. They talked about past road trips, some with their families, while others had been traveling together for a long time. The driver, who I nicknamed Slick, didn't talk much, except to admit that his first road trip with 'the big guy' was before cars even existed. Then they got to teasing each other about how old they were. I tried to listen to everything, just in case one of them would slip and mention something I could use to escape or bribe my way out. The only useful information I got was that Slick was loyal to the mission, but the rest of them were waiting for the riches and the glory that was promised to them as soon as Donovan got what he needed.

CHAPTER TWENTY-SEVEN

After a little more than five hours, we stopped at a gas station of the run-down variety. The machines hadn't been updated in decades, so the pumps had meters with needles instead of display screens. Either because we were on an abandoned road in the middle of nowhere, or because it was so late, the station only had one employee working inside. He looked so engrossed in his cell phone that were they to hold him up for all the cash in the register, he would probably hand it over without looking up. He wasn't going to be the one to save me tonight.

Slick was in charge of filling the tank, Muscles went inside to get snacks and the guy on my left went to the washroom. This left me alone with the guy on my right, who they had called Jim, if I wanted to fight my way out of the car. However, that would also involve me having to outrun Slick once I made it outside. Luckily, the tank was on the left side, which was also where the other vehicle had parked. I was considering whether or not I could hit Jim hard enough to knock him out, when I noticed his leg was shaking, which it hadn't for the rest of the drive.

"I know you guys are going to kill me, so you probably don't care, but I really need to pee, and we are sitting on the same seat," I shared, hoping I hadn't misread the situation.

"You too?" he asked, looking to me and considering it. He was the one who had seemed the least dedicated to the cause in earlier conversations. He was a nervous nail-biter who dreamed of writing the next Great American Novel, but couldn't make it past the prologue before ripping it all to pieces.

I nodded, pleading with him, before he got out of the Hummer and stepped aside so I could follow. I sighed with relief and made sure to look extremely grateful as he helped me get out with my hands still tied behind my back.

"What do you think you're doing?" Slick asked from the other side of the car.

"She's about to pee all over the seat," Jim complained about me, without mentioning that he was about to do the same.

"Be quick," Slick warned before we headed towards the building.

THE RESTROOMS WERE around the side of the station, so Slick and the others wouldn't see what was happening once we rounded the corner.

"Do you think you could untie me?" I asked Jim, playing into the innocent little girl image as much as I could.

"That wouldn't be cool," he shook his head, looking over his shoulder towards the others. He struck me as someone at the bottom of the totem pole.

"It's really awkward with my hands behind my back. Even walking is hard when I have nothing to balance me."

Lucky for me, Jim was more interested in using the men's room than in doing anything inappropriate to me, so he liked the idea of making it easier for me to go in on my own and not take a million years.

"What if your hands were in front?" he offered.

"That would be amazing. Thank you," I told him, swallowing hard, both to show him my fear, and because I was having second thoughts about what I might need to do to get away from him.

He came behind me and was about to untie my hands when he thought better of it. "You can just climb through now," he offered instead of untying and retying my ropes. At least he held onto me, so I could keep my balance while I stepped through the hole my arms made.

I took a look at the building and saw it was unlikely that I would be able to escape through a window while he was outside waiting. For starters, the window couldn't accommodate more than my arm, and Jim was suddenly intent on coming in with me.

"I can use the sink while you...I won't look," he said, and although I believed him about not looking, it was still wrong on so many levels.

Once my hands were in front of me, I pretended to stagger, knowing he would instinctively come closer so I wouldn't fall. As soon as he was within my reach, I put my arms around his head, using the rope pressed against his neck to pull him into me. He struggled, but hanging on the rope gave me leverage, so within a minute or so, he went limp and I let him fall to the ground. In the car, he had mentioned finding prohibition a lot more fun than people would expect, so I was pretty sure I hadn't killed him for good. Not that it made me feel any less like I just murdered someone, nearly with my bare hands.

I heard flushing and remembered that one of the men would be walking out of the restrooms any second now, so without putting much thought into it, I ran off into the field behind the gas station.

· · ·

As I got further away, I could hear shouts and running, so I knew they were following me, but I'd had a head start, and the field was overrun with tall grass and corn stalks. My school athletics wouldn't help against someone with Gabriel's speed, and the vegetation wasn't going to keep me covered forever, but I was convinced that if I could make it to the other side of the field, if I could find someone -anyone- then I would get free.

It rained recently, or they had bad irrigation, because there were puddles along the sides of the rows. Some small enough that I could run over without even jumping, while others looked so deep and wide that I considered hiding in one, as an absolute last resort, if they closed in before I reached what sounded like a highway.

I could see the edge of the field in the distance and sped up to reach it, but I tripped on the uneven ground and fell. Luckily, I managed to put my bound hands out to break my fall, but I still landed with most of my upper body in a puddle.

I tried to use my elbows and feet to push myself off the ground, but my ankle did not appreciate the weight I put on it. I paused and took a deep breath before trying again, this time with less foot and more knee. The ankle was able to bear my weight, and the pain was more like those twists that go away quickly than an actual sprain. I limped a few steps, then used all of my willpower to keep running, knowing they were right behind me. They were gaining on me, and as much as I tried to push the thought out, I knew that it was almost impossible for me to get out of this. I needed to stop a car on the highway and get them to drive off with me before the minions caught up, or I was done for. I was now all wet, in addition to bloody, so even if I found somewhere to hide, I would most likely freeze to death overnight. It was hot summer weather during the day, but I could feel the autumn chill coming once it got dark at night.

I reminded myself that Sam would have died for absolutely

nothing if those guys caught up with me, and used it as extra motivation to push myself harder and keep going. No matter what, I couldn't give up.

CHAPTER TWENTY-EIGHT

I turned my head to look behind me and see how close they were, but I ran right into something solid, yet relatively soft. At first, I just saw the T-shirt, which was black, and I froze. I didn't know if I ran the wrong way or if one of them drove to the highway to catch me from the other side, but I felt so defeated. I could feel the tears coming and pushed them away, preparing myself to at least go down fighting, but all I got from my opponent was a shush. I looked up, recognizing the voice but unable to believe it until I saw his face and knew I wasn't dreaming. I had been so sure it was one of the guys from the other car, but it was Embry I crashed into.

I hugged him, and tears of relief formed as I tried to catch my breath, before Embry gently put me to the side and pulled out his sword. It would have been better if we had both made a run for the highway, but I obliged. I found a wet log on the ground behind me and hoped I wouldn't have to use it.

The minions were only expecting me, a little girl by their standards, running for her life with no weapons and her hands tied behind her back. This gave Embry the advantage, so although my teeth were clenched and my knuckles white from holding onto the log so tight, he managed to cut down the three men who came at us with hardly any effort. The Gifted who were acting against their will had all dispersed when Donovan died, so Embry didn't hesitate to use deadly force. I had to look away, but it was a relief to know that it would take some time before any of them got up and came after us.

"IS THAT ALL OF THEM?" Embry asked me once Slick, Muscles and their friend were all lying on the ground.

"No, there was another car full." I strained, but couldn't hear a thing. "Where's Gabriel? I thought he would...did he not wake up?" I fumbled for words. I had been worried about Embry and Gabriel, but it was with the assumption that they couldn't die. And dying was supposed to break any previously established bonds. Meaning they would come back to me better than new. I was so worried they wouldn't find me in time that it hadn't occurred to me that one of them wouldn't find me at all.

Embry opened his mouth to say something. I was terrified, not sure I wanted to hear his answer, but then I heard Gabriel's voice.

"I took out four of them on the other side, but I think I saw one..." Gabriel didn't get a chance to tell us what he saw one doing. As soon as I heard his voice and knew he wasn't lost to me, I ran to him. I collided with Gabriel like I had on prom night, and with Embry tonight, only this time it was on purpose. Gabriel took me up so my feet were off the ground, dangling for a few moments before he put me down and let me go. He looked about as surprised as I was by my hug, and his own reaction to it.

"I'm sorry, I thought we lost you for a minute." I tried to shrug it off like it wasn't a big deal.

"Cutting off my oxygen won't kill me for good, but I'd rather

245

not have to go through with the coming back to life again so soon," Gabriel made a joke and gave me a smile.

"I'm really glad you guys found me." I tried to keep my emotions in check, but my relief was threatening to come out as tears.

"You're not getting rid of us that easily," Gabriel assured me, straightening up and fixing his jacket.

I gave him a smile before something rustled in the field to my left, making me jump as Donovan broke through the tall grass. "There you are." Donovan looked at me with hatred and determination, so I froze like a deer caught in the headlights, then fumbled my way to the log I had dropped when I ran to Gabriel.

Luckily, Donovan was slow from recently being dead, and the guys weren't as surprised as I was. There was a fierce anger and precision to their moves, as Gabriel expertly karate-chopped Donovan in the back of the neck, which let Embry slice off his right hand once he fell to his knees. I had expected a threatening curse, but Donovan let out a blood-curdling scream instead.

Embry and Gabriel had both killed all the men they'd come up against, except Donovan. They left him to bleed out on the ground, clutching his right arm. It was better to keep him weak and wounded than to let him come back to life in a few hours. I wondered if limbs grew back as good as new when you were resurrected.

Embry put away his sword and came over to me, pulling me into his arms while Gabriel made sure no more men were hiding in the grass.

"The Onstar was genius," Embry told me with an encouraging smile, trying to distract me from Donovan and his stump.

"I knew I told you that I keep having to call them because I lose my keys, but I didn't know if you would be able to figure it out, or convince them you were Sam or..." I said it fast, because my brain still hadn't registered that I was safe. Or at least relatively safe at the moment. But no matter how fast I said Sam's name, it still hit me like a punch to the gut. "I didn't know how else you would find me," I finished, feeling absolutely defeated.

"We've got you now," Embry assured me. He took me in his arms, thinking it was the fear and the adrenaline dropping that made my shoulders collapse.

"He'll never stop until he has her," Donovan told us, laughing to himself and clutching his stump.

My saviors turned to him like they wanted him to take it back, as if that would make the words untrue. I was more preoccupied with his use of the third person.

"He?" I asked. It was one thing to always refer to himself as a collective 'we', but 'he' usually referred to someone else. "Donovan isn't the one we've been running from?" My heart beat faster against my chest.

"Me?" Donovan laughed, a cackling sound worse than his earlier scream. "I am nothing compared to him. None of you would stand a chance if he was here right now. He has powers you couldn't even imagine."

I suddenly understood that all of the 'we's weren't Donovan's grandiose view of himself, but his linking himself to the one with all the power. Donovan was nothing but the weak sidekick to the almighty powerful evil. The thought made me shiver.

"Let's get you out of here," Embry guided me towards an old station wagon they left running at the edge of the field, off the highway I'd tried so hard to get to.

"You won't save her. Just like you couldn't save Annabelle. Like you couldn't save any of them," Donovan called after us like a curse.

EPILOGUE

This time it was Embry who drove. Gabriel let me have the passenger seat so I wouldn't be alone in the back. I was grateful to see one of them had managed to get my bag for me, but the only thing I wanted from it was my blankie, which I couldn't touch when I was covered in mud and blood. I turned up the heating instead.

Embry kept one hand on the wheel, but the other was on the armrest between us so he could hold my hand. The rhythmic rubbing of his thumb on my skin slowly calmed me down.

"We can't defeat them, can we?" I asked eventually, looking to Embry for honesty. If the lowly sidekick was enough to take us down, how could we ever face the real Big Bad?

"Defeating them was not our goal tonight; it was just keeping you safe. We thought we gave you enough time to get away, but then the keychain when we came back told us they had you," Embry explained.

"You gave me enough time," I said quietly, turning to look out the window.

"What?" Embry was confused, and I could feel his eyes on me, meaning they weren't on the road anymore.

"You're driving," I pointed out.

"How did they take you if you had enough time?" Gabriel asked me. I didn't look back, but I knew the vein in his forehead was pulsing.

"I got out through the window and climbed one of the trees to hide. I had just made it up to the leafy part when a woman came through. None of them ever looked up, so...you gave me enough time."

"Why didn't you run and get away from them?" Gabriel asked from the back.

"It wouldn't have worked. That is exactly what they thought I did. They immediately ran off, looking around, but they wouldn't have found me up the tree." I gave them the logical reason before the more honest one. "And I was not leaving you guys." I remembered how unfathomable that concept had been for me, but thinking of Sam brought an overwhelming tightness into my chest.

"But they did find you. Do you not realize that we just died so that you could escape, not so you could hang out and wait for us?" Gabriel was angry and upset with me.

"You don't think I know what everyone has been sacrificing for me?" I asked, the tears burning my eyes. "I saw your dead bodies at the motel, okay? I saw them and even though I knew you were coming back, I still knew it was because of me. And I saw them slit Sam's throat because I said no to joining him. I was there, and I held him, and I know that he died so I wouldn't have to—" I tried to keep talking, but the words became muffled in the tears and I couldn't stop the sobs as I relived Sam's final moments in my head.

"Sam is dead?" Gabriel asked more gently, his anger taken over by the realization of what I was going through.

"Because I said no," I nodded as a fresh batch of tears rolled down my cheeks. I explained to them what Donovan wanted with me, what he planned to do, and how I said no, knowing it would cost Sam his life, but it was a price he was prepared to pay. I told them how I hadn't even realized Donovan was dead because Sam was my main priority, how I hoped Embry would remember that the keys had a computer chip in them, how I tricked Jim into taking me to the bathroom, and killed him so I could run away. They were impressed that I had managed to stab Donovan and kill him, but I couldn't bring myself to show the proper enthusiasm.

"Didn't you see him when you woke up?" I asked, Sam's dead body so vivid in my mind. "We should go back and get him, so we can…" I wasn't sure what I wanted. To have a proper funeral, to bury him, to bring him home to Deanna…all I knew was that we couldn't leave him at the motel, alone.

"I didn't see him," Embry told me, shaking his head before the two of them shared a look.

"Didn't you look?" I asked, figuring they would have gone around to find me before commandeering a car.

"Not long after we woke up and found the keychain, one of the minions drove up in this." Embry nodded to the station wagon he was driving. "We saw him grab one of his fallen friends by the boots and drag him towards the trunk, so we knocked him out to get the keys and came after you."

"He meant discard people," I understood what Slick had been referring to back at the motel. I brought my hand to my mouth when it hit me that Sam was one of those people, the thought making me sick. I closed my eyes and tried to block the images out of my mind before turning to look in the back of the car. I knew it was irrational, but I wanted to see something that would either confirm or disprove my thought. Instead, Gabriel moved so his head blocked my view. I tried to look past him, but he made me look into his eyes.

"Why did you leave the tree?" he asked, changing the subject for me, but also because he wanted to know the answer. I could tell Embry wanted to pull over so he could take me in his arms and try to comfort me, at least a little, but we had to get as much distance between us and them as we could. The hand that wasn't holding mine was gripping the steering wheel so tight that his knuckles were white.

"I fell," I admitted. I knew he was trying to distract me, but I wanted to play along. This wouldn't have been my favorite subject of conversation either, but it was better than what my brain kept replaying.

"You?" Gabriel was skeptical. Once, when Embry had left me alone with him, before I understood that he was quiet, not evil, I had spent almost an entire day hanging out in a tree, watching him search the house and the grounds for me. Embry had found it hilarious when he got back.

"My little monkey?" Embry asked as well. That was the nickname he called me for the rest of the summer, to taunt Gabriel more than anything.

"I had another dream," I said, causing them to exchange a worried glance.

"Who?" Gabriel asked.

"Beth," I admitted.

"What did you see?" Embry pressed, knowing it had to be bad, or at least shocking, if it made me fall out of a tree.

"The prophecy," I admitted, leaving her pregnancy out. For some reason, I felt like now wasn't the time to share it with them. "The reason they're after me and they killed Sam and you guys keep dying and all the ones before me and…"

"It's not your fault," Embry said pointedly.

"Did you guys know that's why he wants me? Because I have the birthmark?" I asked.

For a moment they were quiet, then they looked to each other. I tried to read what their eyes were saying, but had no clue, before Embry answered. "No. We knew that your line was important to him."

"But Annabelle did, I think," Gabriel spoke up. "I don't know if she knew her line would have replicas of her with identical birthmarks, but she was relieved and incredibly happy when she told me that Margaret's only birthmark was a simple brown spot on her knee."

"Why would Donovan's master fight so hard to find Margaret if she didn't have the birthmark? She would have been useless to him as far as the spell was concerned," I asked.

"I don't think he knew Annabelle didn't pass the birthmark on to her daughter," Gabriel admitted. "Maybe he thought it was something that would come to her when Annabelle died, or when she turned a certain age."

"If Annabelle knew, why didn't she warn you?" I asked, beginning to think Annabelle kept a lot of things secret when she should have shared them, or written them in her diary. "I could have removed the birthmark through surgery, or dyed my hair? He never would have known I was a replica if…"

"I think she thought it ended when she let them burn her," Gabriel ventured, cutting me off so I would stop accusing the woman he loved.

"If ever a miracle happens, and I do make it out of this alive, I think I'll adopt," I said, getting a smile from Embry, but it was a sad one, and he knew that mine was fake.

"You're making it out alive," Embry told me like it was the only option.

WE DROVE until we crossed state lines, at which point we brought the station wagon into what I could only assume was a chop-shop, where they would strip it down and repurpose every single piece. Instead of finding new wheels, we walked a couple of miles in the hopes of finding a place to stay for the night.

"Want to kill two birds with one stone?" Embry suggested when we got to railroad tracks with a cargo train pulling out. It looked like the cars were made out of wood that hadn't been updated since the 1920s. It was still in that slow, building up energy phase, the perfect time to jump on board if we were to be reckless.

"You can't be serious." I looked at them, but knew better than to doubt them after spending days in a moving chicken coop.

"Quick, before it gains speed," Embry recommended, so I ran behind them.

Gabriel got to the train first, but he let Embry get in, then waited for me to catch up. Embry put out a hand to sort of pull me in when I got close enough, then Gabriel joined once I was in.

"Any idea where this train is going?" I asked, pulling Gabriel's jacket tighter around me. I was freezing when we gave up the car, so I put on a sweater from my bag, and Gabriel gave me his leather jacket. It did a much better job at blocking out the wind. I went to sit under the one tiny light in our compartment and took out the Chronicles.

"Home." Embry came to sit across from me, while Gabriel explored the wooden crates that surrounded us.

"The plantation?" I asked.

"We can stop by the beach house on the way," he offered.

"We can't." I wanted so badly to go home over the past month, but now I wanted to be as far from the manor and telling Deanna what happened as possible. I still wanted to take Clara in my arms and be comforted by Deanna, but I couldn't stand them hating me. And I would never forgive myself if my death magnet struck again. "It's too dangerous," I only gave them my second reason.

"We have a bit of a breather now, while Donovan recruits a new army. We'll get warnings before he comes back," Gabriel explained, sitting on one of the crates.

"Like last time?" I asked.

"We won't sit around and wait for him to come for us again.

We're going to go home and regroup, get some stuff from the bunker, then…" Embry turned to Gabriel, uncertain about the rest of the plan.

"Maryland has an old army base with a secure underground facility. Even the president can't get into it, but I have a friend who…" Gabriel offered a new location, but I didn't want another prison-like tomb to wait in for the real Big Bad to find me.

"No," I argued, shaking my head before he even finished.

"No?" he asked like he didn't understand the word.

"I don't want to run to a new place to hide. Then wait for him to get close so we can try to run away again." I wrapped my arms around myself. "I don't want any more people dying while I escape, or hide in a not-so-safe house."

"What do you suggest?" he asked like he was humoring me and had no idea what I was talking about.

My current emotional state made it hard to think straight, but I knew exactly what I needed to do. "I want to learn how to take care of myself. Not self-defense against regular guys, but…I want to stand a chance against Gifteds. We need to be ready for *him*."

"How do you plan to do that?" Embry asked delicately.

"I'm going to find out everything I can," I said simply, opening the Chronicles to the section on Beth, since I had finished Cassie's.

"On the prophecy?" Embry asked.

"The prophecy, Donovan's master, the Gifted…anything I can find out."

"Are you looking for something in particular?" Gabriel questioned.

"Anything I can use to defeat him," I said simply. "You've been running for centuries, but now we need to get ready to fight."

The End

***

Sign up to my newsletter to for an Exclusive Owens Chronicles
Novella!
www.amandalynnpetrin.com/prophecybonus

***

Keep reading for a sneak peek at Destiny (The Owens
Chronicles Book Two)

ACKNOWLEDGMENTS

Once more, I thank my mom, who supports and encourages me, then spends hours reading my work and giving me notes and edits to make Prophecy the best book it can be. I couldn't do any of it without her.

To my dad, who doesn't read fiction, but still goes through my novels to give pointers on sports, gambling and whether they're plausible. He constantly pushes me to be better, and I'm forever grateful.

To my grandfather, who religiously reads my blog, and used to print it out so he could keep a copy. Years ago, I applied to a Creative Writing program and left my portfolio on his desk by accident. When I found it, he had not only read all of my short stories, he gave me notes and advice in the margins. I wouldn't trade him for the world.

To everyone who helped me finish the book and supported me along the way, you are superstars and I owe you so much. Mommy, Joanna, J.F, Johnny, Kimberlie, 100 Covers...

To everyone who bought Shards of Glass, who read it, who enjoyed it, who made me believe that I could be a writer... THANK YOU. I appreciate it more than you will ever know.

And to Arsen, who is there for me when I have no idea what to write, and believes in me when I doubt myself.

Thank you all, from the bottom of my heart.

ABOUT THE AUTHOR

Amanda Lynn Petrin is the author of *The Giftedverse* (which comprises *The Owens Chronicles* and *The Gifted Chronicles*), as well as *Shards of Glass*. She graduated with a double major in History and Psychology from McGill University, then spent a decade pursuing an acting career before turning to writing. She currently lives in Montreal, where she enjoys spending time with her family and living vicariously through her characters.

Find her at: www.amandalynnpetrin.com

ALSO BY AMANDA LYNN PETRIN

Shards of Glass

The Owens Chronicles

Prophecy (Book One)

Destiny (Book Two)

Legacy (Book Three)

Etta: A Gifted Chronicles Novella

The Gifted Chronicles

First Life

Second Chance

Third Eye

Find out more at

www.amandalynnpetrin.com

DESTINY

THE OWENS CHRONICLES
BOOK TWO

AMANDA LYNN PETRIN

CHAPTER ONE

THE OWENS CHRONICLES BOOK TWO

"I'll have the three-egg western omelet with sausage, bacon, and ham on the side. Whole wheat toast is fine. Hash browns, beans, and seasonal fruit would be great, with an order of pancakes and black coffee," Gabriel ordered from the diner's waitress while I stared at him in disbelief. He was occasionally hungry enough for an egg, a piece of toast or a bit of oatmeal, but his usual breakfast consisted of black coffee with nothing else.

"I'll have the same, but French toast instead of the pancakes and espresso rather than coffee," Embry told the waitress, who raised her eyes to him in surprise.

"I'll just have…" my stomach growled as if I hadn't eaten in days. I looked to the guys and realized we were starving because none of us had eaten anything but the protein bars from my backpack since before we got to the motel. Plus, they both fought in multiple battles, died and came back to life. "I'll have pancakes with bananas and Nutella, and all the meats they're having." I chose to forego the fruit and granola yogurt bowl for something more substantial.

"Coming right up." The waitress gave us a smile before

moving on to her next table. There was a man sitting alone at it with four stacks of pancakes, each with different toppings. We weren't the first customers to order large amounts of food.

"I didn't even realize how hungry I am." I had to look away when I got the urge to stick my fork into one of the man's pancakes and eat it.

"It comes in waves," Embry explained, as his stomach made the same growl as mine.

"How are we getting to Boston from here?" I asked. The diner menu told me we were in Missouri, which was still a ways from home.

"I saw a used car dealership down the road. Depending on how legit he is, that could be an option," Embry tried to make it sound like a fun prospect, but I had no interest in riding in a car from a shady salesman that would likely fall apart on us.

"We could also hitchhike across the country if staying under the radar is more important than staying alive," I said it in an optimistic way that had Embry shaking his head at me. "I thought we had a breather now, which is why we're going home. If they're still looking for us and ready to pounce, I'm not going anywhere near my family." The guilty feeling in the pit of my stomach intensified when I mentioned Deanna and Clara, Sam's wife and daughter. How could I call them 'family' when I sacrificed Sam so the bad guys wouldn't get me?

"I would never take you in a car that wasn't completely safe, *Tesoro*," Embry assured me. "But we don't want to be obvious about where we are, or where we're going."

Gabriel's main focus was on the other patrons in the greasy spoon. Aside from the man with the mountains of pancakes, the diner had two other occupied tables. One with a man in a suit reading the newspaper while drinking black coffee, and another with a young family dressed like they came from church. The parents looked exhausted, while the children were as excited about their brunch as I would be for Disney World.

"Can I have bananas and strawberries on my pancakes?" the little boy asked.

"And blueberries!" his younger sister exclaimed.

"You can have whatever your heart desires," the dad said, ruffling the little girl's hair.

I got lost watching them, thinking how Sam would never be able to ruffle Clara's hair like that again. Because of me, the only happy family I had ever known was broken.

"If you could go anywhere in the world, where would you choose?" I was surprised when it was Gabriel who asked such a silly question, but I saw concern when I brought my attention back to our table. He'd been watching me watch them.

"Italy," I gave my standard response. "England," I remembered what felt like centuries ago when my best friend Keisha's mom said we could visit her there for Thanksgiving. "Everywhere," I shrugged, my heart no longer in it. I still wanted to see the world, but home was the first place I thought of. My main problem was that home wasn't home anymore.

"I'm sure we'll knock a few places off your list." Embry gave me a smile as the waitress showed up with three plates that went to Gabriel. She came back multiple times to bring two plates for me, three for Embry, as well as some sides she left in the middle of the table.

"Could we go to a library at some point?" I asked, trying to swallow the ginormous bite I took.

"Missing homework?" Embry raised an eyebrow at me.

"Research. If I only read what they wrote, I'll never know more than they knew." I swallowed and took a piece of bacon from the plates in the middle.

"I doubt any of it will be in a library," Gabriel said.

"Libraries have internet," I pointed out as the mother's phone from the other table went off with the Imperial March. I was momentarily distracted by how cute it was that the little boy hummed along. Once she answered, it only took him a few notes to turn it into a song from Mary Poppins. "And there are biblical references and Latin words I want to confirm," I came back to our conversation as if I hadn't left it.

"My Latin is excellent," Embry volunteered. "But we can still check out a library at some point."

The conversation took a lull while we savored our meals. I had my doubts about the hole-in-the-wall diner we encountered by the train tracks, but the pancakes were big and fluffy, the bananas were overly ripe, and they were generous with the Nutella.

"Ready to hit the road?" Embry asked once our plates were mostly empty and he finished his third espresso.

"I'll use the restroom, then I'm ready to go." I stretched as I stood, picking up my backpack with the Chronicles inside and handing it to Embry to watch while I was gone.

"We'll get the bill," Gabriel told me, motioning the waitress over.

THE WASHROOM WAS BETTER than I expected. It was old and stained and falling apart, but you could tell that it had been cleaned recently. That didn't stop me from really lathering my hands when I washed them afterward.

I shook my hands to get rid of the excess water, as the young mother from the other table walked in and headed straight for the other sink.

"Is that one empty too?" she asked me when her soap dispenser came up dry. She held her hands out like they were covered in something gross and sticky.

"Nope, it's all yours," I told her with a smile, going to the paper towel dispenser to dry my hands.

"You're nicer than the last one." Something about her voice made the hairs on the back of my neck perk up.

"The last what?" I turned over and looked into her eyes for the first time. I knew exactly what made me uneasy. "You're one of them." She was wearing blue contacts, but they only made the darkness underneath stick out. "How did you find us?"

"Some wounds heal, but they always leave a scar." She kept her eyes on me as she moved closer.

"What do you want?" I took a step back, only there was nothing but wall behind me. Not even a window to escape from.

"What I want is to get back to my grandkids and enjoy a nice Sunday brunch." Like Embry and Gabriel, she was clearly a lot older than she looked. "But Donovan doesn't believe in coincidences, so the two of us in the same room is apparently too good of an opportunity to pass up on," she sounded bitter. "Everyone's gotta have something to live for," She sighed, giving me the impression that she didn't think too highly of the Big Bad's quest.

"What's yours?" I asked, my voice shaky. "Have you done it yet?" I scoured the room but didn't see anything I could use as a weapon. Everything was either bolted down or innocuous. I could try some of the self-defense Caleb taught me earlier in the summer, but she was almost a foot taller than me and looked like she could be a personal trainer.

"That is so cute. Worried you'll hurt me and I won't come back?" she mocked me.

"We can't all be villains intent on destroying humanity," I tried to hit a nerve.

"Don't let my grandbabies fool you. I've killed infants with my bare hands and still sleep soundly every night."

"Lucky you." I swallowed, taking one last look around. I still felt guilty for the Gifted I strangled so I could escape at the gas station, and the guy who evaporated at the plantation, even if he was trying to kill me at the time.

"Listen, we can do this the easy way, or I can carry you out in a bag. It's up to you." She stood with her hand on her hip.

"You can't hurt me," I said with a conviction I didn't feel. I knew my death was what they all wanted, since my heart was an ingredient in a ritual they had to perform, but I was pretty sure Donovan's master, the real Big Bad, had to be the one to do it.

"I can't kill you," she conceded. "But there are lots of ways to get you to him without taking all the life out of you."

"My friends are right outside. If I scream, they'll…"

"They'll die," she said simply, with a lot more confidence than I had earlier. "And I'm not sure if they'll come back from this." She touched the sink to her left without taking her eyes off me. The stained ceramic went grey as she turned it to stone.

A chill went through my entire body. For a moment I thought about how she must have been a cold-hearted monster in her first life to get a Gift like that, instead of how she was about to do the same to me. On the bright side, unless she could reverse it, turning my heart to stone meant no one could use it to complete the ritual.

I saw her take a step towards me and froze. I closed my eyes so I wouldn't see it coming and put my hands up as if that could somehow protect me from her.

I waited for the blow, but it didn't come. There was a gust of wind and a loud bang, then nothing but a faint ringing in my ears and tingling in my palms. When I opened my eyes, the woman was gone.

***

Find out what happens next in Destiny (The Owens Chronicles Book Two)

269

Made in the USA
Monee, IL
31 January 2023

26794914R00163